FROM DRE
SCREA

I was awoken by a sudden scream.

A scream external to my dream world.

A scream that finally brought me fully awake and sitting up in bed and wide-eyed and trembling as I realized that the scream was coming from below me . . . from the back room of my laundromat.

I calmed down when I realized I recognized the scream.

It was my cousin Sally. But I couldn't imagine what would make her scream like that.

I pride myself on keeping my laundromat spotless, but still, an occasional spider does wander in. But a spider would never cause Sally to scream. Even something larger—such as, God forbid, a mouse, which I'd never had in my laundromat—would not make her scream.

Maybe she's cut herself somehow. Or worse, gotten bleach in her face.

So I hurried downstairs, and I burst in the back room and saw what had made Sally scream.

She kept screaming. But I didn't scream. I stared in shocked, silent horror.

No, I didn't scream. I ran out the back and threw up. And then I ran back inside and grabbed the phone off my desk and dialed 9–1–1.

The Stain-busting Mysteries
by Sharon Short

TIE DYED *and* DEAD

A STAIN-BUSTING MYSTERY

SHARON SHORT

A V O N

An Imprint of HarperCollinsPublishers

This is a work of fiction. Names, characters, places, and incidents are products of the author's imagination or are used fictitiously and are not to be construed as real. Any resemblance to actual events, locales, organizations, or persons, living or dead, is entirely coincidental.

AVON BOOKS
An Imprint of HarperCollins*Publishers*
10 East 53rd Street
New York, New York 10022-5299

Copyright © 2008 by Sharon Short
ISBN: 978-0-06-079328-9
www.avonmystery.com

First Avon Books paperback printing: March 2008

Avon Trademark Reg. U.S. Pat. Off. and in Other Countries, Marca Registrada, Hecho en U.S.A.
HarperCollins® is a registered trademark of HarperCollins Publishers.

Printed in the U.S.A.

10 9 8 7 6 5 4 3 2 1

*To all the wonderful folks of
Antioch Writers' Workshop in
Yellow Springs, Ohio—with
unending gratitude for the workshop's
inspiration and sustenance.*

TIE DYED and DEAD

1

Once upon a time, there were three sisters who were also singers.

The oldest Mayfair sister, Cornelia, sang for money.

The middle sister, Constance, sang for fame.

But the youngest sister, Candace, sang for love.

Not romantic love or passionate love or worshipful love or family love. Just for a pure love of singing, from the heart, because singing was who she was; it was as much a part of her as breathing . . .

For more than half an hour, Cherry had been going on and on about how the Mayfair sisters' lives were like something out of a fairy tale. So I reckon it's not surprising I started entertaining myself by thinking along those lines.

It was either that or listen to her babble on with what I'd come to call Mayfair Fever, or hum along to "Sugar Daddy," playing on the jukebox.

"Sugar Daddy" was one of the Mayfair Sisters' big hits back in the 1960s. The fact that Sally, my cousin/best friend and owner of the Bar-None, had reprogrammed her establishment's jukebox (really a fancy CD player made to look like a retro fifties jukebox) to play only Mayfair Sisters oldies—even though we were smack-dab in the middle of the twenty-first century's first decade—was just another symptom of Mayfair Fever, which had infected all of Paradise, Ohio, and environs for nearly two weeks.

I'm Josie Toadfern, laundromat owner and stain expert. Best stain expert in Paradise . . . and in Mason County. Maybe the best stain expert in all of Ohio. Maybe even in all of the United States.

I can make such a claim with some authority, and not just because I've helped Mrs. Beavy get red wine out of her favorite pink blouse, or Becky Gettlehorn get mustard out of her little boy's best Sunday-go-to-church shirt, or my auto mechanic Elroy Magruder get grease out of his Dickies coveralls.

Besides plenty of testimonials to back up my stain claim to fame, I have a syndicated column—Stain-Busters!—which gives stain removal tips and general household hints.

And on that Friday night a while back, I was thinking about what my next column should be, instead of listening to Cherry—owner of Cherry's Chat N Curl, right next door to my laundromat on Main Street—go on and on about her customers' Mayfair Sisters sightings. I'd already completed a three-parter on the incredible stain removal properties of white vinegar. Next, maybe how to remove coffee and tea stains from mugs? A cautionary reminder about not mixing chlorine bleach with other cleansers? Or ironing tips . . .

And maybe to go with that, a little about the history of ironing techniques and tools. It's fascinating, really. And my current passion was learning as much as possible about the home ironing machines of the 1940s and 1950s, also known as mangles, especially the Ironrite brand . . .

"Ow!"

I looked across the table at Cherry, then back at my forearm—yep, those were fingernail marks—and then again at Cherry, glaring this time.

"Poke me again, and I'm popping those fake fuchsias off of every fingertip," I said.

Cherry ignored my threat, probably feeling safer than she should since she was snuggled up next to Dean Rankle—Mason County deputy sheriff. And her fiancé.

"Josie, have you heard a thing I've said?" Cherry asked.

"No. I've been ignoring you, because you keep talking about the Mayfair Sisters, and I really don't want to hear about them tonight."

"Then you've got to be the only one in Paradise," said Caleb Loudermilk, with an intriguing tone of ruefulness.

Caleb was in the booth next to me, but we weren't snuggling. Caleb's the editor-in-chief (and sole reporter, and ad salesman, and occasional janitor) at the *Paradise Advertiser-Gazette*. I'd already been doing my stain-busting column for the weekly local newspaper when he took over newspaper operations, but he's the one who had the brilliant idea to get my column in as many of the regional newspapers—all owned by the same publishing company—as possible.

We'd also dated for a while at the beginning of the year, but our relationship had settled into an easy friendship after we figured out that our initial attraction was based on a rebound from an old relationship (for me) and a bit of uneasiness at settling into a small town that thinks of second-generation Paradisites as newcomers (for Caleb).

"I've gotten calls from everyone—including the mayor—asking me if I'm going to get a big, exclusive interview with Cornelia and her bankruptcy and tax woes," Caleb went on.

The one who sang for money, I thought.

"Or on the rumors of the feud between the other two—"

"Constance and Candace," Cherry said eagerly, leaning forward, which gave Dean a chance to rub her back—a chance he immediately took.

"Which one wants to relaunch the trio, honey?" asked Dean.

"That's the middle sister, Constance," Cherry said.

The one who sang for fame . . .

"The youngest sister wants to just keep on with her solo folk career, singing backwaters like this the rest of her life," Cherry went on, shuddering as if that modest goal was something that ought to be featured on the current reality TV show *The World's Yuckiest Jobs*. "But, from what I've heard, Candace—"

The one who sang for love . . .

"—was always something of a loner, even when the Mayfair Sisters were a big hit," Cherry said.

"They still seem to be a big hit around here," Caleb said.

"Biggest thing to come out of this area," Dean said. "Well, except for Delbert Whitacre." Dean beamed. Delbert was, after all, Dean's second cousin, once removed.

Caleb looked blank.

"Nascar driver," I said.

"Oh," Caleb said, trying to sound suddenly enlightened, but still looking blank. He shook his head as if to clear it. "Anyway, it seems as if everyone has been calling the newspaper office, demanding to know when I'm going to do an exclusive, in-depth interview. And I'd love to. It would make for a nice surge in circulation, and a nice clip for my portfolio."

Caleb had told me, confidentially, that he wanted to apply to bigger newspapers, but he needed something more than the latest Little League scores, or even witty write-ups about church carry-in suppers to raise money for charitable causes, to even have a shot at breaking in. He'd been doing family history features lately, which everyone around Paradise appreciated, but no matter how well written, those weren't going to be the ticket to better jobs in big cities, either.

He sighed. "But the only thing I can get out of the Mayfairs is the date and time of the reunion concert and auction—"

"Ooh, that's just a week from now, Memorial Day weekend, right?" Cherry asked.

My eyebrows went up, and Dean looked startled, too. Cherry and Dean were each doing their best to save money for their wedding, just a little over a month away, and for their honeymoon in Gatlinburg, Tennessee. They'd reserved the honeymoon suite with a heart-shaped Jacuzzi and king-sized bed. Cherry had shown me the glossy brochure from the Hearts and Roses Inn so many times, my fingerprints were permanently imprinted on the picture of the Jacuzzi.

Not only that, but after their honeymoon, Dean wanted to start a side business, Deputy Dean's Security Systems for homes and small businesses.

So I knew Cherry couldn't afford anything from the Mayfair auction . . . and I also knew she wouldn't have the self-discipline not to bid.

Caleb smiled. "Right. Anyway, I have that, but I still don't have the list of items up for auction to run in Wednesday's paper. I have a feeling I'll get it at the last minute."

And I knew why, but I didn't want to share that, not just yet. I munched a pretzel stick, and then sipped my beer, and turned to stare out the window at the trucks and motorcycles and late-model cars under the lights of the Bar-None parking lot, focusing in particular on a tricked-out red pickup truck, on oversized wheels. It belonged to T-Bone Baker, which I knew because his girlfriend, Rhonda, drove it to my laundromat to bring in their wash. They lived in the Happy Trails Motor Home Park, where Sally lived, and the motor homes there are too small for washer/dryers, so I get a lot of business from Happy Trails residents.

Not that that was particularly interesting. But if I stared at the tricked-out truck, then my face would be turned from my pals—a good thing, since I have a face that can be read by a three-year-old. Which is why I don't play cards. Not even Go Fish with Sally's young sons.

"Now, honeybuns," Dean said nervously. "I think we're busy Memorial weekend anyway. We won't have time to go to the auction, what with last-minute stuff for our wedding. Like, um, the wedding cake. Yeah, we still have to order that, right?"

Cherry gave him a look that could have sliced through a twenty-tier cake. "We've ordered the cake, sweet cheeks. Buttercream icing, with bright red roses to match the brides-maids' dresses, and blue ribbons to match the groomsmen's tuxedos. Don't you remember?"

Dean gazed down at his beer with a look that clearly indi-cated he'd been trying to forget. But despite my, Sally's, and the other bridesmaids' protests, Cherry had prevailed with her July 4–themed wedding . . . which would actually be held on July 5, in order to get the Run Deer Run Lodge for the reception.

Caleb snickered. I elbowed him. Cherry was strong-willed and unreasonable and a pain in the butt at the best of times—and I say that with great love, as one of her best friends. But her pre-wedding jitters had ensured that this was not the best of times.

"Anyway," Cherry said, making the word sound like three, "I need to get to that auction because I'm just betting that the white dress that Candace Mayfair wore in the sisters' farewell concert is up for auction, and . . . I must have it! As my wedding dress!"

Caleb, Dean, and I were struck silent, while Cherry looked pointedly at each of us, daring us to state the obvious.

I looked back at my pals and sighed louder than necessary. I'd been puncturing Cherry's fantasy view of the world and her role in it since seventh grade—not that she'd ever listened. But I'm an optimist. So I tried again.

"Cherry, Candace Mayfair is a size four on her fat days. You, darlin', are a size fourteen on your skinny days. Which, as I've told you many times, you should embrace, because Marilyn Monroe was supposedly a fourteen—"

"And I love your curves—" Dean said.

Caleb was convulsing with either a suppressed sneeze or laughter.

"I don't care! I want that dress!"

"But you said you picked out a beautiful dress at the Medieval Fantasy booth down at the Meet-N-Swap flea market?" Dean sound genuinely confused.

"I did!" Cherry wailed. "But the feathers are molting off the neckline."

I'd told her not to get the dress with feathers. I'd told her they'd probably molt off; that the odor of mothballs was something that, yes, I could probably lessen, but it was still a bad sign; that the feathers would make her sneeze and create a vacuuming nightmare after the ceremony for MayaAnna Lean, who's hunched with arthritis and seventy-plus but still insists that it's always been her job to tidy up the Paradise Methodist Church before and after weddings, and, dammit, it always will be.

But, of course, Cherry had insisted on her own way. As usual.

I decided to try and change the subject before the situation got any more uncomfortable.

"Well, I don't know about that dress," I said brightly, "but let me tell you all about my newest interest. See, I've started researching a book on clothing care history—"

Cherry blanched. "What? You've got to be kidding me."

"This sounds fascinating! Go on, Josie!" Dean said perkily, giving me a grateful look. I knew he couldn't care less about my topic, but he was willing to do anything to get Cherry's mind off a new, too small, and expensive dress. And I was happy to have an audience—even a captive one.

"Well, it really is fascinating," I said. "How womankind has dealt with dirty, wrinkled, smelly clothes throughout the ages is an unchartered bit of domestic history. And it's a unique perspective on domestic life. I think before the permanent-press era makes us all forget, this history and the story it tells should be captured. And I figure with the platform this column is giving me, and my love of books"—a love that Winnie, our bookmobile librarian, can attest to, because I read at least three books a week—"I'm the perfect person to write this book."

"But Josie, you're not—" Caleb started, then stopped.

I knew what he was going to say: college-educated. A historian. Photogenic enough for the *Today Show*.

I ignored him, and went on.

"Why, did you know there's even an organization of people who collect sad irons?"

"What are sad irons?" Dean asked, looking bored already, but trying to sound fascinated. Anything to keep the topic off Cherry spending money they didn't have on a wedding dress that wouldn't fit her.

"Who cares?" Cherry asked, grumpy but already distracted.

"Sad irons," I said, "are heavy, cast-iron, well, irons, that women heated and used to press their family's clothes. Or the clothes of clients. It was such a difficult, labor-intensive job, that lots of women were thrilled with the invention of the ironing machine, or mangle, back in the early 1920s. The most well-known brand was the Ironrite, and they were most popular in the 1940s and 1950s—"

"Oh, Lord, is she going on about that Ironrite machine that's going up for auction at the Mayfair sale?"

I startled, and looked up. There stood Sally Toadfern, Bar-None owner, my first cousin-on-my-daddy's-side and usually one of my best friends. I'd been so caught up in my explanation of the Ironrite machine that I hadn't noticed her coming up to our booth with a fresh pitcher of beer.

I glared at her. Sally knew how much I wanted that Ironrite machine, and insisted on teasing me about it. But that was Sally. And truth be told, I wouldn't change her a bit.

Cherry and Caleb glared at me. Dean sighed and took up my bar-parking-lot vigil.

The Mayfairs' "Sugar Daddy" song ended (*You can be my sugar daddy, I can be your sugar baby, we'll be sweet together . . .*)

"Uh oh . . ." Sally said uneasily.

The Mayfairs' "Easy Lovin'" (*It's not that I'm easy, it's just easy lovin' you . . .*) commenced.

"How do you know there's an Ironrite on the auction list," Caleb asked, "when I haven't been able to get anything out of the Mayfairs for my newspaper?"

"I'm guessing I shouldn't have said that," Sally said, sitting down next to Caleb and giving him a shove, so he pushed into me and I squished against the wall.

"Josie, have you been holding out on us?" Cherry demanded, focusing on me so intently that she didn't notice Dean's head quivering as he shook *no! no!* at me.

I sighed. I should have known I wouldn't be able to keep a secret from this crew. I finished off my beer and then smacked the mug down harder than strictly necessary. I reckon it's a good thing Sally uses cheap plastic mugs.

"OK, fine. I confess. I've known for three weeks now what the items will *probably* be in the auction," I said, "because I've been helping get the costumes ready—"

"Candace's white dress!" Cherry exclaimed. "Please tell me that's one of the costumes . . ."

Dean groaned, put his hands to his eyes, and sank down in the booth.

"—but the family still hasn't decided on whether everything should be up for auction—"

"But I need that information by Monday, noon!" Caleb said. "OK, Monday at five p.m. at the latest . . ."

"—because at one point, back when she was still . . . well . . . herself, Mama Mayfair had a list of items she wanted her daughters to donate to the Mason County Historical Museum. Including some of the costumes—and the Ironrite ironer I'm coveting, although," I concluded rather piously, "I'm at least trying to remember why this auction is taking place to begin with."

Everyone got quiet again, and a little shamefaced.

The Mayfair Sisters were holding a reunion concert before the auction, as well as the auction of their memorabilia, costumes, and childhood home, to raise money for the care of their elderly mother, Dora Mayfair. She was eighty-two, frail, and both physically and mentally ravaged by Alzheimer's disease. Candace had moved back to Paradise a few months before to care for her mother, with professional nursing help, but funds were already running out, and it had soon become clear that poor Dora would be better off in a long-term-care facility.

So the sisters had settled on the concert—to be held at the amphitheater at Licking Creek Lake State Park—and the auction to raise funds.

The concert was the coming Friday night, and had already sold out. We all had our tickets, of course.

And the auction was the afternoon after the concert. It was expected that the modest home on Plum Street would be packed with potential buyers from all over the region, and even some from across the country. Even the Red Horse Motel was sold out for the upcoming weekend, and some Paradisites were renting out rooms. The Mayfair Sisters, after all, had been a big hit in the early 1960s . . . until their sweet—some would say, sappy—love songs just didn't fit the mood of the times, and their act broke up.

The sisters went their separate ways, only Candace staying in the music business, giving occasional folk concerts and more recently—until she went on hiatus to take care of her mother—recording and selling CDs independently.

Meanwhile, the sisters' mama, Dora, had happily continued living on Plum Street as she always had, occasionally chatting with a Mayfair fan who went to the effort to find the sisters' modest childhood home in our little town in southern Ohio. Until about four years ago, when she'd wandered into my laundromat, confused and lost, not sure why she was there or where she'd actually been planning to go in the first place. It was the first alarming clue that she had Alzheimer's, and since then, she'd gotten worse, until it was clear she could not be left alone.

Sally cleared her throat. "Yeah, that's really sad about Mrs. Mayfair," she said. We all had a moment of silence.

Then she said, "And I'm sorry about letting it slip that you're working with the Mayfairs . . ."

"Why didn't you tell me, too?" Cherry said, pouting, at the same time that Caleb said, "You mean you could have given me an inside connection all this time for the story I'm after," and Dean moaned something about don't auctions just take cash or checks and his account being strapped, what with the Run Deer Run Lodge rental and all, and the dress that was already bought, and the red, white, and blue bridesmaids' dresses and groomsmen's tuxes.

I ignored them all and said loudly. "That's OK, Sally, I know you have a lot on your mind, what with Harry, Barry, and Larry"—those are her triplet boys—"and running this place. And of course I told only you because I knew you wouldn't hassle me for favors with the Mayfairs."

"And because Josie needed help with transporting the Mayfair costumes," Sally said, apologetically to everyone else, although I didn't see that she really owed *them* an apology at all.

"Really? You got to see all the costumes up for auction?" Cherry said excitedly.

"Or for donation to the Mason County Historical Society," I said. "That's still being decided—so don't get your hopes up about Candace's white dress."

Dean's expression of tension eased a bit, while Cherry went right back to pouty. Lord, I worried about Dean.

I looked at Caleb. "And as for you getting an interview, well, I can ask tomorrow afternoon. I'm delivering the last of the freshened costumes then. I'm emissary for Mrs. Beavy." She's the eighty-something who runs the Mason County Historical Society, which operates a museum out of the former home of the now deceased owner of the Breitenstrater Pie Factory—but that's another story.

Anyway, I'd promised Mrs. Beavy I'd press the Mayfair Sisters about which costumes they might donate to the museum, so while I was at it, I might as well ask about an interview with the *Paradise Advertiser-Gazette* as well. And see if they were ready to provide that list to Caleb, too.

Caleb looked excited. "Thanks, Josie, you're a pal. But, um, any way that you can move your meeting up to tomorrow morning? I mean, the sooner—"

I shook my head. "No. I have a meeting at Stillwater tomorrow morning."

Stillwater Farms is the residential home of my cousin-from-my-mama's-side, Guy Foersthoefel. Guy is like a brother to me. He's also eighteen years older than me, and he's an adult with autism. He lives in the residential home that his parents, deceased for the past twelve years, carefully chose for him: Stillwater Farms, just a half hour north of Paradise and an hour south of Columbus. His parents, Aunt Clara and Uncle Horace, reared me as a daughter after my parents abandoned me to an orphanage. When Aunt Clara and Uncle Horace died young, just as I was graduating high school and starting to try to figure out what I wanted to do with my life, they left me two things: their laundromat business and Guy's guardianship.

I was only eighteen when I took over both, but I took the responsibilities seriously. Twelve years later, I still do.

"Josie's going to a meeting of guardians and parents where the new director of Stillwater will be introduced," Sally said.

Ohs and ahs, and nods of understanding ensued from Cherry, Dean, and Caleb. They knew how seriously I took Guy's care—and the future of Stillwater Farms. In fact, I'd been on the search committee for a new director at the end of the previous year, but traumatic mishaps on a chick trip with Sally and Cherry to Port Clinton, Ohio, for the New Year's Eve Great Walleye Drop celebration—and my thirtieth birthday—had landed me on bed rest for a while from exhaustion and walking pneumonia. Another long story. But anyway, it had meant I'd had to scale back on obligations, including being on the interviewing committee for the director.

So I hadn't had a chance to meet Levi Applegate, the new director. But I had read his initial résumé and background, and it had made me nervous. He had great credentials. And he had a sister with autism, so I was sure he could empathize with Stillwater's community—meaning residents and caretakers and family members. But his sister was back in New Mexico, so I wondered how long he'd be willing to stay in Ohio. And he had some new ideas about how to work with adults with autism that made me uncomfortable.

"And being reminded of that meeting makes me think I ought to head home for a good night's sleep," I said. I nudged Caleb with my hip. Sally started to stand up, so Caleb could stand up, so I could get out of the booth—but then we all stopped.

"What's your problem, Bubba? Your woman was feeling me up, not—"

The man—a stranger I didn't recognize—in the middle of the tiny dance floor didn't get a chance to finish his statement. The guy he'd called Bubba was really T-Bone Baker, owner of the big, shiny, tricked-out pickup truck I'd been staring at a few moments ago.

And no one made such accusations about his woman, Rhonda. That would be as bad as scratching T-Bone's truck's finish.

Which is why T-Bone was currently whacking the stranger across the jaw.

"What the hell? Not in my place! I run a clean place!" Sally was hollering, and running to break up the fight, such as it was. T-Bone was basically using the guy as a punching bag.

"'Scuse me darlin'!" Dean hollered, clambering over Cherry. He was eager, I reckoned, to get into action he could understand, and away from pleading with Cherry about not bidding on the Mayfair dress.

"What?" Cherry shrieked after Dean. "You're off duty!"

"The law and the press are never off duty!" Caleb said as he ran off to the middle of the floor, pulling out his cell phone with camera.

Cherry glared at me.

"Not my fault," I said, shrugging. "And I still have to get home. Toodles."

I headed toward the Bar-None bathrooms, away from the melee.

But right as I neared the door labeled WOMEN, I heard Cherry shrieking at me, "I want you to find out about that dress, Josie Toadfern!" which made me turn so my back was to the door labeled MEN, and before I could holler back at Cherry, I was suddenly on the ground.

On top of me was a man.

We quickly separated and stared at each other.

He was slender, tall, and interesting-looking, and starting to laugh at our mishap, but suddenly he was just stammering "S-s-sorry," while I was stammering the same thing, and this little voice was whispering in my head, *Oh . . . there you are. Where have you been all my life?*

2

"Well, it's about damned time you connected with the love of your life. So, what do you think about this as a wedding dress?"

In my dream, I stared into the fog, knowing who the voice came from. Sighing, I waited for her to emerge, unsure how I felt about this situation.

The voice was that of Mrs. Oglevee . . . Pearl Oglevee, my long-deceased junior high teacher, who'd taught me *and* taunted me as a student, making junior high history an ordeal. Then she'd retired, and I thought I was free . . . but she substitute taught in my high school. And I had her as a teacher at least once in every single high school class.

Then she was supposed to go off on a Mediterranean cruise, but she died of natural causes, by all accounts. I was reared to respect my elders, so I was somber at her demise, as was proper, but I can't rightly say I was mournful.

And then, about a year ago, when I became involved in the first of several murder investigations, Mrs. Oglevee started showing up in my dream life, again taunting me but also every now and again offering observations that—though obscure—helped me solve the cases.

As luck would have it, my last case was investigating the truth behind Mrs. Oglevee's death, and with the help of Cherry and Sally, I found out that she'd in fact been murdered, by whom, and why.

In my last Mrs. Oglevee dream—five months ago—she'd shown up primly dressed in a tan coatdress and a matching hat, with a small toiletries case. Despite my hollering at her, "Stay!" in a surprising fit of sentimentality, Mrs. Oglevee disappeared into the fog, embarking, I reckoned, on some otherworldly variation of the missed Mediterranean cruise. In any case, she hadn't been back to haunt and taunt in my dreams.

Of course, Mrs. Oglevee had only shown up when I had somehow or another gotten myself tangled up in a murder investigation, the likes of which I blessedly hadn't been involved in since the turn of the year. So I figured that was why she had stayed away from my dream life and gone back to whatever squirrelly corner of my subconsciousness had had the dark humor to spew her forth in the first place. A stress reaction, I'd told myself. I mean, who wants to believe the grumpy ghost of a former junior high teacher is haunting her dreams?

And I hadn't missed murder investigations *or* Mrs. Oglevee, I told myself. Not one bit.

So why was my reaction of "Oh no, not her" tinged with just a wee bit of . . . relief and delight?

I tried to ignore that and hollered into the fog: "What do you want? No one I know has been murdered. I'm not poking about . . ."

I stopped as Mrs. Oglevee abruptly appeared—well, at least her head, arms, and legs appeared. Then I realized the rest of her body was covered in a white dress . . . the very same white dress of Mayfair costume fame that Cherry was coveting as a wedding dress—and that her outline in the dress was blurring into the fog in my dreams.

And I also realized that the dress—which from old magazine photos had been a dream on Candace Mayfair—fit Mrs. Oglevee about as well as I expected it would fit Cherry. Which was to say, as a nightmare of lumpishness.

I moaned.

"Never mind murders. I'm here to ask you what you think of this as a wedding dress!" Mrs. Oglevee preened and twirled.

When she faced me again, I said, "I think that brown orthopedic shoes just don't go with that dress. I think you need white shoes. Even if it is before Memorial Day . . ." I added hastily, to prevent an Oglevee lecture on old-fashioned couture values.

Mrs. Oglevee scowled. "Not for me, you numskull, for—"

"Please don't tell me that somehow you're here on Cherry's behalf," I pleaded. "I've already told her, I don't know if that dress is going in the auction or to the county historical society's museum, and in any case, it wouldn't fit her any better than it does—"

"And not for her, either," Mrs. Oglevee yelled. "I'm just modeling it!"

And suddenly she was in another Mayfair Sisters costume—one of the tie-dyed slip dresses the sisters had worn in their final concert tour, in an ill-conceived effort to keep up with the times.

The swirls of hot pink, orange, lime green, and yellow made my eyes water. I looked down—and suddenly realized that I was wearing the white dress.

Which didn't fit me much better than it had Mrs. Oglevee, or than it would Cherry.

I looked back up at Mrs. Oglevee, who had somehow added a matching tie-dyed scarf, tied around her head. It didn't really work with her iron gray bun.

She smiled at me, triumphant. "That's right. This wedding dress is for you, now that you've met your soul mate." She eyed my midriff. "Although you'll need it let out several inches."

I immediately thought of the man I'd collided with that night at the Bar-None—then quickly disentangled myself from and ran away, speeding home since I hadn't made it to the women's room and I desperately needed to pee.

Then I quickly pushed away the image of the man. Nonsense.

But Mrs. Oglevee's smile widened. "That's right. You know who I'm talking about."

"Oh please," I said grumpily. "I don't know who that man is. I'll probably never see him again. And how would you—would I—would you . . . dammit, how would anybody know he's the love of my life and that I should marry him? No way. I don't care if he's handsome"—well, he was, in a quirky way—"or brilliant or funny or compassionate"—and I'd seen flashes of all that in his eyes—"I am *not* going to tell my future children, 'Oh, how did Mommy and Daddy meet? Well, Daddy had just gone wee at Aunt Sally's bar, and Mommy really needed to wee, but mean old Aunt Cherry distracted Mommy, causing her to literally run into Daddy in her rush to the bathroom.'"

"Ah, you admit you wouldn't mind making babies with this man," Mrs. Oglevee said, with a knowing waggle of her eyebrows.

I crossed my arms—despite Candace Mayfair's white dress being too tight on me even in the sleeves—and said, "Oh, for pity's sake. Listen, how about you come back when and if I ever stumble across another murdered body . . ."

I stopped, as suddenly Mrs. Oglevee was holding a pointer, and a screen slid down from out of nowhere.

Flickering on the screen, as if projected from an old reel-to-reel film, like the ones Mrs. Oglevee had shown in class, was an image of our local police chief, John Worthy.

Except instead of his thirty-year-old image, I was treated to his junior high yearbook photo.

"Exhibit A," Mrs. Oglevee said, "your first boyfriend."

I squirmed uncomfortably, and not just from the constriction of the dress.

"Didn't exactly go well—not even for a junior high romance. Caught him cheating, ratted him out, dug up some ugly business about how the other girl's daddy, the football coach, had fixed it so Johnny-boy made the team even though he wasn't really, well, worthy of playing quarterback—" Mrs. Oglevee paused to chuckle, and I moaned, knowing she was quoting from the school newspaper article I'd written about the scandal—"thus earning you the nickname Nosey Josie. Chief Worthy hasn't quite gotten over you—"

I startled at that.

"—but he's also been nasty to you ever since. Next, a series of unfortunate blind dates, etc., etc."

Four—or was it five?—pictures flashed in a blurry row.

"Now just a minute," I said, "I'm not the first girl to date around—"

"And then we get to . . . him. Owen Collins." Mrs. Oglevee said the name as if she were saying "bubonic plague."

I stared at the picture of Owen, and my heart clenched just a little, even though I knew I was well and truly over him. He hadn't been a scumbag, or deadbeat, or dirty rotten bottom-feeder—as Cherry and Sally liked to tag their exes—but he had had a problem with honesty. Technically, he'd never lied to me . . . but he had avoided telling me crucial truths. I couldn't abide a relationship like that, and I knew I was better off without him. Still, breaking up with him was the first big adult heartbreak I'd experienced.

I sighed. "I learned a lot from that relationship—"

"What, to take the easy way out?"

Owen's face disappeared and was replaced by the yummy visage of Randy Woodford . . . and not just his handsome face. This was a complete body shot . . . with him wearing just a Speedo. Yum, yum. Randy is one of the few men who actually look delicious dressed—or, more accurately, undressed—like this.

"So you went from Mr. Not Ready for Real Commitment to Mr. Stud Muffin?" Mrs. Oglevee demanded.

I sighed again—for a whole different reason. "It was fun while it lasted," I said.

"Did you ever look into his eyes?" she asked.

I tried to think. "Hmmm. Maybe once or twice." I briefly glanced at his eyes in the picture. I knew what she was getting at.

Randy was not exactly bright. On the other hand, Owen had triple Ph.D.'s . . . for all the good that had done me.

I'd occasionally dated Randy while he worked on the renovations on the apartments over my laundromat—I live in the second story over my business, Toadfern's Laundromat (slogan: Always a leap ahead of dirt!). The upstairs had been divided into two small one-bedroom apartments, and for a lot of years, I rented out one while living in the other. At least I rented out the apartment when I could. Not many folks move into Paradise, and those folks that are from here already have houses in town or farms out in the township or mobile homes permanently rooted in the Happy Trails Trailer Court, like Sally.

But, with my big three–oh birthday, a lot of truths finally smacked me upside the head. Such as I'm not going to live anywhere else other than South Central Ohio, because I'm Guy's caretaker. And I don't want to while away years dreaming of white-picket-fence bliss while cramped in a small apartment. So I had the two apartments on the second story of my laundromat building renovated into one. And enjoyed the company of my renovator, hunky Randy Woodford, in the process. Fun . . . but then he met the young woman I hired to wallpaper the kitchen and bathroom. And wooed, proposed, and married her in the space of two months.

I sent a nice gift to their wedding. After all, good skilled carpenter/wallpaper folks are difficult to find.

"Well?" Mrs. Oglevee prompted me.

"Oh, right, Randy's eyes." I smiled wickedly, hoping my next comment would put her into enough of a snit so that she would go away and let me enjoy the rest of my sleep in peace. "Well, he was good with his power tools."

Mrs. Oglevee didn't disappear. She just made Randy disappear—and up popped the photo of Caleb Loudermilk.

"Look, he was mostly a business relationship," I said. "And that's all he is now. And a friend. We enjoy each other's company—but that's it."

"Exactly," Mrs. Oglevee said. "And he's almost just the right mix for you. Handsome enough." Although, I thought, I really wouldn't want to see him in a Speedo.

"Although no one would want to see him in a Speedo," Mrs. Oglevee echoed, and gave me her own wicked smile. I startled. "Smart enough for you. But . . . with plans to move around a lot in life. No designs on commitment any time soon. And no lasting spark between you two . . . just a comfortableness." She pointed at me. "You are afraid of real intimacy, Josie Toadfern."

Then she pointed at the screen, and the image of the stranger from the night before at Bar-None appeared on the screen.

And my stomach flipped.

And that little voice of recognition curled across my brain . . . *Oh . . . it's you . . .*

I rolled my eyes to try to mask my feelings. "I'm not willing to pick out place setting patterns with a guy whose name I don't know . . . who I literally ran into on my way to go pee at Sally's bar . . . and you're telling me I'm afraid? How about more like I'm *not* nuts?"

Mrs. Oglevee tapped the screen and it disappeared, and the little voice said, *No . . . wait . . .* and I shook my head at myself.

"Afraid," Mrs. Oglevee said. "I know you. You've always tried to play it safe—except when it comes to sticking your nose into other people's business, Nosey Josie."

"Now, that's not fair . . ."

"I'm just saying: *You can't find love on your own, true love must find you, but when it does, my friend, what will you do, what will you do, hide your heart inside a stone or to your love be true?*"

And with that she disappeared.

I woke up suddenly, five minutes ahead of my alarm, sweating, and staring down at my Tweety-bird nightshirt to make sure it wasn't the Mayfair white dress.

Where, I wondered, had Mrs. Oglevee come up with such a sappy saying?

And then it hit me. Those sappy words were from a Mayfair Sisters' ballad, but in their warm harmonies, they hadn't sounded sappy at all.

3

I took longer than I really needed to get ready that morning, taking pleasure in my renovated apartment. It had been done for only two months, but you know how it is. It's easy to get used to blessings and start taking them for granted.

So I had a long soak in the Jacuzzi tub—my biggest splurge—and told myself that my Mrs. Oglevee dream was silly, just a stress reaction to the busy day ahead. I surely didn't need a love-of-my-life to be happy.

I went back to my bedroom, not much bigger than my previous one, and moseyed into my walk-in closet. And then backed out. And then walked in again. *Looky here*, I told myself; *you have a walk-in closet!* And then I twirled around for good measure, and dropped my towel down the laundry chute, which led to a strategically placed basket below, in my office in the back room of my laundromat. (One of the perks of living above one's very own laundromat.)

Then I pulled out jeans and a nice white cami and white blouse, navy socks, and brown clogs, and got dressed. It was a Saturday, but I had several important appointments to keep, and I wanted to look a little dressier than my usual T-shirt and sneakers getup.

I told myself to see my walk-in closet as half full—not half empty—and reminded myself I didn't need men's shirts stuffing the closet to be happy.

Then I went to my kitchen, and sat down at the table, and had toast and orange juice.

In the dinkier version of my apartment, I'd barely had room for a dinette. Now I could actually have three people over for dinner—five if we were really close friends—in my newly expanded eat-in kitchen.

Right now my table was a rickety garage-sale find covered with a plastic tablecloth featuring jack-o'-lanterns and witches (half-price sale at the dollar store), and two of the seats were lawn chairs I'd plucked from the curb on Plum Street during the town's semiannual junk pickup day. But someday I'd have a proper table and chairs, I thought—and ignored the voice that asked why, since, truth be told, I usually just met up with my pals at the Bar-None or Sandy's Restaurant and wasn't likely to have need for a real family table.

Then I stared at the beautiful bookshelves that lined my great room. Sally and I had made the bookshelves together—simple pinewood creations—then added trim we'd picked up at a good price at Masonville's Home Depot. We'd painted the shelves to match the walls behind them, a soft moss green, and lightly sponged the shelves with off-white, finishing with triple layers of lacquer. The shelves looked built-in, and I'd given Sally free use of my laundromat, plus a spare key so she could use it after hours, as payment. Considering that she has first-grade triplet sons, she'd seen that as more than fair pay.

And I'd applied the do-it-yourself savings to my second splurge—a skylight, right over the great room.

That morning I stood in front of my bookshelves, running my hands lovingly over the book spines, pausing occasionally to consider a title of a childhood favorite or mystery or romance or fantasy or classic. My reading tastes are eclectic, and I like it that way.

And again, I reminded myself that I was happy. Because I was.

But somehow, stumbling into the semihandsome stranger and my dream of Mrs. Oglevee had me doubting myself.

Finally I left, stepping out my apartment door to my covered small balcony porch, and I gazed around at what I could see of Paradise from my spot smack-dab in the middle of Main Street.

I smiled. It was just a sleepy little town, ragged around the edges from economic changes that had robbed the area of manufacturing jobs, but still home to me and about three thousand other people, all trying to put together lives of worth and meaning. And I had a lot to be thankful for. Decent business. Developing column career. My health. My friends. Guy.

Still.

Before I opened up Toadfern's Laundromat, I went across the street to Sandy's Restaurant, a converted double-wide on the site of the original building, which had burned down due to a kitchen fire thirty years before, and got an extra large coffee, to go, just to celebrate my currently, and probably permanent, happiness as a single.

After I opened up my laundromat, I took a few minutes to sit and enjoy sips of my coffee at my desk in my storage room/office, while reviewing some notes I'd made the day before about a problem.

I didn't tally customers precisely, but I knew about how

many visited my laundromat. And the amount of money I'd retrieved from my washers and dryers on a weekly basis was increasing enough that I noticed.

Maybe my customer tracking was off. It was a good problem to have, in any case.

But not a problem I had time to noodle through right then.

I set my coffee on my desk and triple-checked the last of the Mayfair costumes—which included the white dress Cherry coveted, and the tie-dyed slip dresses like the one Mrs. Oglevee had worn in my dream.

I pushed the memory of that dream aside as I focused on the costumes. Some I'd cleaned and aired out myself; others had needed dry cleaning, so I'd taken them to my favorite dry cleaner's in Columbus. Others had needed mending, and I'd trusted that job to Moira Evans, a seamstress who worked from her Paradise home just a few houses down from the Mayfair home, and who did the finest needlework I'd ever seen. Moira was older and had back problems and a troubled grandson, Clint Evans, who was out of drug rehab yet again and trying to stick out a whole semester up at Masonville Community College, so I knew she needed work.

Anyway, some of the costumes I'd passed directly on to her before cleaning; others just needed my expertise.

By now, all the costumes had been restored and returned to the Mayfairs, except six that had needed Moira's needle-and-thread magic. I'd retrieved them from Moira the previous afternoon—the white dress, plus its silver and gold sisters, and three tie-dyed slip dresses.

I checked the silver and gold dresses first, and then lingered over the pearl white dress. It was far classier than anything I'd imagine Cherry wanting, but then it was so beautiful, I could see how it might break down even her tacky bent. It was lovely, a simple silk sheath, chiffon sleeves, and crocheted lace trimming the neckline. Dora Mayfair herself had crocheted the trim for Candace's dress, as well as for the silver and gold versions Cornelia and Constance wore. I smiled. Somehow, the silver and gold befitted my vision of those two as singing for fame and money, just as the pearl white fit my view of Candace.

Well, to be fair, I'd only met Candace. That afternoon, after my trip to Stillwater, I'd meet the other two. I hoped my opinion of them—admittedly based on gossip and news reports—would change.

And then I thought about poor Mrs. Mayfair and her condition now, and my smile dissolved.

I refocused on inspecting the dress, which had needed only spot cleaning and Moira's fine handwork to resecure the lace trim.

Then I checked the tie-dyed slip dresses. I'd hand laundered those, and Moira had fixed the hems. I finished inspecting two and was looking at the third when I heard the bell jingle over my laundromat's front door.

I grabbed my coffee off my desk and hurried out. I always like to greet people as they come in. I have a growing number of elderly customers, whose caretakers drop off their laundry, which is how I got to know Candace Mayfair a few months before. Plus I have a few customers who have me do their shirts, and sometimes regular customers want stain removal tips, my specialty.

Rhonda Farris—T-Bone Baker's live-in girlfriend—was busily loading one of the triple load super-sized washers with socks and boxer shorts and jeans and T-shirts. Looked like T-Bone's dirty laundry. And Rhonda was crying and cursing under her breath as she did so, wadding up each piece and throwing it as hard as she could into the washer—

not exactly a satisfying way to work off anger. It's not like socks go "thump," no matter how hard you throw them.

"Rhonda?" I approached quietly and said her name softly, but she startled so hard that I jumped and sloshed coffee on my white shirt.

"Oh, Josie, I'm so sorry," Rhonda said. "You know, you should rinse that out with cold water as soon as possible, and if that doesn't take it out, pretreat with white vinegar and—"

She stopped, sniffled, and suddenly we both laughed.

"Well," I said, "I can see my stain tips booklet isn't wasted on you." I'd finally written up my most asked-for stain tips in a little booklet I titled "Josie's Stain-Busters," which I took up to The Copy Shack in Masonville, where I'd had them copied and staple-bound with a green cardstock cover. I especially liked the line drawing, by one of my customer's teens, on the cover: a toad atop an overflowing laundry basket. The booklets had been a big hit.

Rhonda sniffled again, and this time halfheartedly flung socks into the washer. "I wish you had a booklet of tips about what to do about men. Men!"

Mrs. Oglevee's slide show of my romantic flops flashed through my head. Rhonda didn't really want my advice. But maybe she'd benefit from me lending a sympathetic ear. Eons ago, women had talked about such problems down by the river while pounding clothing with rocks, I reckoned. Super triple load washers had replaced rocks, but nothing could replace the need for every now and again bitch-n-moan sessions.

"I was at the Bar-None last night," I said gently. "Anything you need to talk about?"

Rhonda shrugged. "T-Bone and I have been having the same quarrel for the past six months. I want us to get hitched—legal paperwork and all. Dammit, we've been living together two years, and next year I'll be thirty!"

I resisted an eye roll at that; after all, I believed that age thirty was plenty young, and that a woman didn't need a man to feel affirmed.

But apparently Rhonda felt differently. She rubbed her eyes, smearing black eyeliner and mascara over her face. "But T-Bone says we're fine just the way we are, so why mess things up?" She sighed. "I guess it's like my mama keeps telling me—a man won't pay for what he gets for free."

Ugh. I'd never looked at marriage like that. But this was Rhonda's story—and her point of view—and right now she just needed someone to listen.

"So last night, right in the middle of dancing to 'Sugar Daddy'—you know, the big Mayfair hit from back when—"

I nodded.

"—well, I up and told him it was time to fish or cut bait. You know. Get hitched. Or I'd just move out of Happy Trails. And I told him I'd already checked out an apartment in Masonville. And I've got a new job up there anyway—nursing home aide," she said proudly—"and he got mad and told me not to try manipulating him with my feminine wiles.

"Well, I said this wasn't manipulation . . . it was an ultimatum"—Rhonda paused to look pleased with her own cleverness, and I reckoned she'd taken time to work out that line—"and then I walked off the dance floor and sat down at the bar. The only open stool was next to this guy—middle-aged, I'm guessing mid-forties, and he told me he was Terry Tuxworth Jr., like that name should mean something to me.

"So then he said he was the son of Terry Tuxworth, who

had been the Mayfair Sisters' manager, and that he'd heard of the sisters' benefit concert for their mom, and he was in town to convince them to do another recording, maybe a greatest hits and some of the songs Candace sings but doesn't record in her solo act. His dad's company had gone out of business, he said, but he was starting it up again. He even had on a polo shirt with his logo—'Tuxworth Recording'—and gave me a key chain with a fake, miniature iPod that also said 'Tuxworth Recording' on it.

"Well, that got my attention," Rhonda went on. "And then Terry—who was kinda good-looking in a slicked-up kinda way, you know what I mean?"

I nodded, to show that I knew what she meant by slicked up, not that I found that attractive.

"Anyway, Terry bought me a drink, and asked me to dance, and I admit, I kinda got a little, well, hoochie-mama in my moves, just trying to make T-Bone jealous, which musta worked, because T-Bone tried to break up our dance, and then Terry and T-Bone got in a quarrel, and T-Bone punched him out."

I lifted my eyebrows. That must have happened after I ran from the building. "You mean, out? As in unconscious?"

"Well, yeah. Although Terry came around pretty fast and said some wild stuff about nobody should mess with him because he was going to be the Mayfairs' new manager, and that would give him lots of money and power, but by then the sheriff guy—who was holding T-Bone back from killing Terry—had called in the cops, and they took T-Bone in for the night."

Rhonda sniffled again. She'd finally gotten to the bottom of her basket, which contained some of her lingerie. Not just regular bras and undies, but push-em-ups and thongs. And a black pleather bustier.

"Uh, you don't want to put that in the washer," I said, a little awkwardly. Sometimes my customers' dirty laundry makes me uncomfortable. Figuratively and literally.

Rhonda plucked it back out. "But I got whipped cream on it, see?" She started to hold the pleather bustier up. I glanced away. "So how do I get that out?"

"Windex," I said, my voice squeaking a little. "Just spray and wipe."

"Oh. OK."

I glanced back. The bustier was back in the basket, all by itself. I exhaled. "So, are you going to be all right?"

I glanced at the clock. Damn. By the time I rinsed the coffee stain out of my blouse, and ran back up to my apartment to change into a clean top, I'd be late for the introduction of the new director at Stillwater.

"Yeah." Rhonda sighed. "I reckon. But I don't know what I'm going to choose. Do I pick up T-Bone at the jail after I'm done here . . . or meet up with Terry? He said he'd show me a good time, if I'd meet him over at the Red Horse Motel this evening."

The Red Horse was the only motel in Paradise.

I arched an eyebrow at her. "There is another choice, you know."

Rhonda looked confused.

"What?"

"Ditch them both, move up to that Masonville apartment, follow your own dreams, and when a guy who's good enough for you shows up, you'll know it."

4

The reception for Stillwater Farms's new director, Levi Applegate, started at 10:00 a.m. By the time I got to Stillwater, it was 10:15 a.m.

I'd spent a little more time calming down Rhonda, even after Chip Beavy—grandson of Mrs. Beavy, matron of the Mason County Historical Society and Museum—arrived to keep watch at my laundromat. Chip is a student at Masonville Community College, and fills in for me—taking care of orders, greeting customers, and so on—pretty regularly.

Chip's a smart young man, almost done with his business associate's degree, and he wants to be a business manager. I had planned on asking him how school was going, but when I finished up with Rhoda, Chip didn't even give me a chance to say howdy. He launched into a reminder about how his grandmother really wanted to know what the Mayfairs planned to donate to the museum. By the time I put him at ease that I'd try to find out that afternoon, I was already running late.

Then I had to go back up to my apartment to soak my

coffee-stained blouse in a bucket of cold water, and to change. After that, I ran back down to my laundromat, finished checking Moira's handiwork on the dresses—which looked great—and loaded the remaining six Mayfair costumes in the back of my van.

And all that's why I got to Stillwater so late . . . which meant parking in the overflow gravel lot by the greenhouses, near the main road and out of sight from the main buildings.

Usually the very sight of the greenhouses makes me smile, because Guy seems most at peace when he's working in there, methodically planting seeds, or tending to them. Since it was nearing Memorial Day, his job was to tend to the melon seedlings. But all was quiet around the greenhouse at the moment. Soon, I knew, he and a few other residents would be in the greenhouse, tending to the precious plants under the careful supervision of one of their caretakers.

I hurried up the gravel path. As I rounded the curve, the main building popped into view. The building is a two-story farmhouse with the upstairs renovated into office space and a guest apartment, and the main floor into commercial-sized kitchen, meeting/dining hall, and reception area. I trotted up the porch steps and opened the front door, which squeaked, as usual.

Normally that made me smile, too, but I hate being late to anything, especially something this important, and so I unsmilingly hurried in—careful not to let the door bang, since I knew that would easily be heard in the dining room.

Wanda, the receptionist on duty, waved at me. I waggled my fingers at her.

"Glad to see you. Several people were wondering where you were," she said quietly. "One of those mornings?"

I nodded, and rushed over to the door to the dining hall, opened the door quietly, and stepped in.

The head of the search committee was in the last few sentences of her introduction of Levi Applegate, new director of Stillwater Farms. Enthusiastic applause ensued.

I glanced around for a chair—the room was packed—but then, for just a second, I was distracted by the tables on either side of the door, tables filled with muffins and pastries and coffee and tea and juice. My one slice of toast, even with juice and coffee, suddenly didn't seem like much of a breakfast. My hand started floating toward the table. Would it be really rude to grab a big, yummy-looking blueberry muffin now . . . when clearly the table was set up for after the introductions, speeches, and question-and-answer session?

But the applause faded and I looked up, and Levi Applegate strode to the podium.

And my mouth fell open.

Not so I could stuff an illicit muffin in it.

But because Levi Applegate, the new director, was the man I had run into, literally, at the Bar-None the night before.

He started to talk, then hesitated, seeing me at the back of the room—the only person standing, after all.

And then he smiled, amused, regathered his wits, and started speaking. "Thank you so much for your warm greeting," he started, predictably enough.

I snatched my hand back from the food table, turned, and hurried out of the room.

Thirty minutes later, I was twenty minutes into the rhythm of folding towels in Stillwater's spacious laundry room.

Of course, the housekeeping staff is in charge of laundering the home's linens and residents' clothing. Commercial-sized washers and dryers—two each—line one wall, and sorting bins and folding tables line the other. A shelf holds neatly organized supplies.

My aunt and uncle, Guy's parents, helped organize the laundry room years ago and volunteered from time to time to lighten housekeeping's load.

Since I inherited both their laundromat and Guy's guardianship, I've carried on the tradition. And there's a laminated list of my favorite stain tips on the inside of the laundry room door.

Margaret was on housekeeping duty today and had looked surprised when I barged into the laundry room.

"Hey, Josie," she'd said. "The new director's—"

"I know," I said. "No seats. It's all just predictable nicey-nice talk now anyway. Mind if I help for a while?"

She'd given me a long, curious look—I'm usually not so grouchy—and shrugged. "That's fine with me," she said.

I started folding towels.

After a few minutes of quietness, Margaret said, "Hey, Josie, I've noticed that my towels at home have lost their fluff. Any tips?"

"Sure," I said, happy to be on comfortable, familiar turf. "Truth be told, all towels eventually lose their fluff as the fibers wear out—you can't make any towel last forever. How long have you had yours?"

"Just six months! I got a good deal on them at the Dollar Days store, but maybe I wasted money by trying to save money," Margaret said, sounding despondent.

"I don't think that's the case," I said. "A more expensive towel isn't necessarily better. What matters is that the towels are cotton."

"These are," she said.

"Have you been using liquid fabric softener?"

"Yeah!" she said eagerly. "Extra, too!"

I smiled. "Ironically, that's your problem. Too much fabric softener will coat the towel's fibers and grease them down, and make the towel less absorbent. So, instead, wash on warm with minimum laundry detergent, and add some white vinegar during the rinse cycle. That should get out the extra fabric softener. If you're going to dry outside, make sure you fluff before you hang them out, and fluff again after by giving the towels a good shake before folding. But I think it's better to run through the dryer with a dryer sheet. And you can save money and get the same results by tearing the dryer sheet in half and just using half per dryer load. Oh, and don't overload your washer. That's not good for the washer or the towels."

"Wow," Margaret said admiringly. "You do know your household tips. No wonder I hear your Stain-Busters column is taking off."

I tensed, my good mood losing its edge. I knew just what was coming, because I'd been hearing it for a few months now.

"I reckon you'll be pulling up in a new sports car soon, or taking cruises!" Margaret said.

For some reason, people like to think my modest regional success as a household tips columnist means I'm getting rich. The fact I'd had my apartment renovated didn't help, but truth be told, I'd been saving income from my off-and-on renters for eleven years, ever since I moved into the apartment after inheriting the laundry business and building from my deceased aunt and uncle, who'd left them—and Guy's guardianship—to me. Of course, none of us expected I'd inherit all that at the tender age of eighteen.

But life has a way of throwing surprising curves.

The column was a happy curve, but since each column garners a mere ten bucks a pop, even in twenty-seven weekly newspapers, I'm not exactly getting rich, no matter what folks want to think.

Of course, folks also wanted to believe my newfound success meant I was perfectly happy. Well, I wasn't unhappy. But I had my lonely moments. And even though I was steadily working on a new list of goals I'd made over the past New Year's Eve weekend and my thirtieth birthday (which just happened to coincide), I also had my moments of doubts about the future.

But folks—no matter how many times they read in *People* magazine about some star's divorce or heartache or health issues—want to believe that the celebrity life is the perfect life.

It's a human trait. And annoying.

And meant I had to let Margaret down gently.

"No sports cars or cruises any time soon," I said. "My column is fun and earns a little extra money for me, but I'm not getting rich."

"Oh." Margaret sounded disappointed—and a little disbelieving. "Well, will you be OK finishing up here? There's plenty I need to do in the kitchen."

"I'm fine," I said.

Margaret left, and I went back to work, happy to be alone, happy to focus on my towel-folding task. Some folks might think that I'd get sick of laundry, and sometimes I do. But there's something about folding warm, clean towels in particular that's very comforting.

But twenty minutes later I was done.

And it was just 10:40.

The reception would still be going on. I could go back to that, I thought, half daring myself.

But somehow, I couldn't face Levi Applegate, even from afar.

How was it possible that the director whose ideas about working with adults with autism worried me could also be the man I'd literally run into—and felt an instantaneous, deep attraction to? Not just a sexual attraction. Well, yeah. That. But also something deeper. Something I hadn't felt before, not right off like that, not so easily and naturally.

Some—like maybe Mrs. Oglevee—might call it love at first sight.

But my practical nature didn't hold with such silly notions.

How could I feel that about a man I ran into outside a bar's bathrooms? It was too ridiculous.

And how could I feel that about a man whose ideas I questioned, especially when those ideas might have an impact on my beloved Guy? It was too . . . traitorous.

I looked at the clock: 10:42. No more towels. Too early to leave to show up at the Mayfairs'. No point in going back by my laundromat.

On the other hand . . . I knew Guy and the other residents had already been in the greenhouse for two whole minutes. I could go see Guy . . .

I weighed my options.

I stuck as closely as possible to a routine for my visits with Guy, as that seemed to be the least unsettling to him. My regular visiting times were Sunday afternoons. I left right from services at the Paradise Methodist Church, and had lunch with Guy, then spent an hour or so with him after that.

Somehow, I thought he knew just when I was supposed to come, although I wasn't sure how he'd know. Guy can't tell time or follow a calendar. Every now and then I thought maybe I was just projecting that on him; that I wanted to believe he understood when I was supposed to come visit, and that he'd miss me if I didn't. In any case, it always seemed to me that he was uneasy if I came at other times, unless it was while he was preoccupied in the greenhouse. But again, maybe I was just projecting.

I shook my head at myself. Enough already. I patted the stack of neatly folded clean towels. Just five months ago, I'd turned thirty and made a list of goals, and discovered a new-found sense of confidence in my life.

I wasn't going to let some silly emotions over a new director I didn't know, and a silly dream featuring lectures from my long-gone junior high teacher, make me start second-guessing myself.

Guy didn't seem to really notice me as I worked across the table from him in the greenhouse, but I knew that he knew I was there. Guy rarely speaks, and when he does it's in short bursts, a strident tone, and usually he repeats what he's already said, only backward.

So when he saw me enter the greenhouse, he'd hollered, "Josie hi! Hi Josie!" and I'd smiled. When I was a kid, and Aunt Clara and Uncle Horace were still trying to care for Guy on their own, I found Guy's reverse repetition amusing. I'd try to get him to say longer sentences, just to see how many words he could say backward, and ended up distressing him.

Aunt Clara and Uncle Horace had the sense to realize that, as a young kid, I didn't know any better, and had gently corrected my behavior. But I still felt guilty about it from time to time, twenty-plus years later. And the memory made me understand why my aunt and uncle had always been so protective of Guy, who is eighteen years older than me, until they realized for his own safety he needed to be in a good residential home.

Stillwater Farms was—and is—a blessing.

Becky, one of the residents' caretakers, had quietly been watering the peat pots after Guy finished carefully planting each one: sifting in a blend of potting soil and peat, placing three melon seeds in the pot, and then sifting on more potting soil. Someone besides Guy had to do the watering, because he'd get so fascinated with watching the trickle of water come out that he wouldn't stop pouring, and soon there'd be a dirty mess and ruined seeds. Yet this was only true when he was planting the seeds. Once the seedlings sprouted, Guy handled the watering just fine.

It didn't make any sense to me or to anyone else, just like Guy's distress at too much of the color red didn't make sense to anyone but Guy.

Becky let me quietly take over the watering job. I watched Guy place the seeds: three to a pot, placed in a perfect cloverleaf design. And I'd be willing to bet that if we measured, he'd put exactly the same amount of soil in each pot.

He seemed to be ignoring me while we worked, humming in a monotone as he methodically placed the seeds and soil, rocking slightly back and forth on his feet. I watched Guy, feeling as always a surge of protection and love toward him. It didn't matter that, if you looked past the rocking and humming and the somewhat frozen look to his expression and gaze, he looked just like an ordinary middle-aged man— now forty-eight, with a beefy build but pretty fit—thanks to the exercise routines Stillwater staff customized to each individual's needs and abilities--balding, a little pale.

Guy also has diabetes type 2, diagnosed just the previous fall, and it had taken a while to adjust to caring for that disease, as it meant changes in his eating habits and getting used to taking a daily pill—something that might not be a big deal to most people, but that was traumatic at first to Guy.

Of course, if I gazed too long and fell behind in watering the peat pots, Guy got distressed, so I tried to make sure I worked just as methodically as he did. It was always a challenge for me to try to fit into his world, his mode of doing things, and that gave me, I thought, a little glimpse of how alien the "normal" world must seem to adults with autism.

Too soon, though, we finished up. Becky and another caretaker and I helped Guy and the other residents wash up after their duties were complete. I gave Guy a very quick pseudo-hug—just the palms of my hands quickly pressing on the sides of his arms—which he tolerated without fuss. Then he and the others filed out behind Becky.

I walked out last, pausing at the exit to gaze at all the lovely trays of plants—some already seedlings, and some just planted, looking like nothing more than little pots of dirt. I smiled at the sweet little secret those pots held, that soon they'd sprout seedlings. Soon, too, Guy's task would be to thin out the smallest seedlings, leaving the strongest one in each pot. I'd always hated that task as a kid, but it never bothered Guy, and that, in turn, had bothered me. But by now, I'd learned to accept the differences between adults without autism and adults with, and know that adults with autism couldn't really be categorized any more than adults without it.

I glanced at my watch. Enough philosophizing. If I left now, I'd get to the Mayfairs on time, and finally have my day back on track.

Except . . . I stepped out of the greenhouse and right into Levi Applegate.

* * *

Levi suppressed a howl and hopped back on one foot. I'd managed to come down, hard, on top of his right foot, squishing his instep.

"Uh, sorry," I said.

"That's OK," he said, wincing.

"Really?" I asked, arching an eyebrow. "You like having your instep stomped on?"

OK, I admit it. I was being snotty. Bitchy, even. But truth be told, I was hoping that would serve as an antidote to the fact my heart was going double-time, and not just because of the shock of literally running into this man. Again.

Levi looked a little weary, and I felt an immediate sympathy for him. Dammit.

But he wasn't weary enough to let my sarcasm slide by. He arched an eyebrow, too. "No, actually. I really hate having my instep stomped on. Brings back too many bad memories of Miss Elaine's."

My other eyebrow went up. "What? Or . . . who?"

"Miss Elaine's School of Ballroom Dancing. My mother had a theory that every young person should know how to dance. So, when I was a junior in high school, she made me take classes."

I fought back a giggle. Levi was tall and broad-shouldered. He didn't exactly look like a ballroom-dancing kind of guy. More like, I thought, a linebacker.

"And your dance partners were terrible and kept stomping on your feet?"

"No," Levi said. "I was terrible, and kept making them stumble so they couldn't help but stomp on my feet. Plus the other guys on the football team made fun of me mercilessly." He laughed, obviously not traumatized by the memory.

I gulped. "Did you happen to play linebacker?"

Levi gave me a long look. "Well, yeah. OK, I think I've recovered enough to go on into the greenhouse."

For a long moment we stood, staring at each other, until I realized he was politely waiting for me to move out of his way. Embarrassment caused me to blush, which was itself embarrassing, which made me blush even more.

I looked down, stepped widely around him, and mumbled, "Uh, yeah, enjoy looking around."

I started down the gravel path back toward my van, but then Levi called after me. "Hey, maybe you can show me around in here. I don't have much of a green thumb."

I stopped. *Say no, say no, say no,* I told myself. *Be responsible. Get to the Mayfairs' home on time . . .*

"Sure. I'd love to," I said.

Levi grinned and held out his hand. "Thanks! I'm Levi Applegate, the new director here. We keep running into each other but we haven't been formally introduced."

I shook his hand. Funny. He was right; we hadn't formally met, and yet I felt like I already knew him. "I'm Josie Toadfern," I said. "I'm Guy Foersthoefel's caretaker. He's my cousin, but he's really like my brother."

Levi nodded. It was a relief to not have to qualify my statement with "emotionally" or "spiritually." Levi just . . . understood what I meant about Guy really being like my brother.

And fifteen minutes later, I'd run out of things to say about the greenhouse, and its role in Guy's and other residents' lives, and so there we stood, right by the table where I'd watered the melon seeds as Guy had planted them.

"If you want to know more, you'll have to ask Becky," I said. "She's the real expert." I paused. So why hadn't he asked her to begin with?

Levi smiled. "Maybe I will. But to tell you the truth, I just wanted to talk with you a little bit. Wanda told me I might find you here."

"You wanted to find . . . me?"

"Yes. I've heard a lot about Josie Toadfern . . . and been informed that if I'm smart, I should get to know your views about Stillwater," Levi said. "And I like to think I'm at least somewhat smart."

I was complimented that the folks at Stillwater had said such nice things about me, but I was also a bit annoyed with Levi. "Why didn't you just say that instead of listening to me go on about plant pots for fifteen minutes?"

"I've discovered you can learn a lot about a person by sometimes just observing them, and listening," Levi said. "And it's clear that what everyone says is true—this place matters a great deal to you." He gestured widely, and I knew his motion was meant to indicate more than just the greenhouse.

"Yes," I said. "It does. And I understand that you have ideas that are somewhat . . . different . . . than my own about autism, but there are just certain aspects of Stillwater that are just too important to . . . to . . ." I paused. He waited, patiently, not interrupting. Dammit. That was just so appealing and likable, his not interrupting. I hesitated longer, giving him every opportunity to jump in and finish my sentence for me—a real pet peeve of mine. Finally, I finished, lamely, ". . . to change."

Levi smiled. "I'm not exactly planning on tearing down the greenhouse tomorrow, Josie," he said. "But since you could only stay a moment for my introduction—"

"I had to go help in the laundry room," I said lamely, and blushing even more furiously at acting out my own pet peeve.

"And that was nice of you," Levi said. "Anyway. I was hoping we could get together for dinner this evening. You're a very involved caretaker, and you've also done a lot of volunteering to help generate community support for Stillwater, so I'd like a chance to talk about our ideas. Both the ones we share, and the ones that might diverge."

He gazed at me, waiting for my answer.

And truth be told, I was more than happy not to answer. Getting lost in his dark brown eyes was pleasant enough. I could do that for quite a while.

But then I heard the door start to swing open.

"Sure," I said. "That would be fine."

"I could pick you up, or would you prefer to meet? I understand you live in Paradise and own the laundromat there—"

"Toadfern's, on Main Street," I said, interrupting again, and making it sound as if there might be more than one laundromat in a town of three thousand. Or like he might not be able to figure out which business I owned . . . even though its name was my last name.

Levi smiled. "Right. Anyway, I'm staying at the Red Horse Motel, so I'd be glad to pick you up, or—"

The greenhouse door swung open. "Oh!" Becky exclaimed.

Levi shuffled back a little, away from me. I hadn't, until then, realized how closely we'd been standing. A little late, I shuffled back, too.

"That would be fine," I said stiffly, and started toward the greenhouse door.

"Josie?" Levi called.

I turned. He looked even more bemused. Now what?

"Six-thirty OK? And we'll go to the Spring Mill Inn?"

Oh, Lord, I thought. The Spring Mill Inn was the fanciest

place in the area, an old mill and tavern that had been converted to a fancy restaurant, just north of Masonville. Levi had done his local attractions homework . . . and come up with the nicest date place possible.

But this wasn't a date, I told myself. It was just . . . a business dinner.

"That would be a perfect setting for a discussion of my concerns about Stillwater's future," I said stiffly. I glanced at Becky as I started again out the greenhouse door. "Business dinner," I said to her.

"Of course," she said.

I hurried out a little too fast, and the greenhouse door slammed shut behind me, making me jump.

5

Not a date, not a date, not a date, I told myself all the way back to Paradise, focusing on the drive and ignoring the countryside rolling by. Normally I took pleasure in the farmhouses and rolling fields, which at this time of year were just sprouting with soybeans and cornfields. "Knee high by the Fourth of July" was the traditional saying about corn, but with fertilizers, the truth was the corn would be more like head high by the time Paradisites would be gearing up for the annual Founder's Day Fourth of July parade, pie-eating contest, and fireworks.

Not a date, not a date . . . just business . . . that was my mantra as I slowed from sixty to twenty-five miles per hour upon rolling into Paradise, down Main Street. Just past my laundromat, I turned right on Third Street, and then right again on Plum Street, and then parked along the curb at number 47, behind a purple sports car that was not, I knew, the possession of anyone in Paradise. Another car, a red convertible, was parked behind it, and sported the somewhat snarky vanity plate: BYEBYEU.

Just business, just business, just business . . . I was *not* going out on a date that night with Levi Applegate. We were just going to talk about Stillwater Farms . . .

What should I wear?

I shook my head at the question. *Business, remember?* I chided myself.

And it was time to focus on Mayfair business. I glanced at my watch, a nifty Timex I'd picked up at a yard sale just a few houses down from the Mayfairs, four years before, and yes, "it had taken a licking and kept on ticking." The elderly man, Mr. Kansterfeld, who'd sold me the watch for a buck, had been delighted to keep repeating the advertising slogan, especially when I looked perplexed the first time he chanted it, and found out I'd never heard the saying because it had outlived its popularity by the time I was a kid. Then he'd gotten sentimental about the watch, since it had been his wife's, and she'd passed away six months before, and he was selling everything to move to an apartment in Cleveland near his son and his family. A nice family had moved into the old Kansterfeld place and made it their own.

Anyway, my Timex told me I was a half hour late. Still, I paused, staring at the Mayfair house. It was a simple 1940s-era Cape Cod–style house, like all the other homes on Plum Street, with red brick and a small front porch with just enough room for one or two people to knock on the front door, encased in a charming stone arch. I'd been in enough such homes to know the layout: Dormered windows on the top half story meant a huge open space that could be used as two bedrooms, one on either side of the stairs, which would commence right at the entry.

A big picture window meant the living room was at the front of the house, with a small kitchen—not big enough to eat in—and a dining room with fireplace at the back. Arched entryways—no doors—divided the rooms.

A single-car garage had been added to the east of the house, probably in the early fifties, and sometime after that, a breezeway connected the garage to the house and the side entry to the kitchen. And then, sometime after that, probably as the Mayfair Sisters were getting started on their musical careers, the breezeway had been enclosed to make a sitting room. It was a pattern repeated up and down Plum Street.

There was nothing to distinguish the Mayfair house from all the rest, except, of course, the three little girls who had grown up in it had gone on to fame and fortune, at least by Paradise standards. And of course, time had moved on for the occupants, just as it had for Mr. Kansterfeld, and soon other owners—a nice family, I hoped—would move in to the Mayfair house and make history of their own, although probably not as publicly as the Mayfair Sisters.

I tried to recollect what I really knew about them.

They'd had several lighthearted hits in the early sixties while still young. In fact, if I remembered what Caleb had recently written up for the *Paradise Advertiser-Gazette*— cobbled together from public records information since he hadn't succeeded in getting an exclusive interview— Candace, the youngest one, whom I'd just heard singing to her mother, was only sixteen when they made their first recording. The older sisters were eighteen and nineteen. They'd launched their careers with Terry Tuxworth, a buddy of Bob Mayfair, the sisters' dad. Bob and Terry had been army buddies. Bob returned to Paradise after his tour of duty ended, to start a family with his young wife, Dora— they'd married right before he left on his tour—and to work at the granite quarry on the other side of the county.

Terry had returned to Nashville to work in a recording

company, and then launch his own small one-man recording studio, mostly charging people to make vanity records. Bob and Terry stayed in touch and, so the story goes, when Bob died young from a heart attack, Terry came to Paradise for the funeral. By then, the Mayfair sisters were already known in the region as wonderful singers, and sang at churches and revival meetings.

And they even sang at their daddy's funeral. It was during his funeral service that Terry—who'd been getting by with recording minor artists and pay-to-record services—heard for the first time the Mayfair sisters sing "How Great Thou Art" and "Precious Memories" and "Just As I Am."

Shortly after that, with their mother, Dora, acting as their agent, the Mayfair sisters became the Mayfair Sisters and signed a contract with Terry Tuxworth's tiny label, Fleece Records. Dora, who was originally from North Carolina and had moved to Paradise with her family when she was in high school, had made a name for herself as a singer in the school chorus, but had quit singing after Bob went off to war. Still, she'd taught her daughters how to sing.

Terry never bothered with vanity recordings after that, and never signed any other acts, but the Mayfair Sisters went on to fame and fortune, at least until 1969 or so, when their style of music was no longer in vogue, and the Mayfair Sisters became, again, just the Mayfair sisters. By then they'd all married and moved to different towns across the country. Their mama, Dora, stayed in Paradise, still living life modestly, faithfully attending Fellowship Baptist Church, and telling anyone who asked that her daughters were all doing fine, just fine, thank you.

But in the past few years, Dora started being anything but just fine, thank you.

I sighed, getting my pity out of the way. Candace, I knew

from my few visits here, didn't want pity for her or her mother. Her view was that her mother's condition was sad, but since it couldn't be changed, what was most important was making her as safe and comfortable as possible in her remaining time on earth.

It was a view I respected.

My mental meanderings had taken only a few minutes, but still, I was hungry for lunch and eager to get back to my laundromat—at which point I'd start thinking again about dinner with Levi . . . a business dinner, not a date, I reminded myself—so I hurried up the tiny walk that cut through the front lawn to the porch, and knocked on the door, all ready to apologize to Candace for being so late.

But Candace didn't answer the door. For a second I was taken aback; the woman at the door looked like a twenty-some-years-before version of Dora Mayfair, with thick, black, wavy hair, a stocky build, a sharply hooked nose, and even sharper gray eyes.

Then I realized of course this couldn't be some time-warp version of Dora, now a white-haired woman whose muscle and fat had all dissolved, leaving sagging skin on bone, as if she were a doll who'd lost her stuffing, eyes by turns vacant and fearful, currently and forevermore abed in one of the home's dormer bedrooms. I'd just been momentarily confused, because this woman was a come-to-life version of a photo of Dora I'd seen among the cluster of photos hanging over the living room couch. In that photo, though, Dora had looked vibrant in a lovely teal suit, on the afternoon of her youngest daughter Candace's second wedding.

I thought about the photo—which included Candace and her two older sisters, Constance and Cornelia, and mentally aged the sisters. I knew this wasn't Candace—I'd met her several times, and she was petite and ethereal-looking, her lovely silver hair pulled back in a chignon. I decided it was Cornelia . . . the oldest sister, and the one whom I'd mentally tagged just the night before as singing for money.

"Hi," I said. "I'm Josie Toadfern. I don't believe we've met, but—"

"Yeah, yeah, you're the local stain expert who's been working with Candace on getting our old costumes together. She's mentioned you," Cornelia said. "Several times," she added, as if I'd been an incredibly dull topic of conversation too many times, like, say, variations of bread mold.

"OK," I said, "well, I have the final batch of your costumes."

Cornelia didn't shuffle back an inch. She seemed determined to keep me out of the house. "I thought they were all done? The auction is this coming weekend."

"Yes, but these last pieces needed the seamstress—Moira Evans . . . you know her, right? She lives just down the street, on the other side of the Kansterfeld house—well, of course, the Kansterfelds don't live there now. That house was bought by a young couple—Reggie and Sonya Ritter—and they have a little girl, Anna, who's six, and a little boy who's—"

Cornelia sighed so vehemently I stopped. "I don't need the whole history of how this rinky-dink little neighborhood's houses have turned over," she said.

Well. I knew the Ritters because they came to my laundromat on weekends, and I'd reckoned that Cornelia would take some comfort in knowing the life was renewing itself on her childhood home's street, and would do so eventually in her mother's home. But her next words jolted me back to the reality that not everyone felt so tenderly toward Paradise.

"I left this damned nowhere fork in the road forty years ago and hated every visit back home. Just bring in the damned costumes and—"

Before she could finish, we were both startled by angry voices surging into the living room behind Cornelia. The heated discussion tumbled right past us and out onto the tiny front lawn so anyone ambling past 47 Plum Street could have clearly heard it.

FIRST MALE: "We'll see you in court! You've ruined my wife's and Cornelia's careers long enough—"

SECOND MALE (laughing): "You can't touch me! They were full legal adults when they signed—"

FEMALE: "Please, both of you—"

Cornelia turned and screamed, "Shut up!" There was a brief silence, followed by a loud moan, and then over top of that, yet another voice, this one sweetly rising, singing a song I'd heard her sing before, a song she'd told me her mother had written about missing her native state of North Carolina: *Carolina, I hear you calling, but I can't answer, for I've gone a long way away, I knew you only for a moment, but my heart has never strayed . . .*

But the youngest sister, Candace, sang for love . . .

This was, Candace had told me, the only song her mother had ever written, even though Dora had wanted to be a songwriter as a young woman. Now Candace sang the song as a soothing lullaby. To me it was a mournful song, but it seemed to calm Dora.

On previous trips to pick up and drop off costumes, I'd heard her singing before to soothe her mother. Candace's voice was like her, a little ethereal. With today's pop music moving toward belting out a tune with complex backup, lots of folks might find her unaccompanied singing too simple, too airy. But I found her voice haunting and enchanting and soothing.

Dora Mayfair stopped moaning, so I reckoned she found it soothing, too.

"Who's that at the door?" The female voice was both weary and demanding.

"Josie Toadfern," Cornelia said.

"Who?"

"The woman who Candace hired to work on our costumes."

I shifted from one foot to the other. Nothing is much more awkward than listening to yourself being discussed.

"Oh, right, well, have her come in instead of standing there with the door open so the whole world can hear Candace bellowing at our mother!"

Bellowing? I was incredulous. Candace's voice was faint and distant . . . and haunting.

Cornelia looked at me with a rueful smile. "My sister has invited you in," she said. She finally stepped back, opening the door further.

"Um, maybe I should just go get the dresses . . ." I started.

But by then, Candace had stopped singing and come down the stairs. She appeared on the other side of Cornelia.

Candace looked weary, her petite shoulders slumping under a pale blue cotton blouse that was too big on her tiny frame, and that—combined with her silver hair—made her look washed out.

"Mama's finally settled down, if we can all just be quieter," she said, only the barest hint of tension in her voice. Then she smiled at me. "Josie! Come on in."

"Gee, that's two sisters who want you to come in," Cornelia said, "but I agree with Josie. She should just get the dresses . . ."

"Oh, that can wait," Candace said. She smiled at me. "I want to talk with you about the mangle."

That hooked me.

I was in the Mayfair house in a flash.

6

Another flash later, and I was uncomfortably ruing my decision.

I sat on an upholstered armchair that had probably been blue and comfortable when it was new decades before, but was now grayish and lumpy, its inner coils poking me in the butt. The mahogany framing to the chair, though, was still quite beautiful. I wondered if the chair would be part of the auction, and doubted it. The chair could have a new life with some attention from an upholsterer, but that would be expensive, and most people wouldn't take the time. Probably, after the auction was over, the chair would be dumped on the curb for junk pickup . . .

"I wanted all of you to meet Josie," Candace was saying, drawing me away from my attempt at self-distraction.

I looked up at Candace in the other chair, her sisters and one man on the couch, and another man standing behind the couch.

"I think you've met Cornelia," she said. Cornelia glared at me.

I gave a quick, small smile.

"And this is Connie," Candace said, gesturing to the tall, skinny woman with the ash blond hair.

The three sisters were as different in looks as they were in temperament.

Whereas Candace was happily ethereal, and Cornelia's anger was not, I suspected, momentary, Connie had a look of resigned depression.

She sighed heavily. "Please, Candace. I want to go back to being called Constance," she said with a dreariness that implied she held no real hope that anyone would remember.

"My dad always told me how the girls didn't want to use their pet names on stage," said the man standing behind the couch, snickering nastily. He had thinning brown hair, and big glasses that were, literally, rose-tinted. But they didn't disguise the shiner on his left eye. That wasn't my only clue that he was Terry Tuxworth Jr.; he also was wearing a white polo shirt with the words "Tuxworth Recording" embroidered on the left front. A different one, I hoped, from the one he'd been wearing the night before.

I guessed that Terry was wearing prescription sunglasses. His regular glasses must have been busted in his brawl with T-Bone. Given T-Bone's size and usual ruthlessness, I was kind of surprised Terry was able to stand.

Cornelia turned red and scowled.

Ah, I thought. Candy and Connie were fine pet names, but Corny . . .

"And this is Terry Tuxworth Jr.," Candace said, as if there were no tension in the room. "He's the son of—"

"—of the jerk who Mama sold our souls to!" Cornelia exclaimed and jumped up, and started pacing in the tiny space next to the couch. Most of the floor space was filled with boxes marked with phrases like "Christmas China" and "Good Linens."

"Now, Cornelia," Constance said. "We don't need to go airing our dirty laundry in front of our guest."

I edged forward on my chair, about to quip that I really needed to go help my customers with their literal dirty laundry, and that I really should just drop off the costumes and maybe talk about the mangle another time, but I didn't get the chance.

"Oh really?" said the man on the couch. "I think the whole world should know that this fink"—he gestured at Terry—"is trying to hold all of you to the ridiculous contract your mother had you sign!"

Candace sighed, looking, for the first time, irked. I'd seen her several times, and had always been amazed that caring for her mother in such difficult circumstances didn't seem to wear on her. Being around the rest of her family, on the other hand, appeared to be tiring her out. Her eyes looked hollow and dark.

"This is Roger, Constance's husband. He's upset because Terry believes that if we record this concert—as we're planning to do—that his new company legally should get a cut of the profits."

Terry looked at me. "Years ago, Mrs. Mayfair signed a contract on Candace's behalf, because she was underage, and had Constance and Cornelia also sign the contract that my father offered them. They knew what they were doing."

I was confused. They were fighting over the fairness of a forty-plus-year-old contract?

Roger interpreted my expression correctly. "It's not an old contract my wife and her sisters are upset about." I glanced at Candace. She didn't seem upset about that, I thought. She was focused on her mother. "It's a current contract—because the language in the contract they signed years ago says that Fleece Records—which went out of business—"

"No! It just went on hiatus for a while," Terry said. "I inherited it from my father, and I brought it back as Tuxworth Recording!"

"About two months ago," Cornelia said angrily, "when you found out we were doing this benefit concert for our mother!"

"Anyway," Roger said, extending the three syllables in a tone that fully expressed his opinion of all this bickering, "the original contract assigned all rights, forever, to Fleece Records or any of its holdings and concerns—"

"That would be Tuxworth Recording!" Terry exclaimed.

Roger ignored him and went on. "—of the Mayfair Sisters' works. 'In perpetuity' is, I believe, the exact phrase. However, this recording is not-for-profit to help Dora . . ."

"Except the recording will help get the Mayfair Sisters' names back in the mainstream!" Terry glanced around the room, with a look of contempt. "Why, just the publicity from the concert and auction alone is already doing that!"

I looked first at Terry. Was he really begrudging the Mayfair Sisters' efforts to help their mother, if he couldn't somehow get a piece of the action?

Then I looked at Candace. She'd been singing her own folk ballads, and doing a recording every two years or so, and selling to her fans under her own label via her Web site.

She smiled at me. "The contract didn't say anything about each of us individually recording."

"Not that she's making more than a few pennies," Terry said, snorting.

Candace shrugged. "True. But that's not why I'm doing it."

The youngest sister, Candace, sang for love . . .

Constance thumped her fists against her thighs. "Well, I'll admit it! I want to start again as a solo act! And I'm all for anything—even this auction—if it will help me get noticed again." She started crying, putting her face to her hands. "I should have done it long ago. If she can do it, I can."

Roger put his arm around his wife and looked embarrassed. "Now, honey . . ."

Oh, for pity's sake, I thought. *The middle sister, Constance, sang for fame.* Even when her mother was so ill in the final stages of her life, fame was what Constance was after. But the truth was, Candace had always been the strong, lead singer, and Constance and Cornelia had been backup. Cornelia had sung lead on a few of the Mayfair Sisters' songs, and done all right. But Constance . . . she had only sung lead on one of the group's songs, and that song was considered the group' weakest.

Constance would be better off singing backup, in a group.

"Couldn't you just change your act's name if you want to record as a group again?" I asked.

Terry scowled at me. "You think these gals have enough talent to start over under a new name? Besides, the contract is for them singing as a group—under any name. And the only way any of them could make it is playing on nostalgia for groups of their kind—nostalgia that's on the rise right now, and that won't last long, so we all ought to cash in while we can. My father had enough foresight to put language in the contract to prevent that kind of dishonesty."

"Dishonesty!" The word fairly exploded from Cornelia's tightly pursed lips. "You have the nerve to talk about dishonesty? Your family lived high on the hog off of our recordings . . . eighty percent . . . in perpetuity!"

My eyebrows went up at that. I recalled the purple sports

car parked in front of the house. The car was probably Terry's. Even if his father hadn't recorded any other groups, if he really took 80 percent of the Mayfair Sisters' earnings, and invested it wisely, then there was no reason that he—and his descendants—wouldn't be living well.

But now, apparently, Terry Jr. wanted more . . . and wanted to cash in on this concert.

Then I thought about that number—80 percent. It was hard to believe anyone—even a simple woman like Dora Mayfair—would have agreed to that kind of deal.

Especially with a company called Fleece Records.

Even if that company was owned by her deceased husband's old army buddy. Even if she was a desperate widow, with three talented daughters.

I wondered what I wasn't hearing about that deal. About what, perhaps, even the Mayfair sisters didn't know.

Cornelia jumped up and started pacing around the boxes. "No way! If we get back together as a group, then it won't be with Tuxworth Recording. I still say we can go to an entertainment rights attorney and make a case in court that since Candace was underage, the contract was never fair for any of us. Then use this concert"—she gestured at the boxes in the room—"to relaunch our act—a nostalgia tour! Maybe even a Broadway show!—to get the money we deserved all along." She stopped right by Terry, and poked him in the shoulder. "In fact, I think we could make a case that your company owes us repayment!"

The oldest Mayfair sister, Cornelia, sang for money.

Terry went pale.

Constance looked up, smoothed her hair, and sniffled. "And think of all the press we'd get if we sued Terry! Why, we could be in *People* and *Entertainment Weekly* and on *Entertainment Tonight* . . ."

Fame . . .

"That's the spirit, honey," Roger said.

Constance grabbed something off an end table, held it to her mouth, and breathed in. An inhaler.

Roger looked worried. "You OK, honey?" Constance ignored him and put the inhaler back on the end table. Roger looked at me. "Stress," he said, "makes her asthma worse."

Terry thumped the back of the couch, causing Roger and Constance to jump. "No way," he said through gritted teeth. "That contract is legal and binding. And—" He stopped, suddenly smiling. "There are plenty of reasons you don't want to take this to court because believe me, you'd get some notoriety you don't want. I'd say ask your mother about that, but even if she still had her wits about her . . ."

I gasped.

Candace jumped up. "Leave," she said quietly, but in a tone that had greater force than any degree of shouting. "Leave this house, and do not come back."

Terry had the good sense to start shuffling toward the door. "Fine. But I'll be back for the auction. And no one is going to outbid me on your memorabilia or this house. And I'll turn this place into a museum that will draw tourists from all over the country, and make even more money!"

I gasped again as Terry moved toward the door. I wasn't sure just how much money he thought he'd make from a museum, but I knew that lots of people wouldn't like his plan. This auction was disrupting our sleepy little lifestyle in Paradise enough as it was.

Plus I knew that the Mason County Historical Museum was counting on a few donations from the Mayfair Sisters to set up a permanent display—and the twenty or so folks heavily involved in the museum wouldn't like that competition.

Terry paused at the front door. "Think about what I've

said. You really want a comeback act, it'll be through me. I'll even be willing to renegotiate the percentages we split." He let the front door slam as he left.

"Maybe we should talk with him," Constance said.

Cornelia sank back down on the couch. "Yeah, maybe if we split fifty–fifty . . ."

"No!" Candace's voice was sharp, at least for her. "I agreed to a reunion of our group just for Mama's sake, to help raise money for her. I am happy with the singing I'm doing—and the way my life's gone."

She looked at me. "I'm sorry you had to witness this whole conversation," she said. "I really just wanted to introduce you to everyone and make sure it was fine with my sisters if we gave you the mangle as a thank-you token for your work on our costumes."

I gaped at Candace. "But . . . you've already paid me for the work, and—" I stopped, stunned by Candace's generosity. She knew I'd fallen in love with the ironing machine—an Ironrite model 95. The Ironrite brand was the most popular ironing machine in the 1940s and 1950s, a machine the size of a large sewing machine or washer, at which the user would sit and feed through clothes or tablecloths or fabric to prep for sewing or other linens, and let the two rollers iron the fabric.

The idea, in the 1950s, was that the machine would save women time . . . to spend, of course, on other tasks to make their home lives even cheerier.

Since I'd been toying with a book on laundry history, I'd come across the Ironrite and all manner of information about ironing history, and then when I took on the Mayfair costume repair job, I'd seen the old Ironrite in the Mayfairs' basement, during my first meeting with Candace about cleaning and repairing the costumes.

She'd been surprised that I knew what it was and said it had been her mother's pride and joy for years . . . until synthetic, permanent-press fabrics made ironing far less necessary, and women's lib did away with the idea of household tasks as the only way women could find fulfillment.

Now most people had no idea that ironing machines like that have ever existed, or that they'd been nicknamed mangles as a reference to devices used once upon a time to remove excess water from clothes, with a similar technique . . . a kind of pejorative term for the ironers used by people who were nervous about the possibility of getting hurt using the machines, or who were just plain jealous they couldn't afford one. Ironrites were the big-screen HDTVs of their day.

Anyway, Dora Mayfair's mangle was in perfect condition—and even came with the matching "health" chair. (Supposedly it promoted health by encouraging good posture.) And I'd admitted to Candace that I'd be bidding on it at the upcoming auction.

"That old hunk of metal?" Cornelia asked.

"Oh, I'd forgotten it was down there," Constance said.

"Sure, it's fine with me if Josie has it," Cornelia said. "The real money draw will be the costumes."

"Um, about those . . ." I said. "Mrs. Beavy, from the Mason County Historical Society, wondered if you had decided about which items you might want to donate for the display . . ."

"Oh yes!" Constance said. "We've boxed up some costumes, photos, and other memorabilia."

I was relieved.

"Of course," Cornelia said bitterly, "we won't get paid for any of those items."

"But the display will be a permanent tribute to our fame," Constance said.

Candace sighed. "OK. Roger, you'll help Josie get the museum box out to her van—and the Ironrite?"

"Sure," he said.

I looked at Candace. "Thank you so much! I can't tell you how . . . I'm just so excited about the Ironrite . . . I have the perfect spot for it in my back room, and I'll use it for table-cloths and other linens my customers bring in . . . plus it's such an exciting piece of history . . ."

I stopped. Cornelia's and Constance's expressions showed they were starting to have second thoughts about letting me take off with the mangle.

But Candace smiled kindly. "I also found some of Iron-rite's promotional items. Turns out Mama had the paper-weight and the salt and pepper shakers."

I'd read about the company's promotional items—and how some women in the forties and fifties loved to get them, even if they couldn't afford the Ironrite itself—which in to-day's dollars would cost about three grand.

I already knew I'd love to have the whole collection, but I said, "Candace, I'd love to look at them, but I really don't think I can take that much from you, since you've already paid me for the costumes."

"Come on, Josie," she said. "Let's take a look. Roger, you come with us and help us pack up whatever Josie wants."

"OK," I said. "I'll take a quick look. And then I'll get the final batch of costumes from my van."

Twenty minutes later, I sat down on the rear bumper of my van and stared down Plum Street. I couldn't bring myself to open the van, pull out the costume bag, and go back into the Mayfair House of Emotional Horrors just yet, as if nothing had happened, as excited as I was about the museum dona-tion and the generous gift of the Ironrite, the chair, and the promotional items. Roger had been quiet while we were in the basement, and when we came back up, Cornelia and Constance were no longer in the living room.

Still, I needed to regather my wits before returning, so I gazed down the street, focusing on the once-Kansterfeld-now-Ritter house. The Ritter boy—who is three and named Joe, as I was about to tell Cornelia before she cut me off— rode his tricycle up and down the tiny driveway, while his mama trimmed the shrubs below her home's picture window into neat little boxes. She looked up every few clips to make sure Joe hadn't wandered from the driveway to the street.

Then the door to the house across from them opened. It was Moira Evans's house. A young man slammed the door and hollered back at the house in a half-sob/half-scream, "I said I'd pay you back! I don't know why you won't believe me! I need that money!"

Clint Evans, I surmised, Moira's grandson.

He got on his motorcycle and roared off.

By then, Joe Ritter had ridden his tricycle closer to his mama. They stared after Clint for a moment, before Joe went happily back to riding up and down the driveway, and his mother shook her head before getting back to her gardening. Her head shake seemed to say, *Here we go again*.

I felt badly for Moira. She wasn't particularly likable—she was usually surly and gruff—but I figured that had as much to do with her back pain as anything else, as well as trying to help a grandson who apparently was quite a handful.

I thought about checking on her, and then changed my mind. She'd just be embarrassed to know what I'd witnessed.

The whole scenario made me sad—as did the scene inside the Mayfair house.

Now, I'm enough of a realist to know that every family has its difficult moments.

But what I'd witnessed in the Mayfair household bespoke of more than just passing difficulties brought on by the stress of the upcoming performance and auction or even Dora's ills.

We Paradisites had always just assumed that time passed by the Mayfair Sisters' style of music, and they had chosen to simply let go of their gig, but now I wondered. Maybe something darker and deeper had driven them apart. What had Terry meant about Dora Mayfair knowing something?

And since the Mayfair Sisters had long faded from the headlines, there was no reason to think otherwise. In fact, Paradisites young and old just reckoned they were living in luxury, satisfied by their earlier fame and fortune.

But . . . obviously not. Candace seemed at peace with her life and modest solo singing career, but Constance and Cornelia were bitter and wanted more fame and money.

I pulled my mind back to the present, and gazed again at the Ritter house. Joe had abandoned his tricycle now and was kneeling next to his mama, and she watched carefully as he placed a flower in the ground under the big shady maple. Impatiens or begonias, I reckoned.

A week from this Saturday, life on Plum Street wouldn't be made up of such simple, ordinary details. Caleb, through the *Paradise Advertiser-Gazette*, had been reminding folks for weeks that Plum Street would be barricaded, with no vehicular traffic. Hundreds of people were anticipated to attend the auction, not just from Paradise, but from all over the country.

The Friday night concert would draw lots of locals who both remembered the Mayfairs and wanted to relive their music, but the auction at the house would draw serious collectors of memorabilia.

Obviously, the Mayfairs wanted the money for their mother's care, and there had been some uncharitable gossipy whisperings around town that it was a shame the sisters wouldn't just use their own funds to help their mama, and donate all their costumes and memorabilia to the Mason County Historical Society. I'd heard it at Sandy's Restaurant, and in my laundromat, and, truth be told, I thought the same thing.

But maybe they didn't just want the money.

Given the unfairness of their original contract, maybe they *needed* it.

Then I shrugged. I had spent so long sitting on the rear bumper of my van, my own rear bumper was going a little numb. It was time to unload the last of the costumes, and load up the boxes of donated memorabilia and the mangle.

I turned and stuck my key in the back door to unlock it, but discovered it was already unlocked. I frowned at that, shaking my head at myself. I'd been in such a hurry that morning, running late after hearing about T-Bone's fight with Terry Tuxworth Jr., that I hadn't locked the van!

I glanced at my watch. Two o'clock. Well, at least I wouldn't have to hurry before my date—no, my *business dinner*—with Levi Applegate, but still, I suddenly felt in a hurry.

So I jerked open the back door and rushed to grab the garment bag . . .

And then my hand froze in midreach and my breath caught in my throat.

The garment bag was right where I'd left it, chained on the rack I'd fixed in the left side of the cargo area, except the bag was unzipped.

And hanging next to the pearl white, silver, and bronze farewell concert gowns was . . . nothing.

The three tie-dyed slip dresses were gone.

7

Truth be told, I panicked.

I slammed shut my van's door, rushed around to the driver's side, hopped in, and took off.

Two minutes later I was back at my laundromat. I'd hurried there thinking that surely I must have left the tie-dyed slip dresses in the storage room. After all, I'd been delayed by listening to Rhonda Farris talk about T-Bone Baker's fight with Terry Tuxworth Jr. the night before at the Bar-None. I'd been in a hurry to get to Stillwater, so maybe—just maybe—the tie-dyed dresses were still on the rolling clothes rack.

But . . . no. A quick look around the storage room only proved the dresses weren't where I recalled leaving them, and a thorough search of the storage room proved I hadn't moved them elsewhere in the room and then forgotten.

So I rushed out to the front and found Chip about to help Mr. Garvey—an elderly, widowed man—with his laundry baskets.

"So, how's your grandmother, Chip?" Mr. Garvey asked.

"Just fine, sir," Chip was saying, when I rushed up to him.

"Chip!" I said, making him startle so hard that he jumped and made Mr. Garvey's boxers—neatly folded on top of the basket—hop. "Sorry." I took a moment to look at Mr. Garvey and greet him. Then I looked back at Chip. "Have you seen three tie-dyed slip dresses around the laundromat?" I tried to sound casual.

"Uh . . . no," he said. "Should I have?"

"Why, yes," I said, just in case he'd seen someone walking out the front door with them. "I left them hanging in the back storage room."

Chip shrugged. "Haven't been back there." He started to walk toward the door, but I grabbed his arm.

He gave me a puzzled look, and Mr. Garvey looked startled. "Uh, sorry," I said. "I'll finish talking to you when you come back in."

As they went out the front door, Mr. Garvey was saying, "Tell your grandmother I'll be by around five-thirty this evening . . ."

That was enough to distract me for just a moment—Mr. Garvey and Mrs. Beavy, both eighty-somethings, were dating?—but then I went right back to worrying about those slip dresses. I stood by my laundromat's front door, barely noticing my other customers, and practically pounced on Chip when he came back in.

"Did you see anyone else go back to the storage room?" I asked.

Chip's expression showed that he was concerned about my mental health. "No, Josie." He walked around me back to the chair behind the front counter. "No one has gone back there, and just now is the first time I've stepped outside all day. Is there something wrong?"

I thought about my answer. On the one hand, I wanted Chip's help. On the other, I didn't want word to get back to the Mayfairs that their dresses were missing before I had a chance to return to the house . . . and I knew if someone in my laundromat overheard me admit that to Chip, word could travel back that fast to them.

"Uh, no," I said, feeling a flush creep up my face. Chip looked disbelieving. "I mean, I've just misplaced something . . ."

"Three tie-dyed dresses?"

"Shh!" I hissed at him. I went behind the counter and sat down in the other metal folding chair. "Yes," I whispered, "but I don't want word to get around. The Mayfair Sisters' dresses . . . I thought I'd put them in the van, but they're not there! Are you sure you didn't see anyone go back there?"

Chip shook his head. "I didn't. And I think I'd notice someone walking out with three tie-dyed dresses."

I glanced at the book on the counter, a book I knew he'd been reading: *The Zombie Survival Guide: Complete Protection from the Living Dead* by Max Brooks.

It was Chip's turn to blush. "OK, I admit I've been reading off and on," he said. "But you've always said that was OK as long as the customers were taken care of."

I nodded. "And it is."

Chip looked relieved. "I couldn't swear nobody went in there, but I didn't see anyone. And no one would have any reason to go back there."

I took a deep breath, trying to calm myself and think. "Chip, do you think you could make a list of the people who've been in today?" I asked.

Chip immediately looked happier. "Yes, I think so. I mean I know pretty much everyone who comes in here."

"OK," I said. "You do that now, while I go back to my desk and try to think."

He pulled some paper off the back of a receipt pad and started jotting names. I went back to my office, pausing to say hi to a few of the folks in my laundromat, at least the ones who weren't trying to entertain their kids or weren't lost in reading paperbacks.

Back at my desk, I sat down and tried to think carefully. I closed my eyes, reviewed each moment of the day so far.

Yes, I remembered putting the three tie-dyed dresses in the garment bag with the pearl, silver, and gold silk dresses. At least I was pretty sure I did. The morning was a blur because I had been in such a hurry.

But even if I hadn't, if I'd left the dresses here, they were now gone. I knew for a fact I had locked up the back entry of the laundromat—I'd had to get out my key to unlock it just minutes before—so no one could have come in the back and taken the dresses, even if I'd left them here. Well, except the people who had spare keys.

Which were Chip, in case of emergencies, and Sally, so she could do her laundry after hours.

But who would want the dresses—besides the Mayfairs—anyway?

I opened my eyes and started jotting notes.

Number one—someone who would think they could sell the dresses on eBay.

But then . . . why wouldn't they have taken the silk dresses, which were much more valuable? There were plenty of photos of the Mayfair Sisters wearing those dresses in their farewell concert but none, as far as I knew, of them in the tie-dyed dresses. I had only Candace Mayfair's word that the tie-dyed dresses had been worn, very briefly, near the end of the sisters' career as a trio, as a way to try to fit in to the changing music and times.

I stared at my note.

Wow. Short list.

OK, who else?

Well, the Mayfair sisters themselves knew the dresses were in the van, and for that matter, so did Terry Tuxworth.

Terry would have had plenty of time to take the dresses, but again, why would he want to? And why would he take just the tie-dyed dresses? Unless it was simply to make a fuss, cruelly add a bit more tension to an already tense time.

Constance and Cornelia also would have had plenty of time to take the dresses, maybe wanting to hurry along their work for the day. But that still didn't explain taking just the tie-dyed dresses and leaving the others.

I tapped the eraser end of my pencil against my pursed lips while trying to think creatively.

Then it hit me. The seamstress, Moira, lived on Plum Street. Maybe she'd seen my van, and suddenly remembered that she hadn't completed repairs to the tie-dyed dresses. After all, I hadn't finished examining the dresses that morning, so for all I knew, she'd failed to complete a hem repair, or something.

But there were problems with that theory.

For one thing, I'd hired out the repair work to Moira because she was a painstaking perfectionist about her work. For another, Moira was sixty-some years old, had a bad back, and was fifty pounds overweight. Let's say she'd decided to snatch the dresses back from my van. Even as long as I'd been in the Mayfair house, she wouldn't have been spry enough to dash out to my van, get the dresses, and get back to her house. When I left the Mayfair house, I'd have seen her still hobbling back to her house with the dresses. And she lived alone, so she couldn't have sent anyone out to do the snatching for her.

Unless she'd asked her grandson, Clint, to do the snatching. But he'd been pretty upset when I saw him leaving her house. I figured most of their visit had been, sadly, taken up by an argument.

Which meant that either I'd left the dresses here, and someone had taken them from the back room—which seemed very unlikely to me, although I'd look over the list Chip gave me carefully.

Or for some reason, Cornelia, Constance, or Terry had snagged the dresses.

My vote was for Terry.

But one thing was certain. I had to go back to the Mayfairs and, as my aunt would have said, face the music.

Unfortunately, I knew that music wasn't likely to be the sweet lullabies that Candace sang to her mother.

I wasn't sure what offended Cornelia and Constance more— my question about whether they'd taken the dresses, or the idea of them—as Cornelia put it—crawling around in the back of some smelly van.

"I'm quite sure Josie's van is spotless," said Candace.

We were all, again, in the tiny living room.

"Of course it is," I said, unable to keep from sounding offended myself. "And odor-free. I run a laundromat, for pity's sake. I would never deliver my customers' clothing in—"

"In any case," Constance said, "it seems most likely that Terry took the dresses—like you said, Josie, just to shake us up. I can't think of anyone else who would have taken them and left the other dresses. No reason to."

"Well, do you know where Terry's staying?" I asked. "I want to call and ask—"

"At the Red Horse, I think, but don't worry about it," Candace said. "Even without those dresses, we'll raise enough money for our mother."

"But . . . those dresses would probably have fetched another thousand, at least!" Cornelia exclaimed.

"But what if he tries to embarrass us with those dresses?" Constance wailed. I stared at her. What did she think he was going to do with them? Show up at the concert in drag? "That would be bad publicity. Or what if we do find out he took the dresses and brought charges against him? That would be bad publicity, too!"

"I think we should call the police," I said.

"No! No police," Constance said. "We don't need the negative publicity—not just before the auction."

"I have to say I agree with her," Cornelia said, sighing. "Even though the dresses are valuable."

Both Constance and Cornelia looked at Candace, who nodded.

OK. So no reporting the missing dresses to the police.

Roger put his arm around Constance. "Dear, you look tired. Why don't you and Cornelia head back, and I'll catch up with you after helping Josie get the mangle in the back of her van."

"Oh no," I said, "I couldn't possibly accept the Ironrite now."

"Of course you can!" Candace said. "I'm sure it's not your fault that the dresses are missing."

That just made me feel worse. Of course it was. I was responsible for them, and they'd been stolen.

"Good idea," Cornelia said. "We need plenty of rest this week before our concert. This whole business with Terry has been so exhausting."

I glanced at Candace, who looked worn to the bone. And who didn't complain a bit. And who would, I knew, give a spectacular performance next Friday. I wondered if she'd always been the quiet, put-upon little sister, while the older two were spoiled.

Then I looked back at Cornelia and Constance. "You're not all staying here?"

"Of course not." Cornelia looked horrified at the very idea. "This place was too crowded, even when we were kids. And with all this chaos . . ." She gestured to the boxes.

"Ah," I said. "So you must be staying at the Red Horse, so if you happen to see Terry . . ."

"Oh, heavens, not the Red Horse," Constance said, looking even more horrified than Cornelia had managed. "That place is so musty. I couldn't handle it. Plus, all the fans would be bothering us. We'd never rest. We're at a bed-and-breakfast in Masonville. Come on, Cornelia, I'll ride with you in your rental." Yet another car that was parked in front of the Mayfair house, but not as distinctive as a purple sports car or a red convertible with a BYEBYEU vanity plate, so I hadn't really noticed it.

The two women turned and headed out the front door, without so much as a backward glance at Candace or Roger . . . or bothering to run upstairs to say good-bye to their mother.

"Well. I'll help get the Ironrite in your van, Josie," Roger said—although he stared at the door. He sounded bitter, and I knew it had nothing to do with helping me. If he hadn't been with Candace and me when we'd been inspecting the Ironrite earlier, I'd have wondered if he took the dresses from the van—a little passive-aggressive revenge at being taken so for granted by his wife.

"Thank you, Roger," both Candace and I said. He smiled, a little.

"I need to feed Mama," Candace said. "Come up and see us before you go, Josie?"

I glanced at my watch. Five o'clock, already!

I was barely going to have time to get ready for my date . . . dinner business meeting . . . with Levi.

But I nodded at Candace. It was clear that it would mean so much to her if I visited with her mama.

Besides, I didn't need to primp to please Levi, right? A quick shower and a change into something simple . . . my cap-sleeved pale blue dress, for example . . . would be enough.

'Cause this was *not* a date.

"Is that you?" Dora's pale blue eyes were wide and anxious and seeking as she stared up at me.

I glanced across the bed—Dora's thin frame barely made a bump under the spotless white blanket—at Candace, unsure what to say.

Candace gave a slight nod to me, and I took that to mean that I should pretend to be whoever it was Dora was asking after.

I smiled, nervously, at the thin, small version of Dora Mayfair, who had known very well for years that I'm Josie Toadfern. "Why, yes," I said. My voice shook a little. I hadn't been prepared to see how much Dora had receded from reality, in just the two weeks since I'd last visited with her. And what would happen if she suddenly realized I wasn't this mystery person, but just Josie? "I—I just wanted to drop in and see how you were doing."

Candace had edged a spoonful of vegetable soup toward her mother's lips, but Dora swatted at Candace's hand, and the soup spilled on the blanket.

I gasped, but Candace didn't look the least upset. And

Dora didn't seem to notice my gasp. She glared at Candace. "Go away! Can't you see I'm talking with her? Finally!"

Dora looked back at me and smiled, as if she hadn't just swatted and snapped, but had been peaceful all along.

I took a deep breath. I could do this. After all, I was used to interacting with Guy and his fellow residents at Stillwater. Not that autism and Alzheimer's are the same thing, of course. But they both require caretakers' patience . . . and a separation of emotion from the individual's actions and words. There was no point in Candace taking her mother's reaction to the soup personally, just as there was no point in my taking personally Guy's lack of affection and stiffness if I gave him a hug that, to him, was overwhelming.

I knew this, yet sometimes felt tremendous sadness that Guy and I couldn't relate in a way that felt normal to me, that I constantly had to adjust what felt comfortable to me to be around him at all.

And I knew that Candace had had to make the same mental adjustment . . . although for her perhaps it was more heart-wrenching, because there were moments still when the mother she'd known as Dora would reappear, just for a moment.

Candace knew I understood, because of my experiences with Guy.

Maybe that's why Candace and I connected so immediately several weeks before, when I'd first taken on the task of cleaning and repairing the Mayfair Sisters' costumes.

"I can't stay long," I said to Dora. "But I'm glad I could see you for a few minutes."

Dora's hand was thin and shaking as she patted my cheek. "You look different than I thought. But pretty."

I smiled. "Thank you. You look nice, too."

Dora brightened, but her hand fell back to the top of her

blanket. The effort to pat my—someone's?—cheek had worn her out.

"Candace has brought you some soup. It looks really good," I said.

Dora looked at her daughter, confused. Then she looked back at me. "Candace? But . . . I want to visit you. Finally . . ."

I smiled. "And I think the soup would really be good for you," I said.

She nodded. If I . . . or whoever I represented to her . . . thought so . . .

I slipped down the stairs as Candace started feeding her mother the soup.

Roger had finished loading the Ironrite into my van. We stood on the front lawn. He took note of my expression, and the quiver in my voice as I thanked him for his help.

"Kinda shakes you up, doesn't it," he said. "Seeing Dora."

I nodded.

"I really admire what Candace has done for her mother," he said. "I think the only break she gets is when the night nurse comes. She takes a walk around town, then."

I nodded. I'd seen her once or twice, passing my building, which was just a few blocks away.

"But Cornelia and Constance . . ." Roger stopped, shook his head. "I'd better get going."

I watched him through the front picture window as he walked quickly to his red BYEBYEU convertible. He drove off just as Candace came out the front door.

Candace gave a little wave, although Roger couldn't possibly see it. I looked at her, worried about how weary she looked.

"Are you going to be OK?" I asked, hating to leave her alone, but knowing I had less than an hour to get back to my laundromat, get the Ironrite unloaded into the back room, and get ready for Levi's arrival. Maybe I should call Stillwater, cancel the *business dinner*, and stay with Candace.

She smiled tiredly. "I'm fine. The night nurse will be here in about forty-five minutes. Mama ate her soup and is napping again. Thanks for going along with being whoever she thought you were. She does that with us sometimes, too. It really upsets Cornelia and Constance." Candace shrugged as if to say that, on the other hand, even the least little things seemed to upset her sisters. "The nurse and I will bathe Mama tonight, and help her walk around a little bit—she can't walk on her own anymore—and then I'll have time to myself for a little bit. I usually just allow myself one walk at night, but I might drive up to Masonville and take in a movie."

"That's a good idea," I said. "Listen, I'd be glad to launder the blanket for you . . ."

"Not necessary," Candace said, patting my arm. "I've really appreciated all the times you've kept me company when you didn't have to. I'll just wash the blanket here. The washer and dryer in the basement are old, but they should hang in for the next three days until—"

She paused, her voice catching. Three days. I guessed that was when Dora would be transferred to the nursing home.

I gave Candace a hug, tentative at first, but she seemed grateful for the gesture, so I made the hug a little firmer before pulling back.

"She'll be fine," I said gently.

"I know," Candace said. "It really is time for her to go to the nursing home. Even with in-home nursing help, this has become too much for me to handle alone. I've neglected my own husband and family."

"Will they be coming for the auction?"

"Oh yes, they'll be here to help me transfer Mama on Wednesday. We felt the auction commotion would be just too much for her. And then they'll be here for the performance. We're not staying for the auction, not any of us. It's just too hard to watch," Candace said. "My two sons are grown, of course, but they plan to be here too, with their wives and children. I have five grandchildren. My family loves my mother as much as I do." She wiped her eyes, and smiled ruefully. "They just don't . . . get along well with my sisters."

Well. I liked Candace's husband, sons, daughters-in-law, and grandchildren already.

"They'll be a comfort to you, then," I said.

She nodded.

I lingered, wishing in the meantime I could offer something more of value to her.

Then I brightened. "Oh! By the way, just rinse the soup from the blanket in cold water," I said. "And pretreat with dishwashing detergent before laundering. I find that's a good all-around pretreatment for food stains. And, um, call me if it doesn't work, and . . ."

I was about to add that I was sure the tie-dyed dresses would turn up, but Candace's gaze was already straying toward the front door of her childhood home. She was anxious to get back to her mama and be caretaker for these last few days.

8

"Have you thought about the possibility that someone took the three tie-dyed dresses from your van while you were at Stillwater earlier today?"

I stared across the table, and not just because I was stunned I hadn't thought of the idea.

Levi Applegate—who had just asked the obvious—looked good in the candlelit Spring Mill Inn and in his carefully pressed gray suit and mauve dress shirt—no tie, just the top shirt button undone, just a little tuft of black chest hair peekabooing. The hair on his head was black, straight, and neatly cut in a style that would look either too military or too good-little-boy on most men, but that fit his angular face and intensely dark brown eyes perfectly. The fact that his upper lip had a soft curve, à la photos of young Elvis—a fact I hadn't noticed until sitting across from him at the polished oak table—had done me in.

Or maybe the fact that he had—without pretense or show—held my chair for me as we were seated had done me in.

Or could it have been that he noticed the waiter's slightly

overbearing tendency to try too hard to be pleasing and managed to help the waiter correct course with a few well-chosen words—something along the lines of "Thank you for checking on our water glasses, but please leave the pitcher here"—rather than just enduring the constant interruption (which I would have probably done) or snapping something too sharp or critical (which I would have also probably done, depending on my mood).

It didn't matter.

I was done in . . . meaning I found Levi Applegate, the new Stillwater director I'd been planning to grill mercilessly, completely sexually, emotionally, and spiritually attractive.

Yeah, he looked good in the suit and shirt and candlelight. But I also found myself thinking about how good he'd look in, say, just a swimsuit and sunlight. Or a bathrobe and bedroom light. Or . . .

I shook my head. I was starting to sweat more than the water pitcher, which we ignored as we ate our salads and talked.

I needed to think—and act—more coolly.

After all, I was wearing my light pink silk blouse, which was quite fetching with the black skirt with polka dots in various shades of pink and the black mule sandals, but which would soon just be embarrassing if sweat wicked from my armpits to my blouse bodice and sleeves.

Never mind those other images. It's just the romantic candlelight that's getting to you. And the red wine . . . I finished a bite of filet mignon and sipped more wine. *And the fact that Levi is seriously . . . hot.*

"Well, that's an interesting premise," I said.

Levi looked amused, and I flushed—why did this man make me flush so much? And even stutter occasionally?—because I knew I had sounded precociously prim.

"I—I m-m-mean, I hadn't thought about someone taking

the dresses from my van," I said, "which kind of surprises me, because usually I think of every possibility in these kinds of situations . . ."

I trailed off as Levi's eyebrows lifted in amusement compounded by surprise. "These kinds of situations?"

Oh, Lord, I thought—and I meant that prayerfully. What would he think of me if he knew I'd been involved in not just one, but five murder investigations?

You don't care what he thinks of you, remember? You're just supposed to address your concerns about his viewpoint on autism, remember?

No, I hadn't remembered. The topic hadn't come up. In fact, so far this evening we'd talked about how I'd come to be a laundromat owner and stain removal expert and now household hints columnist, how he liked Ohio so far but how different it was from New Mexico, how I'd gotten involved with the Mayfair sisters, which led to long asides on our tastes in music (eclectic for both of us, with his leaning more to jazz and mine leaning more to new country and folk and gospel, but with plenty of overlap), which somehow looped back to how crowded it was at the Red Horse—he was staying there and really liked the proprietors (damn! Another reason to like him, since Greta and Luke were among my favorite people)— and how he knew he wanted to buy a house now that he was Stillwater's director, but he was torn about where to house hunt since Masonville was closer to Stillwater, but the homes were more expensive, whereas Paradise was much more affordable, but an extra hour away from Stillwater (double damn! He really was planning to settle in the area, then, so I couldn't dismiss him as yet another guy who would come here, realize he wasn't *from* here, and take off after a year or two), which finally led somehow to me telling him about the stolen tie-dyed dresses.

"By these situations," I said, "I just meant that usually I'm good at figuring out all the possibilities that could explain a perplexing situation."

"OK," said Levi. "So why do you suppose you didn't think about the possibility that someone took the dresses from your van while it was in the Stillwater parking lot?"

Oh, great. Now the man was taking my ideas seriously, without being patronizing.

Plus he had this deep yet mellow voice—a deepness that was totally natural and not forced (I hate it when guys force their voices to be deeper than they actually are, as if this makes them naturally sexier and no one will notice) and that somehow managed to envelop me.

If Levi didn't watch it, I thought, I was going to leap over the table—lit candles and filet mignon and sweating water pitchers be damned—right on top of him.

I wondered if he'd mind?

I gave my head another little clearing shake. "Let's say someone did take the dresses from my van. That assumes the person knew the dresses were in my van that morning. That they followed me. Which means that they had some really compelling reason to take those particular dresses, since the three satin dresses were left alone. And that I'd left the van unlocked, since there were no marks around the van's back door lock." I smiled triumphantly. "So, try unraveling that!"

"Hmmm," he said. "I'll need to think a minute . . ."

The waiter came by and asked if we were ready for our plates to be taken—which, considering both our plates held only the skins of our baked potatoes, the parsley garnish, and the juice from our filet mignons—seemed pretty obvious.

But Levi rewarded our young waiter with a smile, and said, "Perfect timing! Yes, I think so." He glanced at me and

I nodded, appreciative that he didn't just assume I wanted my plate taken. After all, I might want to lap up my steak juice or munch the parsley.

The waiter asked about dessert, and Levi said, "Ladies first."

Damn! Would I look greedy if—after such a huge meal—I ordered the chocolate decadence cake? Should I go for a sorbet? A cappuccino?

Who cares? You're not *interested in him, anyway.*

Riiiight . . . Well, in any case I was sure when we finally got around to discussing Stillwater, I'd find his attitudes unacceptable and a turn-off—and since chocolate was supposed to stimulate the same chemicals as romance, I decided chocolate decadence was a tasty substitute for real decadence . . . and ordered it. With a side of vanilla ice cream. And a large coffee, decaf.

Levi grinned, looking genuinely pleased at my gusto. "That sounds wonderful. I'll have what she's having."

"Are you sure you locked the van?" Levi asked after the waiter left with our dinner dishes and dessert orders.

My wineglass was still half full, so I took another sip while I thought. "No," I finally admitted. "I mean, I know I slipped in the key to open the back when I finally went for the dresses, but by then I was so rattled about the scene at the Mayfairs and the gift of the Ironrite that I didn't really pay attention to whether or not the lock clicked."

"OK, so the dresses could have been taken from your van at Stillwater. Now, are you sure no one could have figured out the dresses would be in the van?"

"I didn't tell anyone."

"That's not what I mean," Levi said. "You have friends and know lots of people in the area. I noticed that last night at the Bar-None."

I flushed again. Of course he hadn't forgotten the woman

who'd barreled into him as he was trying to leave the men's room.

I decided to just be blunt. "How could you notice that from me literally running into you?"

Levi smiled. "I'd noticed you before that."

I stared at him.

And he . . . shook his head as if to clear it.

"Oh," I said, my voice squeaking.

"Anyway, I'm guessing you have many friends and acquaintances," he said.

Was he blushing, too? It was hard to say in the candlelight.

"True," I said.

"And so they'd know your habits. You could have mentioned that you were glad to finish the costume restoration project and eager to deliver those dresses. Any number of people would know—without your mentioning it—that you'd be at the meeting this morning at Stillwater," Levi said. "After all, Guy is important to you and you probably speak of him often. And the news of this morning's meeting isn't exactly a secret. It was in the newspaper and, so I've been told, even mentioned on the local evening news last night. So word could have easily spread about your finishing up the dresses and planning to deliver them—the Mayfairs are celebrities and people love to talk about celebrities, or even about knowing people who know celebrities—and it wouldn't be hard to figure out that you'd be likely to have the dresses in the van before you went to Stillwater."

I thought about what he'd said, and decided that he was right. "OK, I'm impressed," I said. "You've made a good case. But that means someone must have desperately wanted those dresses—and just those tie-dyed dresses. Why?"

Levi shrugged. "About that . . . I have no idea." He smiled. "I actually think you're right about Terry Tuxworth taking them as a spur-of-the-moment attempt to rattle the sisters. What did the police say?"

"It wasn't reported," I said. "The sisters were adamant— they didn't want negative publicity over three dresses. Which I found kind of . . ." I trailed off.

"Odd? Me, too," Levi said. The waiter brought our desserts. We each took our first bites . . . and moaned in unison, then looked away from each other. Yeah, I was blushing. My guess was that Levi blushed, too.

"Well, if you want, I can try to track down Terry Tuxworth tonight—since apparently we're both staying at the Red Horse—and see what I can get out of him," Levi said. "Indirectly, of course."

"Really?" I said. My natural curiosity was thrilled. Not to mention that I was pleasantly stunned—and delighted—to suspect that Levi might be just as nosey as me.

"Sure," Levi said. Then he smiled. "But that would mean, of course, getting together again for me to tell you what I found out. How about breakfast?"

I looked at my chocolate decadence cake, only half eaten. I didn't think I'd be hungry again for a week. In fact, I was going to have to ask to have the dessert boxed . . . and I'd already been planning on having leftover decadence for breakfast.

And yet, as I thought this, I said, "Sure. If you're thinking of buying in Paradise, you'll want to get to know Sandy's Restaurant. Best eggs and biscuits and gravy and sausage and pancakes . . ."

"OK, OK," Levi said, laughing. "I'll come by around nine a.m.?"

"Better make it earlier," I said. "I go to services at the Paradise Methodist Church on Sundays at ten."

"OK," Levi said. "Let's make it eight—and I'll go with you to church."

I stared at him.

"If that's OK," he added. "If I'm going to live in Paradise, I'll also need a place to worship."

"That's fine," I said. "You're . . . Methodist?"

"Reared Catholic," he said, "but I lapsed long ago. I regularly attended a Methodist church in New Mexico, although I never joined."

"Fine. Eight it is. But I want a full report on Terry Tuxworth with my biscuits and sausage gravy," I said.

Because, really, it's just a business breakfast . . .

And while our chocolate decadence leftovers were boxed, and we sipped coffee, somehow the conversation turned to why I was excited about the Ironrite currently sitting in the storage room at the back of my laundromat (Roger had helped me unload it and set it up and I'd had a whole half hour to get ready before Levi showed up—promptly at 6:30—at my door), and that led to the research I'd been doing for a book of the history of laundry—which Levi thought was a wonderful idea, since it's a little-explored area of domestic history and would give a unique perspective on women's lives throughout history—and we bounced around title ideas and he told me not to be so nervous about the community college course (Composition 101) I'd signed up for during the summer term at Masonville Community College because if my column was such a success I was sure to do well in the class, and somehow from there our conversation turned to area hiking paths since Levi is an avid hiker.

We kept chatting like that all the way back to my laundromat/home, and Levi insisted—in spite of the floodlight off the back of my building that shines down on the parking lot—that he'd walk me up the steps to my entrance.

He waited until I'd unlocked the door to my apartment,

then said, "See you tomorrow morning," and gave my hand a lingering, but gentlemanly, squeeze.

It wasn't until after I'd switched into my Tweety-bird PJs that I realized we'd never gotten around to the business discussion of our business dinner.

"No way," I said, moaning, and sorry I'd finished off the chocolate decadence just before bed, while trying to decide what I would have done if Levi had given me a good-night kiss.

I mean, that would have been a bit pushy, since our dinner was business only, and I'd just met him, and I was sure I would end up not liking him . . .

By the time I'd finished the chocolate decadence, I'd given up fighting my feelings, and admitted to myself that I wished he had kissed me.

By the time I'd finished brushing my teeth, I was wondering what might have happened if I'd asked him in.

I'd hurried to bed, skipping my usual routine of reading first for half an hour, fearful of where my thoughts would go to next.

But it seemed that I'd been asleep only a few blissful minutes when who should appear in a dream but Mrs. Oglevee.

And she'd pulled down the screen she'd had up the night before, and was tapping Levi's larger-than-life face right on the nose. Plus she was again stuffed into the pearl satin Mayfair dress Cherry coveted as a wedding dress.

"No way," I moaned again. "We're not discussing Levi. He was charming, yes, but how do I know he wasn't just being nice since he's the new Stillwater director? I mean, all that interest in me was probably to deflect me from talking about my concerns about his views—"

"Then why take you to dinner at all?" Mrs. Oglevee demanded, glaring at me. "If he just wanted to deflect you, he would have put you off, been inaccessible, found someone else to take out to celebrate his first official day in his new job."

That gave me pause. Had he taken me out as a way of celebrating? He hadn't said that.

And who else would he take out, anyway? There were several female staff members who were available, but he couldn't date them for ethical reasons.

Still, I felt a surprising surge of jealousy . . . and then my stomach did a twist as I thought of two community volunteers who were just the right age for him . . . and who were single, skinny, and pretty . . .

I moaned.

No. No, this was not jealousy, this was chocolate decadence, and I started to tell Mrs. Oglevee as much, but I was awoken by a sudden scream.

A scream external to my dream world.

A scream that finally brought me fully awake and sitting up in bed and wide-eyed and trembling as I realized that the scream was coming from below me . . . from the back room of my laundromat.

I calmed down when I realized I recognized the scream.

It was Sally.

But I couldn't imagine what would make her scream like that.

If she were being attacked, I knew I'd hear cursing along with the screaming, and plenty of scuffling as she fought back.

I pride myself on keeping my laundromat spotless, but still, an occasional spider does wander in.

But a spider would never cause Sally to scream. She'd either stomp it into oblivion, or gently scoop it up on paper and take it back outside—depending on her mood. Even something larger—such as, God forbid, a mouse, which I'd never had in my laundromat—would not make her scream.

Maybe she'd cut herself somehow. Or worse, gotten bleach in her face.

So I hurried downstairs, confident that I wasn't in any danger, eager to help my cousin, who I was sure had just injured herself somehow while doing a late-night load of laundry while her boys spent the night at their grandparents'.

And I burst in the back room and saw what had made Sally scream.

She kept screaming—a hysterical ahh! Ahh! Ahh!—even after she saw me.

But I didn't scream. I stared in shocked, silent horror.

There sat Terry Tuxworth Jr. in the health chair in front of the Ironrite.

But he definitely wasn't healthy.

He'd been bashed on his head. There was blood on the floor and, I assumed, on the too-tight black T-shirt he wore. Some small part of my brain tried to distract me with the thought that the T-shirt didn't seem his style.

And then two tie-dyed dresses, the missing slip dresses, had been turned into a noose of sorts, the hems tucked through the arm loops. I noted the little detail that one of the loops was broken, but still, an effective noose had been made, and then pulled over his head. Someone had then fed the hem ends of the dresses into the Ironrite, which had been started up, the rollers pulling the dresses—and Terry—toward the mangle, resulting in him being strangled to death.

No, I didn't scream.

I started to wonder where the third dress was, but before I could get far with that thought, ran out the back, and threw up every bit of chocolate decadence in my brightly lit parking lot.

And then I ran back inside—trying not to glance at Terry—and grabbed the phone off my desk and dialed 911.

9

"Why," I asked for the third time, through gritted teeth, "would I have given a key to someone I met only once?"

I was at the Paradise Police Department, answering Chief John Worthy's questions in the one and only interrogation room—a beige, bland space that might bore a suspect to death, but wouldn't intimidate a stray cat. And, yeah, I knew from the *Paradise Advertiser-Gazette* that an abandoned litter of kittens had been kept in here, just last week. The ammonia scent wafting from the corner behind me served as olfactory evidence.

The Paradise Police Department, being small in terms of budget, personnel, and square footage, required certain compromises . . . like no dedicated interrogation room. It was also a conference room, furnished by a long conference table and twelve chairs. I sat on one side, and Worthy and Officer Amelia Grayson sat on the other.

"I'm asking the questions!" yelled Worthy.

"You're asking the same question, over and over. 'Why did you give Terry Tuxworth Jr. a key to your laundromat,

Josie?' And I'm telling you, for the third time, I did not give a key to Terry Tuxworth." I spaced the last words out slowly and evenly, like I might be explaining to a child how to put the quarters in the washing machine pay tray.

"Then how could he have gotten in?" Worthy asked, looking triumphant at finally having come up with a new question.

I sighed, closed my eyes, put my head to my hands, and rubbed my eyes with my fists.

I was weary. I wanted to go . . . somewhere . . . and brush my teeth and gargle. But not back to my home. My beautiful, newly renovated home . . . right over my beloved business . . . now turned into a gruesome chamber of horrors.

I wanted to weep . . . and no, not for Terry Tuxworth Jr., as terribly selfish as that may sound.

Instead, I let my fists fall back to the table with a heavy thud. The sudden movement and sound made Chief Worthy jump, although Officer Amelia retained her composure. So far, she hadn't said anything during the interview. I guess she was just there so I couldn't complain later that Worthy had thumped me upside the head.

Or, maybe, given how I was feeling—and how my expression reflected it—to protect Worthy from me thumping him.

"I dunno," I said. "You're the chief of police. You're Mr. Brilliant Guy. You're the one who has been ragging me ever since we broke up in junior high school as being a dummy screwup. So why would you think I could answer that question?

"It wasn't forced entry. I noticed that much. But I also know I didn't give Terry a key. I've told you—only two people besides me have keys to my laundromat: Sally Toadfern and Chip Beavy. Sally has a key so she can use my laundromat in off hours in exchange for doing occasional odd jobs for me, since she's an excellent carpenter in her spare time." Plus because I felt sorry for her that she was a single mom of young triplets.

But I didn't think I needed to say that for the tape recorder.

"Chip has a key because he works for me on an occasional basis, and because it makes sense for someone to have a key in case of an emergency.

"I came back from my evening at about ten-thirty p.m. I was asleep by eleven. And woke up to the sound of Sally screaming at about eleven-forty-five.

"Which, since there were no cars in my building's lot when I returned at ten-thirty, means Terry had to arrive sometime after that."

"Would you have heard a car pull into the lot, from your apartment?" Officer Amelia asked her first question.

Both Chief Worthy and I looked at her, surprised. I reckoned she wanted to actually collect some facts, and get Worthy off his power trip of berating me about why I'd given Terry a key, when I hadn't.

I felt immediately calmer, and shot her a look that offered both gratitude and caution: *Watch it, girlfriend. Worthy doesn't like even a hint that he might be challenged.*

"Excellent question," Worthy said, sounding just a tinge grumpy, and taking over the interview from Amelia. "Would you have?"

I thought about it. "Not necessarily. The building is very well insulated, for one thing. So I don't hear a lot of noise from the street, or if I happen to be up in my apartment while my laundromat's open, from the laundromat, either. Plus I was pretty tired from a long day. I had a quick snack"—the leftover chocolate decadence, which I now regretted eating—"and took a shower—I definitely wouldn't have heard anyone pulling up during the shower or while I blow-dried my hair—and I was asleep almost immediately after I went to bed."

I thought a second longer. If I'd have stayed up to read as I usually did, I might have heard something. I might have heard Terry's car pull up while wolfing down the chocolate decadence, but that had taken only a few minutes. My activities after that involved enough noise to block the faint sound of someone pulling into the parking lot.

So, Terry had arrived between 10:30 and 11:45 without my being aware . . . and been murdered in a most gruesome and odd fashion.

I shuddered as the image of Terry and the Ironrite came to mind.

"Yet you woke to the sound of Sally screaming," Worthy said. Was that a tinge of accusation in his voice?

I sighed. "Yes. I did. When I had the two apartments renovated into one, my bedroom ended up right over the back room which doubles as my office. And I had a large walk-in closet added to my bedroom, complete with a laundry chute that leads to a laundry basket by my desk. The basket, in fact, is between my desk and the Ironrite.

"I tend to leave both my closet door and my laundry chute door open." I didn't mention that the laundry chute door being open was for convenience, and the closet door being open was a habit dating back to a childhood fear of monsters-in-closets, which somehow I convinced myself would vanish if the closet door was open a crack. I'd gotten over the fear but not the habit. "So Sally's scream would have shot straight up to my bedroom. Plus, you know as well as I do, that when Sally screams, it's not exactly wimpy. She's used to yelling over the top of her bar patrons' voices and over her triplets. Not that this is a new skill. As you might recall, she and I were on the volleyball team together. And she was skilled at screaming even then."

"So you heard Sally scream, and you went downstairs and found Terry Tuxworth, who had somehow quietly entered your laundromat without, as you say, forced entry . . . but with a key. Which you claim you didn't give him." Worthy looked at me pointedly.

Oh, Lord. We were right back to the key. I started to protest again . . . but then I was struck by the implication of the way Worthy phrased his statement. Terry Tuxworth had had a key to my laundromat. The officers at the scene must have found it on or near him.

But I knew I hadn't given him a key.

And as I'd just said, only two other people had keys to my laundromat: Sally Toadfern and Chip Beavy.

So if I hadn't given Terry a key, then one of them . . .

Worthy grinned as he saw realization dawn in my expression.

"Sally has her key," Worthy said. "She showed it to us."

Officer Amelia gave him a startled look. Had her chief just shared testimony from one witness to another? Yes, yes he had.

She was new to the department, although not new to the area. But young enough . . . or I suppose Worthy and I were old enough . . . that she wasn't aware of our long-standing feud.

"We haven't talked with Chip yet," Worthy was saying.

I swallowed, my throat suddenly dry. "He wouldn't have given Terry his key, either," I said.

"Do you have your key handy, Josie?" Worthy asked.

Did I? I had to think a second, sort out the scenes that had played out since I'd awoken to Sally's screams ricocheting up the laundry chute and into my bedroom.

I'd stumbled downstairs, sure Sally had hurt herself some-how. Instead found Sally screaming in horror and standing near Terry, who was horribly tethered to the Ironrite.

I'd run out and puked.

Then I'd gone back in and dialed 911.

Sally and I had stood outside and shivered—just from nerves; the night was fairly warm—until police and emergency workers arrived. That had taken only a few minutes.

There had been a flurry of activity after that: initial questioning . . . then, yes.

Officer Amelia had asked both Sally and me to come to the station. Sally and I could have taken her truck or walked to the police department—it was just a few blocks down from my laundromat—but Officer Amelia offered to drive us, since we were so shaken up.

Officer Amelia had waited while I went upstairs to lock up my apartment—that wasn't part of the crime scene—and I'd grabbed my purse. I was sure I'd dropped my keys in my purse, even though I didn't remember doing so. It was the kind of automatic thing I wouldn't remember even under cheery, normal circumstances.

"My laundromat key should be on my key ring in my purse," I said.

"Check," Worthy said.

I picked up my purse and sat it on the table. I unzipped it—it was a large, beige, bolo-style bag that could—and did—hold my wallet, tissues, various grooming items like Chap Stick, and a comb, and a paperback because I never went anywhere without one.

And for this evening, a lipstick and small body wash spray for my dinner out with Levi.

I felt a pang.

I wished I were back at the restaurant with Levi. What if I had invited him in? Would we have heard Terry arrive, heard something that would have alarmed us, prevented Terry's horrific demise?

I fished out my keys, splayed them out for both Worthy and Officer Amelia to see. I pointed to one of the silver ones.

"That's it. My laundromat key."

"It looks just like the one Sally showed us," Officer Amelia said quietly.

"The *copy* Sally showed us," Worthy said. "And if you made copies of the keys for Sally and Chip, you could have made one for Terry."

"I didn't," I said. And there was no reason Sally or Chip would have . . . was there? My stomach flipped.

"And you didn't just happen to have an extra copy you loaned Terry, while you were at the Mayfairs?"

I'd already explained about my visit at the Mayfairs, receiving the Ironrite, meeting Terry. I'd tried to keep my value judgments about the Mayfairs out of my statement, though.

Although it seemed pretty obvious that any of the Mayfairs would have had a good motive to kill Terry: to get out of the contract that he claimed still bound them to him.

Except Candace wasn't interested in recording with him.

And why in the world would they have chosen such a strange way to kill him? No one lures someone to a laundromat in order to knock them out and then imaginatively strangle them with a mangle/slip dress combo.

Plus Cornelia and Constance had been adamant that they didn't want even the negative publicity of the missing slip dresses.

No, this had to be a sudden, spontaneous crime of passion. Someone spotted Terry at the laundromat. That same someone came in, argued with him, hit him on the head, and then strangled him. While I slept above.

But . . . if I had heard Sally's screams come up the chute, why wouldn't I have heard the struggle between Terry and his attacker?

Maybe the attack had been so sudden, Terry hadn't had a chance to react.

Which eliminated the idea of an argument, and implied an amount of premeditation.

And of course, if Terry was knocked out, he wouldn't have struggled against being hooked up to the Ironrite.

I shuddered.

"I didn't," I said, "give Terry a key. He didn't ask to use my laundromat, and truth be told, I'm surprised he'd have gone there. He didn't strike me as the sort to do his own laundry."

"Fine," Worthy said, surprising me. "Tell us about the Ironrite."

"Like I said, it was a gift from the Mayfairs, a thank-you for the work I've done on their costumes—"

"No, I mean how, in your opinion, it could have been used as a murder weapon. Was it a dangerous machine?"

I considered the question. "Not ordinarily," I said. "The machines were nicknamed mangles, which comes from a machine that was used to get water out of clothes. Some people were afraid they could hurt their hands if they got caught in the rolls, but the machines came with a pretty foolproof release device, and the rolls fed cloth through slowly.

"So probably the word 'mangle' was as much a nickname out of jealousy because these machines were expensive in their day. Anyway, Stephen King even wrote a short story about a demonically possessed folding machine called 'The Mangler,' which was made into a pretty cheesy movie.

"But obviously, the Ironrite wasn't demon-possessed," I went on. Although it would take a person who was at least demonically deranged to come up with the way Terry had been murdered. I cleared my throat. "From what I saw, someone put the loops of the dresses around Terry's neck, then fed the hem ends into the ironing machine—and let the machine keep pulling until he choked to death. The machine wasn't sophisticated enough to stop on its own if it got jammed. So whoever did this just kept the machine on. Or maybe, when they saw that the material was tight enough around Terry's neck, they turned it off and let nature finish up what they'd started."

"Would the machine be hard to use?" Officer Amelia asked. "Could anyone figure it out?"

"The machines don't have the most intuitive design," I said. "So unless someone had used it before, they'd have had to take a few minutes to figure it out." Minutes in which Terry could have come to . . . but he hadn't. "On the other hand, I did leave the user's manual that came with the machine on top of the machine."

"Had you plugged it in or started it up after you got it?"

"No," I said. "I was in a hurry for . . . my evening appointment . . . after Roger and I brought the machine back to my laundromat."

"So you didn't know if it worked?"

"Candace assured me it did. She said she'd just started it up to be sure before giving it to me, but that it hadn't been used in years." I bit my lip. Did that make Candace look bad?

Then I thought more about what I'd said. Someone had to take the time to plug in the machine, start it up, and figure it out before, well, feeding the slip dresses into the machine.

I shook my head at the murder method.

It was too . . . weird . . . to seem spur-of-the-moment.

Yet who premeditates a murder and thinks they'll kill someone in the most bizarre way possible? Why not just lure Terry out for drinks—I was guessing that wouldn't be hard, from his behavior the night before at the Bar-None—then offer him a drive home but instead knock him out and shoot him? We were in the middle of rural territory . . . cornfields and woods and even caves. Plenty of places to hide a body where it wouldn't be discovered for weeks.

But this murder seemed designed to be discovered and to make headlines.

And I thought of something else.

The missing tie-dyed slip dresses.

It was incredible—but it just then hit me as the shock of the evening started to wear off and my questioning, logical brain kicked in. Whoever had stolen the dresses from my van also had to be Terry's murderer.

I cleared my throat. "Um, I haven't yet told you something . . . about those tie-dyed slip dresses . . ."

10

And that is how I ended up nearly talking my way into being held on suspicion of murdering Terry Tuxworth Jr., a man I'd met one time.

Oh, I wasn't actually *held*.

But as I started talking about the tie-dyed dresses and how they'd been taken from my van, which I was sure I'd left unlocked, and how my best guess was that Terry Tuxworth had taken them to spite the Mayfair Sisters, a startled look emerged on Officer Amelia's face.

And then that same look flashed across Chief Worthy's face.

And those looks said: *Hmmm. Who had opportunity? Josie. After all, the crime occurred at her place of business. We have only her word that she went to sleep after her evening out. Sure, she gave out two copies of her laundromat's key, but she herself has a key, of course.*

And those looks further said: *Hmmm. Who had means? Josie. After all, who has a passion for and thorough knowledge of the Ironrite? Josie. Yeah, the machine was in the Mayfair*

home . . . but the sisters were happy to give it away, and Josie
would have had no trouble operating the machine, whereas
anyone else in a fifty-mile radius would have had at least
some difficulty knowing how to operate it.

As for motive . . . well, I didn't have a motive and of
course I didn't kill Terry, but I reckoned the police thinking
would be: What if Josie woke up to hear Terry in her laundromat, went to investigate, became angry when Terry
wouldn't say how he had a key? Maybe Terry mouthed off at
Josie. Terry was already known in town for easily angering
people (witness the events at the Bar-None). Maybe Josie
became angry and bashed his head.

Or maybe she'd been angry over catching him with the
slip dresses.

Or (and I could just see Worthy in particular coming up
with this one) perhaps Josie, who's had quite a string of bad
luck with boyfriends, flirted with Terry and he spurned her.

In any case, motives aren't necessary for charging someone with a crime . . . I reckon because motives are as easy to
come by as fuzz on a sweater.

I knew I was in trouble when Worthy suddenly became
friendly: "Well, Josie, you've answered a lot of questions.
We'll probably have to ask you a few more, though, OK?
And just as a formality, if you could tell us your whereabouts earlier in the evening, any witnesses . . ."

"I had dinner with Levi Applegate!" I announced with
such gusto that the chief and his officer just stared at me.
Those looks told me that they now knew that I knew that
they suspected me . . . and even though I was perfectly innocent, I felt guilty. And terrified. After all, you didn't have
to *be* guilty to be *found* guilty.

Of course, it wouldn't surprise anyone that my fingerprints were all over my laundromat. And both Sally and I

had entered the back room where Terry had been murdered, so it wouldn't surprise anyone if a stray hair of mine was found on Terry.

But that meant that I couldn't be eliminated as a suspect, either.

Unless physical evidence was found on Terry during autopsy that pointed conclusively to the killer.

But what if it didn't?

The circumstantial evidence—means and opportunity—would point to . . . me.

"Levi Applegate," I said. "The new director of Stillwater Farms." I retraced my steps through the whole day. My time, thankfully, was all accounted for, up until the hour or so before Terry's murder.

"We both had filet mignon," I said, "Levi and I. And chocolate decadence for dessert." My stomach turned. It would be weeks—well, days, anyway—before I'd be able to face chocolate again. "We went to the Spring Mill Inn and—"

"That's fine," Worthy said cheerfully. "We'll just double-check with him. Standard procedure. Nothing to worry about."

Oh, I was worried, all right.

Really worried.

"What'm I gonna do if I'm locked up, even for suspicion?" I wailed. "I mean, it'll take a few days—I'm thinking, what, two or three? 'Cause the FBI is going to be involved, you know it will, in a high-profile case like this. And the medical examiner will have to do an autopsy. But if he—" I knew the county medical examiner was a he because Dr. Richard Pritchard (yes, that was his name. I think his mother must have given birth to him with either no medical comfort . . .

or too much) was also one of Paradise's two family practitioners. "—if he doesn't find clear proof of someone else as the murderer, then I really think I'm going to be booked on suspicion. Just because I know so much about the damned Ironrite machine!"

"Well, plus Terry was murdered in your laundromat, and it is fairly amazing you didn't hear any commotion but you heard my scream," Sally said.

I glared at her. She was driving us back to her trailer at the Happy Trails Park. I couldn't stay at my place, even if I wanted to, because of the police and evidence technicians still swarming over my laundromat, which would be closed for at least two to three days, I'd been warned, while it was carefully combed for evidence.

Not that I wanted to stay at my place right now. I hadn't even been able to bring myself to go back to my home for a change of clothes and a toothbrush.

So I was going with Sally back to Happy Trails. Her sons were off for the weekend with their grandparents, she told me, at an amusement park. So there was plenty of room for me at her mobile home, at least for one night. Until the boys returned on the next afternoon after church, it would be just her and me and Bozo. (Bozo was a beagle/Labrador mix as far as anyone could tell, and Sally had found him one night licking out a bourbon bottle by the Dumpster behind the Bar-None. She immediately adopted the scrawny fellow as a pet for her family—and as protection—and after getting the health all-clear from the veterinarian up in Masonville, brought him home and introduced him to Harry, Barry, and Larry as Boozer, their new dog. Fortunately, Harry misheard and called him Bozo, and we all finally convinced Sally that Bozo was a better name for her children's pet than Boozer, after pointing out the permanent mental damage they'd suffer if they had to introduce their dog Boozer at pet show day at the elementary school.)

"You know I didn't kill Terry Tuxworth," I said. "Why would I?"

"You wouldn't," Sally said, quietly.

"But what if I'm convicted, anyway, just based on means and opportunity? That does happen, you know."

"Not in the age of DNA testing," Sally said.

"Oh yeah? My DNA is all over the murder site . . . because I own it! Unless someone else's DNA is all over the place, that's not going to help me. And even if someone else's DNA is all over the place, if there are no other suspects, then what?"

"Any number of people could have killed Terry," Sally said. "The Mayfairs. T-Bone. Other people who Terry pissed off in just the short time he was here. Anyone who was unhappy with his loudly announced plans to buy the Mayfair house and turn it into a museum—which is about half the population of Paradise."

"So lots of people have motive to murder Terry . . . at my laundromat? With my . . . mangle? And two of the missing slip dresses?"

Sally was quiet.

"Exactly," I said, as her truck bounced over a rut at the entrance to Happy Trails.

Happy Trails, I thought, needed its entrance repaved.

Sally needed new shock absorbers for her truck.

And I needed a lawyer.

"Oh, Lord," I wailed. "What'll happen to Guy if I'm put away for murder?"

Mrs. Oglevee wasn't saying anything.

She was just inserting coins in a washer coin tray. Not sorting her darks from her whites. Not loading clothes.

Just inserting coins into one washer after another.

As soon as she finished inserting coins into a washer, it would disappear, only to be replaced by an identical washer.

And each time a new washer appeared, her outfit changed.

Waitress, prison guard, schoolmarm. Dressy, casual. Cold weather, warm weather. Her outfits changed in dizzying succession, like she was a geriatric version of Barbie set on auto-change. She even morphed briefly into a bikini.

That caused me to yelp.

"What are you doing?" I hollered, in my dream.

Mrs. Oglevee looked over her shoulder at me, glaring. Her bikini morphed into a ski suit. Thank the good Lord.

She clucked her tongue. "Josie, Josie," she said, shaking her head, just like she used to back in our junior high days. "You should do better accounting."

She went back to hurriedly putting coins in the washer trays as fast as she could. The washers and her hands were nearly a blur now.

What was she trying to tell me? Mrs. Oglevee never shows up in my dreams unless she wants to nag me about something I wasn't, in her opinion, understanding.

"What?" I asked, grumpily.

But Mrs. Oglevee was too busy, now, inserting coins in the washer—her hands a blur, her changing outfits a blur—to pay any attention to me.

Suddenly I felt a heavy weight on my chest, which made it difficult to gasp at the sudden realization of what Mrs. Oglevee was trying to tell me.

But I gasped anyway.

And woke up to find the source of the weight on my chest staring at me: Bozo.

He panted, happy that his new buddy had woken up, and drooled, right on the oversized "Drip by drip is really hip! Donate!" T-shirt (from the county blood center) that Sally had loaned me as a nightshirt.

I hollered—but not at Bozo. I yelled Sally's name loud enough to shake the trailer.

"But I only gave copies of your laundromat key to three people!" Sally said, sniffling every other word.

We were sitting at Sally's tiny kitchen table, which was still covered with a wreath-and-holly-themed vinyl tablecloth, never mind that we'd be coming up on Memorial Day the next weekend.

Even though she'd insisted on brewing coffee before our little chat—a delaying tactic, of course—Sally's coffee grew cold in her cup. She hadn't taken a single sip. Just sniffled.

I'd gulped down my coffee while glaring at her, hardening my heart to her sniffles.

"I trusted you with that key," I said. "You knew it was just for you to do your laundry after hours."

Sally stared down at her mug. "I know," she said, so sadly that I almost felt sorry for her.

"Well? What were you thinking?"

She looked up. "I gave a copy of one key to Mrs. Langenheimer," she said.

Sally didn't have to explain why she might have been so moved. Mrs. Langenheimer, who lives two trailers down from Sally, has arthritis and works as a bookkeeper for a tool and die shop up in Masonville. If she could get her laundry done after hours with full access to the washers in my laundromat, that would save her weekends for resting up.

"OK," I said as gruffly as possible.

"The other one went to the Rhinegolds," Sally said.

"What? But I already do all the Red Horse Motel linens."

Sally nodded. "Yeah. But their little washer and dryer in their house"—the motel was 1950s mom-n-pop architecture, meaning the motel had been built out on either side of the original house, making the original structure look like it had sprouted wings—"went kaput, and they knew if they brought in their personal laundry, you'd insist on doing it for free."

I started to argue that that didn't make Sally's actions right, but instead sighed. "That's true. But I don't see what's wrong with that."

"Pride," Sally said. "Everyone needs to keep their pride."

I felt myself starting to soften toward Sally. Aw, I thought. She just wanted to help out a struggling neighbor lady and our good friends the Rhinegolds . . .

Stop it! I told myself. I always do that . . . go ooey-gooey marshmallow far too fast and easily. Sally had violated my trust by passing out copies of keys to my laundromat like free passes. And somehow or another Terry Tuxworth had ended up in my laundromat, murdered.

I took another sip of coffee and narrowed my eyes at Sally. "Who else. You said you gave out three copies of the key."

Sally mumbled something.

"What?" I snapped. "Out with it!"

"Rhonda Farris!" She said the name so loudly that Bozo barked.

I stared at Sally and finally said, "Rhonda? T-Bone Baker's girlfriend?"

Sally nodded.

"But . . . Rhonda was just in my laundromat Saturday morning!"

Sally looked up at me. "I gave her the key yesterday afternoon. She came into the bar, told me she was going to leave T-Bone Monday morning. She'd taken your advice, she said, and was going to take a job and apartment up in Masonville, and before she did, she wanted to get all her clothes clean. She'd caught up on T-Bone's"—I nodded, remembering that she'd had only his laundry the previous morning—"but wanted to make sure she had, well, a clean start."

Sally cleared her throat. "More coffee?"

She was nervous, I could tell, that this situation was really going to harm our friendship. I didn't want it to, but I couldn't forgive her, not just yet.

I shook my head at her offer and pushed my mug away. Sally looked crestfallen, and I hardened my heart even further.

"You have seriously violated my trust," I said, "whatever your motives."

"I know, I know," Sally said quickly, tears rushing to her eyes. "And Josie, I am so, so sorry—"

I held up a hand. "Not now. I am not interested in apologies right now. I am interested in figuring out how Terry got in my laundromat, and I have to assume it was because of one of the keys you gave out, unless Chip's betrayed me, too."

Sally's face crumpled, and tears started down her face.

I looked away. "I will talk . . ." I paused, to clear my throat of a sudden lump. "I will talk to him later. In the meantime, I need to think very carefully about how Terry might have gotten ahold of one of those keys, because hopefully that could lead us to the killer, or at least some clues about the killer. Because right now, my life is on the line as the most likely suspect, from the police point of view."

"Well, I can't imagine Terry got the key from Mrs. Langenheimer," Sally said. "There's no reason their paths would cross. But I suppose he could have gotten it from Rhonda. He was flirting with her pretty heavily Friday night, letting her know he was at the Red Horse. Maybe she decided last night, after breaking up with T-Bone, that she'd pay Terry a visit . . ."

"And then he decides to do his laundry?"

Sally looked hurt. "Well, it could happen. Postcopulation rituals vary from couple to couple."

I arched an eyebrow. "Postcopulation rituals?"

Sally shrugged. "Harry," she said, citing the most precocious of her triplets, "has been asking a lot of, well, you know, questions lately about where babies come from. I've been putting him off while I study up on proper terminology."

"Just tell him babies happen when mommies and daddies—" I stopped, too late. Wrong path.

"Love each other?" Sally asked wryly. Her ex-husband had taken off shortly after the triplets were born, shocked at the sight of three little blue bundles of joy . . . and responsibility. She'd been courageous ever since, with the help of her ex in-laws, who loved their grandsons and Sally.

I sighed. It wasn't going to be easy to stay hard-hearted with my cousin and best friend.

"Look," I said, "I doubt anyone, including Terry, considers going to the laundromat along the lines of, say, a cigarette."

"Or rolling over and going to sleep," Sally muttered. She shook her head as if to clear it. "Anyway. It doesn't seem likely Terry got the key from Rhonda, either, although that would be convenient, since T-Bone threatened Terry. So that leaves the Rhinegolds." Sally leaned toward me. "My bet is that Terry demanded laundry services and they directed him to your laundromat, like they do all their customers. He probably hassled them so much about not having on-site laundry services that they loaned him the key that I'd loaned them!"

I stared at Sally, thinking: *Have you lost your mind?* My

facial expression must have reflected my thoughts, because Sally's triumphant look faded.

"Because Terry desperately wanted to do his laundry late last night? Because he's just that kind of guy? A neatnik who takes care of his own laundry? Are you kidding me?" I snorted. "My guess is he hasn't done his own laundry in years. Especially not at a laundromat, on a Saturday night, nearing midnight. No. You know what probably happened? Just like you made copies of my key for three people, those people may well have made copies of their keys for who knows how many people. All kinds of people could have keys to my laundromat by now . . . anyone in town, in fact!

"It's more likely that instead of Terry going to my laundromat on his own, someone lured him there—"

"But his car was in your parking lot!" Sally protested.

I ignored her. "—maybe even getting him to drive, and knew that the Ironrite was there, and knew just how to kill him with it, not caring—maybe even hoping—I'd get the blame just due to circumstance—"

"Which brings us right back to the Mayfairs," Sally said eagerly. "Who else could it be? So we need to start investigating—"

"I'm not investigating," I said, standing up. Sally stared up at me, shocked. I'd been the one dragging her and Cherry into investigations over the past year. "This isn't some lark, Sally," I said. "It's my life on the line. So today I'm going to church. And tomorrow I'm hiring an attorney."

11

After that brave proclamation, I realized two important things: (1) I didn't have my van and (2) I didn't have a change of clothes.

So I was beholden to Sally to get a ride back into town. She realized the problem, too, and offered to give me the ride without me even asking.

We were silent on the way into town. I was, I admit it, stewing, not even willing to give Sally a little credit for having at least given keys to my laundromat to people who really seemed to need them. She hadn't just passed them out willy-nilly. The folks who'd used the laundromat had been quiet and neat and clean.

But I really had no way of knowing if they'd given the keys to other people, and what if those people had in turn passed out keys to others?

I'd have to have my locks changed.

And in any case, Sally had betrayed my trust.

When we pulled into my laundromat building, I felt a little pang at seeing the yellow police tape tied around the front doors. I hopped out of Sally's truck without saying thanks or good-bye, slamming the door without looking back, and went around to the back of my laundromat. The police tape was on the back door, too.

How long before my business was no longer a crime scene? How long before customers could return . . . or would they even want to return? How long before I felt comfortable in my laundromat, in the back storage room/office, in my apartment?

I came back around to the side of my building. Sally's truck was gone. I felt a pang of disappointment, but what did I expect?

She'd confessed the truth, apologized, and I wasn't ready to accept that apology just yet. I couldn't really expect her to hang around for more guilt from me.

I went up the metal staircase. My hand shook as I unlocked my door.

I hurried through my shower, my change of clothes, my teeth brushing, not pausing at all to enjoy my beautifully redone apartment.

I locked my apartment door as I left, checking and rechecking several times that it was secure, and then drove to church by myself, belatedly thinking that maybe I should have invited Sally to come with me.

Not that she would have come, I thought defensively. Sally doesn't, she says, cotton to organized religion.

By the time I arrived at Paradise Methodist Church—the only Methodist church in Paradise, although we do also offer Catholic, Lutheran, Baptist, Presbyterian, and several nonaffiliated options . . . but only the one bar (Sally's)—the congregation was singing the "Gloria Patri."

I slid into the last pew on the left aisle, not wanting to cause a ruckus by sitting where I usually do, a few pews forward.

". . . as it was in the beginning . . ." I joined in. My voice wobbled.

". . . is now, and ever shall be . . ." There was a rustling, as someone on the right side of the church started shuffling out of a pew. Who was causing such a commotion, I thought, annoyed.

". . . world without end . . ." Suddenly Levi Applegate was beside me.

". . . amen, amen . . ." we all finished up, including Levi.

But the pastor hadn't even gotten through the first sentence of the prayer when I started crying quietly.

By the prayer's amen, Levi had handed me a hanky—fresh, clean, white, and pressed, which somehow made me cry even more.

Because how was I supposed to resist a man who was sexy and adorable, who somehow made me feel like I'd known him a whole lifetime—instead of just twenty-four hours—and who came equipped with fresh white hankies for womenfolk in distress?

By the end of service, I'd pulled myself together, but I didn't want to talk to anyone. I knew all the folks rushing toward me as soon as service was over had heard by now about what had happened the night before at my laundromat, and I knew they'd be curious and have a lot of questions. Even if those questions were served up with kindness and good intentions, I just didn't feel like facing them quite yet.

The irony didn't escape me. Ever since junior high, my nickname has been Nosey Josie. I haven't resisted sticking my nose into other people's business, or eavesdropping at my laundromat—or anywhere else in town, for that matter—or asking carefully phrased questions. But I just wasn't ready to be at the receiving end of that.

Levi read my expression perfectly, and proclaimed loudly—even before Eva Rae Gallup could get to me—"Well, Josie, we'd better hurry if we're going to go on that picnic!"

And then he grabbed me by the elbow and steered me out of the crowd and to his car.

"We're going on a picnic?" I said, once I was in his car and we were pulling out of the church parking lot.

"We are now," Levi said cheerfully. "Make up for that missed breakfast."

"Oh no!" I yelped. "I'm so sorry . . . I clean forgot . . ."

"Understandable, considering the circumstances," Levi said. He pulled up to a stop sign. "Where we headed? We need a place close by to pick up picnic fare."

"Um, turn left," I said. "So you know about what happened last night?"

"I knew last night, several hours after the murder," he said. "But I'll tell you more about that later. In any case, I wanted to call you, but realized I didn't have your number. The Red Horse owners, though, assured me you'd be fine. You're very resourceful, they said. I went to Sandy's Restaurant as planned, and when you weren't there, I checked at your apartment, and when you weren't there, either, I just went on to church. I figured I'd either catch up with you there, or sometime at Stillwater, but I'm glad I found you there."

"Me, too," I said. I pulled his hanky out of my purse, and carefully folded it. "I can launder your hanky before I give it back to you."

"No need," he said, plucking the hanky from my hand and tucking it into his inner suit pocket. "I'll do it when I do the rest of my laundry . . . at Toadfern's Laundromat, when it reopens."

I was glad he felt so confident about the future of my business . . . and of my life.

"Turn left up here, and then take a right into Elroy's Gas Station," I said.

Levi glanced at me, clearly puzzled, but did as I asked. When he'd pulled into one of the three parking spaces in front of the "quick mart" part of Elroy's Gas Station, I said, "Here we are. Best place for picnic fare."

"Um . . . I like cheese crackers as much as anyone, but I was kinda hoping . . ."

I laughed, and immediately felt amazed by that. An hour before, I'd have sworn I'd never feel like laughing again. "Around here, we're the land that fast-food development forgot. We have Sandy's Restaurant. We have home cooking, which normally I'd be glad to offer—"

I stopped, again feeling a tremor over how violated my home felt to me now. Levi patted my hand.

"And on Sundays, we have Elroy's mama's fried chicken. Through the week, Elroy just has hot dogs and chili available for takeout, but on Sundays, to serve the church crowd, his mama fries up several batches of chicken."

Levi lifted his eyebrows. "Does she happen to make potato salad, too?"

I nodded. "And for dessert, we can get a local treat— Breitenstrater's mini pies. They come in peach, apple, and cherry."

Levi smacked his lips. "Let's hurry, before the rest of the church crowd gets here."

We took our picnic fare out to Licking Creek Lake State Park, bypassing the turnoff to the small amphitheater where the Mayfair Sisters would be performing in just a few days, and continuing down the main gravel road to the man-made lake.

Elroy, upon meeting Levi and learning we were going on a picnic, had given us each a Big Fizz soda, plastic forks, paper plates, paper napkins, and a clearance Easter paper tablecloth—festooned with bunnies and crosses, in an unselfconscious mixing of secular and religious—which was originally $1.99 but marked down to 50 cents. It was a nice gesture, and Elroy had waggled his eyebrows at me as we were leaving, to show his approval of Levi, who in turn was gracious enough to pretend not to notice either Elroy's eyebrow waggling or my blushing.

At the lake—which we had to ourselves except for an occasional jogger or dog walker, since it was still too cold even in May for lake swimming—Levi and I spread out the paper cloth and our picnic fare.

We happily munched away while I filled Levi in on the history of the lake—how the creek had been dammed up to create a man-made lake, with the hope that the recreational activity would draw business to the area, and how that had happened but not to the extent hoped for—and then carefully cleaned up our trash. A wind had kicked up, and we didn't want to litter the beach, even if it was gritty sand that did not invite barefoot strolls. This stuff was definitely not imported from the white sand beaches of Florida.

Then we fell into a comfortable silence.

And I realized how obliged I usually felt to talk, to fill silences, with everyone I knew . . . but not with this man I'd known for twenty-four hours. Well, more like thirty hours. But still. That, ironically, made me uncomfortable.

Levi must have sensed that because he broke the silence by saying, "I ought to fill you in on what happened last night after our date."

Date. He said date. Not *business dinner.* But *date.* As if we'd been dating for months now.

"I got back to my room at the Red Horse, took a quick shower, went to bed," Levi said. "Next thing I know, I'm waking up to the sound of a woman shrieking in the room next to mine. Terry Tuxworth's room."

I gasped.

"I'd only met him last night, when I came back to change before our date."

There was that word again. Somehow as gasp-worthy to me as the fact Levi had been booked in the room next to Terry's.

"He was hurrying up to his room just as I was opening my door, and complained to me about the fact there were no laundry facilities at the motel, and how he just couldn't believe that. What kind of crummy motel was this, he said.

"Well, I didn't like that. The Rhinegolds have been very sweet to me, and they seem like a nice couple. So I said, 'Didn't pack enough for your trip?' Which made him even more annoyed." Levi paused to grin. "He started to say that of course he'd packed enough for his trip, it wasn't like he needed to wash his undies, it was just . . . and then he stopped, and let himself in the room. That was my only encounter with him, and he didn't seem very nice."

"I only met him once, too," I said, "at the Mayfairs, and I had the same reaction. But go on. What happened after you awoke last night?"

"I put on my robe—"

Did he sleep in the nude? I wondered, then shook my head to refocus.

"—and ran outside. The police were trying to calm a woman who was clearly startled—nearly hysterical—in Terry's room that they'd let themselves into with a pass key from the Rhinegolds. I saw the Rhinegolds standing in the parking lot and went over to them. They explained that they'd already heard, before the police even arrived, about Terry Tuxworth's murder at your laundromat.

"I guess someone working at the police station called her sister, told her about it, and the sister called a friend, who is friends with Greta Rhinegold, and knows she doesn't sleep much anyway, and called her even though it was so late."

I nodded. "We hear these days about social networking on the Internet," I said, "but it's got a long way to go to catch up with Paradise's grapevine."

Levi smiled. "At least the Rhinegolds were prepared for the police when they arrived. All they wanted to do was look through Terry's room in case there were any clues that would help them.

"Instead they found Rhonda Farris—that's who the Rhinegolds said she was," Levi finished.

"Rhonda! She is—was—T-Bone's ex-girlfriend. Terry and T-Bone fought at the Bar-None night before last—"

"—the night we met," Levi said, and smiled, as if we'd been properly introduced at a tea party, instead of meeting because I'd plowed into him.

I blushed and cleared my throat. "Anyway, they fought over Rhonda. She was at my laundromat yesterday morning, telling me about a job offer she had up in Masonville, and how she wanted to take it and leave T-Bone. I encouraged her to do that. I guess, on the way out of town, though . . ."

"Maybe this information will help make T-Bone a suspect, depending on what Rhonda told the police," Levi said helpfully.

"You've already figured out I'm a probable suspect?" I asked.

Levi looked chagrined. "It was, ah, well . . . the talk at church before service. I got there earlier and overheard several people talking, and I guess I shouldn't have kept listening, but it seems that same woman at the police department told her sister, who told . . ."

I burst out laughing.

Levi lifted his eyebrows. "You're taking being gossiped about as a possible murder suspect very well," he said.

"It's just . . . since junior high, I've been known around town as Nosey Josie. I tend to eavesdrop and listen in when I shouldn't and ask questions about things that aren't really my business because I'm so curious. And now the tables are not only turned—with me being the subject of everyone else's curiosity—but I suspect I've met someone just as nosey as me!"

Levi blushed, and I couldn't help but notice how that made him even more appealing. And he said, with feigned innocence, "Me? Nosey?" He chuckled. "I admit it. I am. But I think that's a terrible nickname for you. You should never be called Nosey Josie. How about . . . Lovely Josie?" And with that, he took my hands in his, and stared at me . . . hard . . . with those deep brown eyes of his.

I held his gaze. Putting aside I'd only met him yesterday, here was a man who was good-looking, with his black hair flecked with gray and his dark eyes; who seemed like someone I'd always known; who knew how to read my expressions; who was comfortable to be silent around; who was nosey like me; who carried clean, white hankies; who was game to picnic on Elroy's mama's fried chicken, albeit purchased at a gas station, and proclaim how good it was.

There had to be something wrong with him.

Maybe he was a bad kisser.

And then I remembered what *was* wrong with this scenario.

Levi was the director of Stillwater Farms, where my cousin Guy lived. And back when I was still on the director search committee, I'd run across an interview with him that had made me wonder about his views of adults with autism and how those might impact Guy . . . and the other residents.

"Josie," Levi said, his voice dropping low, which made a gentle heat start within me, "when I came here this weekend, I expected to be introduced to the Stillwater community. I expected to start searching for a home in Masonville or Paradise. I expected to figure out things like where restaurants and churches and groceries and, yes, laundromats are.

"My first night in town, I went to the local bar, hoping for a bourbon and water—"

Oh, Lord! His favorite drink was the same as my favorite drink!

"—to help me relax after the last leg of a long drive from New Mexico, and after putting my goods in storage and returning the U-Haul trailer in Masonville. I expected to have that drink, go back to my motel room, and get a good night's sleep before my next morning's formal introduction.

"I did not expect to literally run into a woman who makes me feel so . . . at home with myself. Who sparked, yes, lots of curiosity and interest. Who stuck in my head so much I couldn't sleep that night, after all."

My eyebrows went up at that—and so did my internal heat.

"I didn't expect to ask her out on a date the next day, or to spend an hour before that date carefully reviewing Stillwater's policies about fraternizing." He grinned. "By the way, we're safe. If we both worked there, we couldn't date, but there is nothing in the rules against Stillwater employees dating relatives of residents—"

I pulled my hands away, and my heart panged at how disappointed that made Levi look. "But, Levi, you need to understand . . . Guy means the world to me. And I was on the search committee, at least up until New Year's Eve when a, ah, mishap meant I had to cut back on my activities to get better." No point in telling him just now about how Sally, Cherry, and I nearly lost our lives in Lake Erie while in the middle of investigating the truth behind Mrs. Oglevee's death. "But I read several articles that quoted you, and a piece you wrote about—about—" I stuttered to a stop, not sure where I wanted to go with this.

"About how I think those of us who view autism as a neurological disability should listen to our friends across the aisle in the autism rights movement?" Levi asked gently.

I nodded.

To those outside the autism community, the phrase "autism rights movement" might sound like rights for those with autism to get the care and treatment they deserve.

But it's actually a movement by a variety of people—including some higher-functioning adults with autism—to put an end to thinking of autism as something to cure, or as something difficult for families to bear, but instead to see it as "neurodiversity," meaning that people whose neurological makeup is different should simply be accepted as who they are.

Which I suppose is fine if you're an adult with, say, a mild case of Asperger's.

But what about people like Guy, who have severe autism and mental retardation, and can't function on their own?

I didn't see Guy as a terrible burden to bear. I accepted him for who and what he was. But at the same time, I welcomed any intervention, so long as it was humane, such as his work in the greenhouse, that enabled his functioning.

Of course, I didn't have to spell all this out for Levi. He knew exactly what my concerns were.

"In my view, autism and Asperger's manifest like thumbprints—as unique as each individual who has the disorder," Levi said. "The conditions are so complex. I know how you feel, how overwhelming all the points of view are. I have a sister with Asperger's who happens to be highly functioning, and who holds with the neurodiversity view, although not to its most extreme. We disagree on a lot. But by listening to her perspective, I also learn how to take a fresh look at the complex issues around these disorders. I just don't see how any of us help each other with an us-them attitude. That's all I was trying to say in my interviews and my essay."

I nodded. "That makes sense."

"I'm glad," Levi said. "And your concern is a good one. We can talk about it more another time, but first . . ."

And then he pulled me toward him and kissed me.

Damn.

He was a good kisser.

A fine, imaginative, exciting kisser, and I kissed him back as we toppled to the Easter paper tablecloth.

We'd have kept kissing for a lot longer, I'm sure, if we both hadn't been startled by someone throat clearing.

We broke off from our kiss and stared up at Sally Toadfern.

Who was grinning down at us.

"Guess what!" she said excitedly. "I just talked to the Rhinegolds, and they admitted to me that late last night they gave their copy of the key to your laundromat to Terry Tuxworth Jr.!"

12

A half hour later, we all gathered at Sally's Bar-None. By "we" I mean Sally, Winnie, Caleb, Cherry, Levi, and myself.

Back at the gritty man-made beach, I would have been happy to turn my back on Sally and resume kissing Levi. As far as I was concerned, we were just getting started, but Sally insisted on explaining that she'd sought out all the people whom she'd given copies of my laundromat keys and interviewed them.

And then, she added, she'd assembled the usual people who help me with my investigations into murder and mayhem, who were waiting for us over at the Bar-None, just so we could all figure out a plan of action.

Levi shot me a curious look: the usual people? My investigations into murder and mayhem? Plan of action?

Sally saw his questioning look and was about to launch into an explanation but I cut her off with a quick "Fine!"

No point in scaring the poor man away, even if I didn't know a thing about him yet . . . except he made me feel more comfortable in my own skin than I ever had before. That he had gorgeous eyes. That he carried hankies.

And that he was a good . . . no, great . . . kisser.

Nope, sure wouldn't want to scare him away.

So that's how we ended up at the Bar-None, which Sally opened up special just for us, seeing as how her bar closes on Sundays, just like my laundromat and most every business in Paradise, except Elroy's Gas Station, on account of his mama's takeout fried chicken. Plus people always need gas.

Anyway, we pushed together several freestanding tables to make a conference table of sorts.

While Sally got us drinks—Big Fizzes and sweet teas and lemonades—I introduced Levi to everyone. He was sitting on my left, Cherry on my right, Caleb and Winnie across from us, with a spot saved for Sally.

"He's cute!" Cherry whispered to me, a bit too loudly.

"Hush up," I whispered back. "I can see that."

I caught Caleb's eyes, and started to look away. We hadn't dated in a while, but still . . .

Caleb gave me a little smile and a nod and a look that said, *Good for you!*

What? Did everyone assume that, just like that, Levi and I were an item?

But I didn't fight it. I just gave Caleb a small smile and nod back, and a look that said, *Thanks*. He didn't need or want my sympathy. What Caleb wanted, more than anything right now, was a big, juicy story that would launch him from the *Paradise Advertiser-Gazette* to a nationally recognized newspaper or magazine.

Sally distributed the drinks—I took a long, savoring sip of my sweet tea, which I like as an alternative to Big Fizz Cola every now and then, especially since Sally's hit on the perfect recipe.

As Sally took care of finishing passing out drinks, I caught a bit of Winnie's and Levi's conversation. He was easily charming Winnie with talk about books about autism and Asperger's that he'd love to donate to the library system.

Winnie caught my eye as Sally sat down across from me, flashing me a look much like Caleb's. I just smiled. The rational part of my brain wanted to scream: *I just met this guy yesterday! And it doesn't matter anyway, because I'm probably going to jail soon, which is just as well because my apartment and business now feel too sullied for me to ever return to!* I've got to be the only person in the universe with timing this sucky: love at first sight simultaneous with being a suspect in a murder committed with a vintage ironing machine.

Of course, the irrational part of my brain wanted to scream: *Yippee! Isn't he adorable! And sweet!*

But I didn't get to scream anything, because Sally quickly called our meeting to order.

"Now, we all know Josie's possibly in a world of trouble over this murder, which took place at her laundromat last night," Sally said, "and it's all my fault, because I gave copies of keys to her laundromat to three people, and somehow one of those keys either got into Terry's hand or into his killer's hand, because the idea that Josie killed Terry is just ridiculous."

Everyone murmured agreement with that. Well, how nice. These folks didn't think I was enough of a lunatic to kill someone just because that someone was in my laundromat after hours. Too bad none of them worked for the Paradise Police Department.

"Well, I just gave out those keys because I was only trying to help," Sally said.

Damn! Why did she have to use that phrase? That's what I always said whenever I tried to help someone, and in the process just made the situation worse. And whenever I said, "I was only trying to help!" I meant it, and felt so bad about myself.

How could I not feel a pang of forgiveness for her?

I glared at Sally, still trying to feel mad, but Sally just gave me a smile that said, *I'm so sorry and I'm trying to make it right.*

I sighed. I'd been at church that morning, hoping for solace in my time of trouble, but most weeks I just went because I needed to be reminded about the whole we-mess-up-but-we're-forgiven-anyhow dynamic that, I hope, plays a role in the universe. I'd messed up plenty of times, and folks had forgiven me. So . . . now I knew, just as it was my time on the cosmic calendar to be the focus of curiosity and a murder investigation, it was also my time to do the forgiving.

"Sally," I said, "I love you. And I know you were just trying to help. And . . . I forgive you."

Tears jumped to her eyes, and most everyone murmured some variation of "Awww . . ." as we briefly clasped hands. Hugging across the table would have upended our sweet teas, after all.

I pulled my hands back and added, a mite grumpily, "I appreciate everyone wanting to help, but I don't see what we can do."

"Investigate," Sally said firmly, wiping her eyes quickly. "Do a little, ah, legwork on behalf of the Paradise Police Department."

Cherry leaned across me and said to Levi, "See, Josie used to date John Worthy, who is the chief of police, back in junior high school. Well, he wasn't the chief then, of course, he was just another kid in junior high, but he's never quite forgiven Josie for writing up a story about how he'd started dating the football coach's daughter just to get a good spot on the team, and he's the one who started her Nosey Josie nickname, and he always believes the worst of her." She tut-tutted. "Some people just never grow up."

Levi tried to hold back a laugh, which ended up coming out as a half snort, and I elbowed Cherry hard enough to make her yelp a little as I said, "Thanks, Cherry."

"Well, as silly as it may sound, it's true. Worthy never wants to believe the best about anyone, especially Josie," Sally said. "So, anyway, I got to thinking, what if I tried to figure out what happened to those keys? What if Josie was right, and copies were made and passed along, or something?

"So I talked briefly to Mrs. Langenheimer, who lives two trailers down from me. Of course, she assured me that she hadn't given the keys to anyone, which I knew she would because she doesn't talk to anyone but me." Sally paused as we all pondered the loneliness of Mrs. Langenheimer.

"I should bring her a cake," Winnie said. "Pineapple upside-down cake. Next week, after all this is sorted out."

"Good idea," Sally said. "And of course she hadn't met Terry Tuxworth at all. In fact, she didn't know he was in town and she only vaguely remembered the Mayfair sisters. But I just wanted to be thorough. Then I went on over to see T-Bone the next street over."

Cherry gasped. "You didn't give T-Bone a key to Josie's laundromat, did you?"

Sally frowned at her. "Of course not! First off, he'd never do his own laundry, and second of all, he'd have made so much noise he'd have woken her up."

"It is true," I said a bit prissily, "that I never heard people sneaking into my laundromat in the middle of the night . . . until last night, of course."

"Death is noisy," Winnie offered sympathetically.

"At least murder is," Caleb said. His effort to fight off a smile was making his mustache twitch.

"Death should be, too," Winnie said. "'Do not go gentle into that good night. Fight, fight against the dying of the light . . .'"

Winnie is a librarian who runs the Mason County Bookmobile and is always trying to remind people of the classics.

Sally cleared her throat. "*Anyway*, of course I didn't give T-Bone a key. I reckon I have more sense than that. But I did give his ex-girlfriend, Rhonda Farris, a copy of the key."

"That was the woman in Terry Tuxworth's motel room, next to my room," Levi said.

Cherry gasped. "Ooooh la la! Those motel room walls are mighty thin. Hear anything?"

I kicked her under the table. Cherry gasped again. Sally ignored her.

"T-Bone didn't know anything about the key, he said, but he knew all about Rhonda meeting up with Terry. She made a big deal of it, he said, bragging about it as she threw her stuff into the back of her hatchback."

Caleb whistled. "Wow. How did T-Bone seem? Was he angry-sounding as he told you this? He sounds like the best suspect in this case."

Sally shook her head. "'Fraid not. He was sort of apathetic about the whole thing, like he was already over Rhonda leaving him. Maybe because Jolene Watson was there."

"Ew! That trailer trash?" Cherry exclaimed—then looked at Sally. "Sorry. You know I didn't mean—"

"Whatever," Sally said. She—and I—were used to Cherry's gaffes.

"Well, anyway," Cherry said, having the good grace to look embarrassed, "Jolene comes in every now and again to my salon to get her hair and nails done, and she's always dressed trashy, and always complains that the job wasn't done right, and never tips."

Cherry's red faux-tipped fingers grasped the plunging neckline of her tiger-print spandex top, and she wiggled to pull it up a bit, just to show she was a whole lot classier than trashy Jolene, even if adjusting her clothing to prove it made her DD girls seismically shift in the process.

I was kinda glad Levi wasn't getting the full view. Not that my sister Cs were exactly blocking his line of sight.

"But T-Bone did give me Rhonda's new phone number and address," Sally said. "I haven't had a chance to contact her yet."

"And that leaves the Rhinegolds," I said a mite impatiently.

"Yes, the Rhinegolds," Sally said. "Now that's where this starts to get really interesting. See, late last night, about eleven, Terry came into the motel office and rang the bell, pulling the Rhinegolds away from the Masonville local news." The Rhinegolds, like me, live in an apartment over their business. "He demanded to use their washer and dryer—right then. Greta said he looked panicky and distraught. She told him their personal washer and dryer was on the fritz and wasn't available for motel guests, anyway, and that she always directs guests to Toadfern's Laundromat."

"That's true," I said. "The Rhinegolds have been good about directing people to me." Of course, the next closest laundromat is twenty miles up the road, in Masonville. Still. Referrals are referrals.

"And Greta told Terry that your laundromat would be open on Monday," Sally went on, "but that just wasn't good enough for him. He went into a rant about how he'd never stayed at a motel that didn't have 24/7 access to a laundromat and he was going to check out and make sure he got word out in the press that anyone coming to Paradise, Ohio, for the Mayfair Sisters' final concert and auction shouldn't stay at the Red Horse, if they didn't call you and tell you to let him in."

"What an idiot," said Caleb.

"And bully," added Levi.

The two men looked at each other and grinned as if they'd been pals their whole lives. I resisted rolling my eyes.

"Why didn't they just call me," I asked. "I'd have been glad to set Tuxworth straight and give him directions to the no-service 24/7 laundromat up in Masonville, if that's all he wanted—and to tell him to back off my friends."

And then, I thought, maybe Terry Tuxworth's sorry butt would still be alive . . . or at least murdered elsewhere.

A sudden uncomfortable silence had hushed everyone at the table. An alarm went off in my head. What was going on?

Finally, Winnie said, an awkward warble to her voice, "Well, Josie, see, word had spread around most of the town about your date with Levi, here, and I'm guessing the Rhinegolds just didn't want to disturb you."

I glanced at Levi, and immediately a blush rushed up my face, because he was grinning. And then he waggled his eyebrows at me.

I closed my eyes and put my head to my hands. Let me get this straight, I thought:

1. Word spreads around town I'm on a date with the new, hot director of Stillwater Farms—even though it's really a business dinner.
2. Terry Tuxworth Jr., the son of the Mayfair Sisters' despised manager, appears in the Rhinegolds'

    office, demanding access to their washer/dryer or
    my laundromat.

3. The Rhinegolds don't want to disturb me because,
    hey, I'm on a hot date with the new, hot director of
    Stillwater Farms and, who knows, I might be
    having hot sex with a man I've known less than
    twenty-four hours . . . so they give Terry the key to
    my laundromat.

4. Terry goes to my laundromat to do his laundry and
    ends up murdered with a bizarre combination of the
    Mayfairs' vintage Ironrite ironing machine and the
    Mayfairs' slip dresses, which mysteriously went
    missing from my van earlier in the day. And . . .

5. I didn't even get to finish kissing . . . never mind
    having hot sex . . . with Levi.

Gee, in all that, surely there was something we could all work with to remove me from the suspect list of who-killed-Terry.

I thought for a few more moments and then opened my eyes, and found everyone looking at me expectantly.

I looked at Sally, and she gave me a small smile, encouraging me to share whatever grand plan I'd formed on the spot from her news.

"Does anyone else think it's really weird that Terry was so desperate to do his laundry so late at night?" I asked.

Everyone nodded and looked at me eagerly.

I went on: "Well, it's also weird because I didn't see a laundry basket near Terry, and I would imagine that if the police found a laundry basket of men's clothes sitting out, they'd have thought that it was at least possible that it was Terry's. But I never saw any of the investigators walk out with a basket. Did you, Sally?"

She shook her head. "I sure didn't, Josie."

"But why would he be at the laundromat? There are plenty of other places he could go to meet someone that would be more private. And the lights were all on in the front and back rooms. So Terry must have had something he desperately needed to wash.

"And it's likely the police didn't think to check the washers since, as I said, there were no baskets of laundry near Terry."

"So you're going to break into your own laundromat and check the washers and dryers?" Cherry asked. "OK, you'll need a flashlight, all black clothing, a ski mask . . ."

"Cherry," I said, "it's Sunday afternoon and the only thing keeping me out of my own laundromat is yellow police tape. There are no police guarding the place. I think I'll just walk in and . . . look."

"But you'll need a lookout," Levi said. "And I need to take you back to town to get your car from the church, anyway."

I looked at him, and he smiled again at me, and all the protests I was about to give about not needing a lookout melted away.

"Fine," I said. "Levi can watch at my apartment in case any cruisers happen to roll down Main Street past my laundromat, while I take a look in the washers and dryers—just in case.

"Now, the other thing that's odd is the fact that the three tie-dyed slip dresses went missing from my minivan at some point yesterday." I explained that in more detail to everyone, and finished with, "And of course the next time I saw them, they were used in combination with the Ironrite to strangle Terry."

I shuddered at the memory of finding him like that.

"Maybe Terry took them just to shake up the Mayfair sisters, a sort of juvenile spiteful prank," I said, "and the killer just used them because they were handy."

"That's a pretty creative leap," Winnie said. "Kinda like Picasso putting the bike handle bars at the back of the bike seat to make a bull sculpture."

We all looked at her.

She shrugged. "Just saying."

"Or maybe," Sally said, "Terry took them because there was some stain that provided evidence to some crime and he wanted it washed out."

"But I didn't see any stains on the dresses, and in any case, I laundered them," I said. "That was part of my job."

"On a tie-dyed dress, it might be easy to miss stains," Sally said. "Maybe if you didn't know where to look for it, you wouldn't see it."

"Well, then, why would he want to wash it out?" Cherry said.

"Well, now, I don't know, but—"

"It seems possible there is something about those dresses that made someone take them and then use them to kill Terry, instead of them just being handy," Caleb said soothingly. He'd seen me, Cherry, and Sally get into a squabble often enough, and he was trying to keep us from that. "I could interview the seamstress who worked on the costumes . . ."

"Moira Evans," I offered.

"Right, Moira Evans," Caleb went on, "just telling her I wanted her thoughts on working on the costumes for the auction." He paused, thought about that. "Yeah. That could be good—since I can't get an in with the Mayfairs."

"And maybe she'll have something to say about the slip dresses that will give us a clue," Caleb concluded.

"And I will research the Mayfair family history in depth," Winnie spoke up.

We all looked at her.

She smiled. "You never know what you might find by looking into someone's past. We know the official story of the Mayfairs, and what people around here know, but this Terry Tuxworth Jr. . . . maybe there is something about his family's past relationship with the Mayfairs that will give us a clue."

I looked at Winnie appreciatively. "Kinda like putting together pieces of a bike in a different way to come up with a sculpture?"

Her smile widened. "Exactly."

"But what about me? What do I get to do?" Cherry wailed.

I looked at her pouting face and smiled. "Why, Cherry, isn't your business closed on Sundays and Mondays?"

"Yes," she said.

"And don't you know Rhonda Farris much better than I do?"

"Ummm . . . well . . . yes." Cherry stared at her faux fingertips as if suddenly tempted to gnaw them off.

"Great! You get to help me track down Rhonda and get her to tell us everything she can about Terry's last night alive."

Cherry rubbed her hands together, the faux fingertips clacking together ominously. "Oh, goodie! A road trip to dig up gossip."

I made a mental note to myself: Before leaving Monday with Cherry . . . call a lawyer.

13

"I like your friends," Levi said.

After leaving the Bar-None, Levi drove me back to the Methodist church, where I retrieved my minivan. Then he followed me back to my laundromat/apartment—not that he needed to in terms of keeping from getting lost. But it was nice of him to assume a ladies-first position anyway.

We parked and I led the way up to my apartment to figure out how to best proceed with Levi as my lookout and me as spy in my own laundromat.

But first we were sitting on my couch in my newly renovated apartment, each of us self-consciously and primly at opposite ends. I'd made us cups of coffee—instant, but the good instant, with hazelnut flavoring, just like in Belgium (so it said on the can)—not because we really needed refreshments after the picnic and Bar-None, but because it was only polite and because it gave us something to do with our hands.

Which, personally, I needed, because what I wanted to do with my hands was jump on Levi and start running them through his thick, black hair . . .

I took a sip of my Belgian hazelnut coffee and recomposed my thoughts.

"I like my friends, too," I said. "Of course, I've known most of them my whole life."

Levi laughed. "You're thinking I move too fast, aren't you?"

Oh, Lord. We'd been in my apartment long enough for me to make two cups of instant coffee, and already the conversation was turning awkward.

"I'm just not sure how you can know you like people or not after spending about an hour around them," I said, a bit tensely.

"Your friends are eager to help you in a time of need," Levi said. "Lots of people would be put off by a friend being suspected of murder and would distance themselves. Instead they want to help you, as best they can. What's not to like?"

"You make a good point," I said, "but Cherry can be bossy, and Sally can be thoughtless, and Winnie can over-mother-hen, and Caleb's mostly out for his career."

I took another sip of coffee and gave Levi a so-there! look.

"Ah," he said. "So it turns out your friends are human instead of perfect demigods. Well, now that I know that . . ." He lifted an eyebrow and sipped coffee—a touché gesture.

"Well, it's nice to know you judge people based on qualities like their loyalty to their friends," I said. "Still, you seem to dive into relationships awfully quickly."

Ha! Take that!

Except . . . Levi put his coffee mug down on the coffee table . . . and clasped his hands in his lap and looked at me . . . hard.

"Are we still talking about my fledgling relationships with your friends?" he asked.

I gulped, midsip, too much hazelnut-instant, and instead of it making me think I was transporting to Belgium, far, far away from my troubles in Paradise, Ohio, the heat of the coffee hit the back of my throat, made me cough and swallow at the same time in a funny—and by that I mean weird—convulsion, and ultimately spew coffee through my nose.

Levi whipped out his hanky.

I tried to daintily dab up the coffee from my face as if this was a common, normal thing to do. Levi, meanwhile, had gently taken my coffee mug and put it on the coffee table. And moved closer to me on the couch.

"Are you OK?"

He asked this with complete seriousness, no hint of laughter in his eyes or face.

"I am fine," I said, folding the handkerchief in squares. I stared at it for a second. He took it from me and put it back in his pocket.

"I'll launder that later," he said. His right arm went up on the couch and his right hand ended up behind my head. I felt warmth coming from him that was so tempting . . .

"That's what you said about the last handkerchief," I said grumpily. "How many do you carry? Do you do magic tricks with them? Make origami out of them?"

Levi laughed, and I caught a whiff of his breath—fresh and pepperminty in spite of the coffee. He had, I realized, eaten a mint between the church and my apartment. Maybe because he wanted to continue the kissing session we'd started on the beach?

I hoped so and yet I hoped not and yet . . .

I felt dizzy.

A sensation that worsened as Levi suddenly looked serious. "Josie, you make me laugh, and—"

"I reckon that's another quality you value in people you've just met—"

He gently put a forefinger on my lips. "Let me finish," he said, "before I lose my courage."

He moved his finger away, and I felt a little disappointed. And even more attracted to him because he'd just admitted that what he wanted to say would take courage.

"You have no reason to believe me, but no, I normally don't move so quickly to get close to a woman I find attractive," Levi said. "In fact, until I got here, my plan was to sink all my energy into my new job at Stillwater. I can't wait to get to work, to really immerse myself in the Stillwater community, and to see how I can work with others at Stillwater to share just how special it is. It should be a model community for other areas."

I nodded enthusiastically. I knew just how he felt.

Levi smiled. "I'm glad to see you feel the same way, but I'm getting off point. My point was that I had promised myself I wouldn't date for a year after I got here."

Disappointment weighted me down. "Oh. Because of your new job?" My voice squeaked.

"No," Levi said. "Because of Estelle. My fiancée. Well, former fiancée. Through a friend, she'd found out about a job I qualified for to manage a new outpatient counseling service at a hospital in an upscale area. The pay would have been at least twice as much.

"I explained to her that I was dedicated to the autism/Asperger's community. She knew that when we started dating. But she told me it was my duty to move on and earn more, especially as a husband, and that otherwise I was wasting a perfectly good psychiatry degree.

"And when I told her that, no, for me working outside of the autism community would be wasting a perfectly good psychiatry degree . . . she dumped me."

We stared at each other a long moment. All kinds of emotions—outrage, sadness, and, yes, even glee that Levi was free now to date—swirled in my head.

Finally, I said, "So . . . you're on the rebound. And you promised yourself you wouldn't make any romantic moves . . . in your raw state."

Levi nodded. "More or less. It's been six months since I broke up with Estelle, and I think I'm over it. What really rocked me was I thought I was a good judge of character, but I was really blindsided by Estelle. So I'm not exactly raw, but I don't exactly trust myself yet, either, or at least I didn't, and then I met you and we went out to dinner . . ." He shook his head, pulled his hand back to his lap. "You know, I just can't explain what's happening here."

Love at first sight? I thought . . . but didn't say. It sounded so juvenile and corny.

"I can see from your eyes," he said, "that you've been hurt, too."

Oh, let me count the ways. But saying that would have been too bitter . . . and amazingly, bitter was not at all what I was feeling. I was feeling . . . joyful. And peaceful. Yes, peaceful, that however our relationship developed . . . into friendship or something more . . . would be fine.

"I'm thirty," I said. "So it would be surprising if I hadn't been hurt. But what I've learned is that honesty in a relationship is crucial to me. I don't mean knowing each second what the other person is thinking. I mean about what the person really wants, what's important to him."

Levi grinned. "So . . . I shouldn't tell you it was kinda cute when you squirted hazelnut coffee through your nose—"

I swatted him on the arm for that.

"—but I should tell you that what I really want is more of this . . ."

And then Levi leaned over, pulled me to him, and kissed me long. And hard. And long.

After that, I snuggled up against his chest. Was it weird to think about how neatly I fit against his shoulder, with his arm around me, so soon after meeting him for the first time?

Then I decided to just put aside my concerns about how quickly we seemed to be falling for each other. Who said emotions must fit a timetable: attraction on first date, more attraction on second date, affection only on third date?

After a while, Levi said, "Josie, I could stay here with you for hours, just like this, but . . ."

I sighed. "I know. I have to go look through the washers and dryers in my laundromat, just in case Terry left a clue there."

"You've got your cell phone, right?"

"Yes," I said.

"How about this? I'll watch through the window up here for police cars, just in case one cruises by. You go down to your laundromat. We'll be on our cell phones."

I giggled. "Kinda like walkie-talkies?"

"Exactly."

"So . . . how did you get into the laundromat business?" Levi asked casually, as if he wasn't on his cell phone up in my apartment staring out the front window on the lookout for police cars, and I wasn't in my own laundromat searching through washers and dryers for . . . who knew what.

Something, anything, that would turn police attention away from me.

So far, I'd found one stray sock, dirt-stained—how many times did I have to tell people to presoak white athletic socks in hot water, dosed with laundry detergent and Borax, before laundering?

That wasn't exactly going to get me out of my own hot water.

"I was reared by Guy's parents, my aunt and uncle," I said. "They worked at other jobs and ran this laundromat and lived modestly to make sure their money would go as far as possible to take care of Guy." Levi was trying to keep me calm by talking to me, I realized, and I was more than happy to go along.

It felt so wrong, and creepy, to feel so nervous in my own beloved establishment. But my skin had started crawling and my stomach turning as soon as I entered the back room. The Ironrite was gone—how had the police managed to fit that in the tiny Paradise Police Department evidence room? Or maybe they'd taken it to the Mason County sheriff. The place was completely cleaned up, as if no bizarre murder had taken place here at all. The only evidence that the police had been in my laundromat at all was the yellow police tape still on the front and back doors.

But still, I saw in my mind's eye a flash of the image of Terry Tuxworth Jr., grotesquely tethered to the Ironrite machine with the two tie-dyed slip dresses. Would I ever be able to walk into my laundromat's storage room/office without seeing that? And where was the third dress?

"Guy's parents—your aunt and uncle—sound like wonderful people," Levi said.

"They were," I said. Twenty washers down, five to go. I'd already checked the dryers and found nothing in them . . . not even another sock to go with the lonely stray I'd already fished out and draped over the washer lid so it could dry before I tossed it into the lost and found. Not that I expected anyone to claim a single sock from the lost and found. People left perfectly good jeans without claiming them. But the honesty streak runs deeply within me, so I dutifully pile up left-behind clothing items in my lost and found box behind the front counter, and then donate whatever looks still useful to my favorite thrift shop in Masonville, and toss the rest. That happens on June 1 and December 1. The policy is clearly posted by the front door.

"But," I went on, "my aunt and uncle died young. Well, they didn't seem young at the time—in their late fifties, early sixties—but they were. And I was definitely young—eighteen—when I inherited this laundromat. This is what I've done ever since."

Twenty-one washers down, four to go.

"You've made a success of it," Levi said. "Especially with your stain-busting column. And you were talking about the history of laundry book. I think that's a great idea."

Washer twenty-two. Still nothing. I was getting to the back of the laundromat. Washer twenty-five was closest to the door that opened to the storage room/office. My heart started pounding.

If Terry had something he'd wanted to desperately wash, in a hurry, that's the washer he'd use. I'd started at the front of my laundromat, telling myself I just wanted to be thorough.

But truth be told . . . I was nervous about what I would find. I just wanted to put it off. I still wasn't sure if finding something would help me, hurt me, or make no difference.

"I don't know," I said as I checked washer twenty-three. "Even if I could write a book like that, who'd want to read it? I mean, really, a history of how women—and let's face it, until recent times, it's been mostly women doing the wash and often still—have managed laundry issues?"

"But wouldn't that be sort of a quirky domestic history that could give great insight into how women have viewed their roles in the family and society—and how they've been viewed—through something so basic? And how those roles have changed?"

I sighed as I opened washer twenty-four. If Levi kept being so supportive . . . and kept being such a good kisser . . . I'd be seriously in love with him by the end of the week.

Did men ever marry women in jail? I'd only ever heard of it working the other way, women marrying men in jail . . .

I closed washer twenty-four, moved to washer twenty-five, and stopped, staring at it.

Last chance to find . . . something. . .

"Uh, Josie," Levi said, sounding suddenly nervous. "I see a police car . . ."

Could I have had worse luck?

"I just have one washer left to check . . ."

"Hurry up!" Levi said. "I think the cruiser just pulled into the parking lot . . ."

I lifted the lid of washer twenty-five and smelled, before I saw, what was in there.

The smell of blood is acrid, distinctive. In this case, it was overpowering. My stomach turned.

But I finished opening the washer lid and stared in.

And saw stuffed on the right side Terry Tuxworth Jr.'s white polo shirt—the one Terry had been wearing at the Mayfairs when I met him the day before, the one emblazoned with his company's name.

But it was soaked in blood.

"Josie? Josie? Talk to me!" Levi was saying.

I heard a knock at the back door of my laundromat.

"Come down. Please," I said, my voice a bare squeak. "I'm going to have to talk to the police . . ."

14

Twenty minutes later, I was sitting in the one and only interview room at the Paradise Police Department with Chief John Worthy across the table from me. Officer Cook—the young officer who'd knocked on the back door of my laundromat and stopped to see what was happening—was sitting next to him, fidgeting nervously, staring at the tape recorder I'd agreed to as if the recorder might explode at any moment.

I think Officer Cook's job was to refresh tape/batteries as needed.

As usual, Chief Worthy was not looking pleased with me. This time, it was partly because his pleasant Sunday afternoon off had been disturbed.

Levi had helped me explain everything to Officer Franklin Cook, who was one of only two officers on duty, and the only one patrolling. Officer Cook conferred with the officer on duty at the police station, and they agreed that this—my discovery of a bloody shirt clearly labeled as Terry Tuxworth Jr.'s—in my laundromat was something that the chief would want to know about, even if it interrupted his plans for a Sunday afternoon barbeque.

In fact, Chief Worthy was in his khaki shorts and a plaid shirt. All he needed was a kiss-the-cook apron and a spatula.

He was also not pleased with me, because, well, he hadn't been pleased with me since junior high.

"How do I know you didn't plant that shirt in your washer?" Worthy demanded.

To my credit, I resisted rolling my eyes.

"If I had," I said, "I'd have gotten blood on myself and clothing or elsewhere at some point. It's not like there were a few drops of blood on that shirt. It was blood-soaked. Which is strange, since I remember seeing blood on Terry Tuxworth's head last night, and some on my office's floor, but nothing close to that amount. Anyway—"

"You crossed police tape, going unauthorized into a scene of investigation," Worthy started. "I could book you right now for tampering—"

"Uh, Chief," Officer Cook said. "Um, actually I stopped by Ms. Toadfern's laundromat because I noticed the crime scene tape still on the front door, and realized it shouldn't still be there. We, uh, just forgot to take it off after finishing up, and since I know a lot of folks will want to come to the laundromat tomorrow morning . . ."

He trailed off as Worthy turned to glare at him.

Oh, Lord. I wasn't up to opening up my laundromat in the morning. Even if from the police's point of view Toadfern's Laundromat was ready to go back to business as usual, I wasn't ready for that.

Plus, I was planning to go with Cherry to find and talk to Rhonda Farris the next morning. Now, more than ever, I was determined to find out what Rhonda knew about Terry.

I'd have to make up a TEMPORARILY CLOSED sign and put it up in my laundromat, which didn't make me happy, but when Worthy looked at me again, I had a gotcha grin waiting for him.

"Hmmm. Looks like you missed a few details. Not just taking down the tape and letting me know I could reopen. But the bloody shirt. It didn't occur to anyone to look in the washers and dryers?"

Officer Cook had the good grace to look shamefaced, but Worthy just leaned forward and glared at me. "Why would it occur to you to look there . . . unless you already knew Terry's bloody shirt was there?"

I sighed. "I guess I have to spell this out for you. First of all, other than the hour I was home after my dinner date"—hah! There! I'd said it!—"with Levi, I have been with someone every hour since I awoke yesterday morning, well before Terry was murdered.

"And if somehow, for some reason, I managed to murder Terry in that hour, why would I stuff his shirt in a washer? That doesn't make sense. And even if I had, how would I have managed to keep that amount of blood from getting on other things—like me, or on items in my laundromat?

"No, I think it's more likely Terry was desperate to wash that shirt to cover up something he did, and someone caught him in the act, and murdered him."

"Now, why would you think that?" Chief Worthy asked, a patronizing tone taking over his voice.

I almost said, *Because I'm a hysterical little ninny who just loves to make up hysterical little stories, don't you know.* In a purely sarcastic tone, of course.

But instead I told him what I'd learned about Terry showing up around 11:00 p.m. at the Rhinegolds' office and demanding to use their washer and dryer and then, upon learning that their machines were on the fritz, bullying the key to my laundromat from them.

"OK," Worthy said slowly. "I will talk to the Rhinegolds about that." He sounded reluctant to go to that much effort. "But I still don't understand what made you look through the washers and dryers, especially when you had to cross police tape to do it."

"It's not like the tape has special people-crossing sensors that make it zap someone painfully when she crosses it," I said.

Officer Cook snickered.

Chief Worthy gave him a harsh look, and the poor officer quickly resumed his sincere, playing-by-the-rules look.

"And as to what made me think to look in the washers? Well, I'm sure it's not shocking to you that last night's grisly scene has been playing in my head over and over. And something—besides of course Tuxworth tethered to the Ironrite—didn't seem right to me after I learned that he'd been so adamant about using a washer. And I realized there was no basket of laundry near him. So I realized he must have only brought one or two items in with him, and he must have some reason to have been desperate to wash them.

"The officers last night wouldn't have thought to look in the washers, because of the absence of a laundry basket, and besides, a man like Tuxworth wouldn't generally do his own laundry, especially on the road. He'd just pack his dirty clothes back home and have a service, or his housekeeper, take care of them.

"So I decided to have a look. Good thing I did, I reckon."

Officer Cook had the good grace to let a flash of admiration at my sleuthing logic cross his face, but Chief Worthy glared at me even harder.

"Your theory is that Tuxworth hurt someone enough that

they bled all over his shirt, and he wanted to destroy the evidence? Why would you think that?"

"He was more than willing to get into a fight with T-Bone, of all people, Friday night at the Bar-None. T-Bone bloodied his nose—"

"Aha! So that's the shirt! No big deal." He looked relieved. Back to the Sunday barbeque!

This time, I couldn't resist an eye roll. "Oh, please. There isn't a schnoz out there that would produce that much blood. Besides, Terry wasn't wearing a white polo Friday night. He had on a black long-sleeved shirt. No, this is blood from someone else. It's the only thing that makes sense."

"OK, let's say you're right. Terry gets in a fight with someone, bloodies them up, and the blood gets on his shirt. What's the big deal?"

"Have you gotten any calls of complaint about Terry getting in a fight last night?"

"That would be information not disclosable to a private citizen," Worthy said. Even Officer Cook looked like he wanted to roll his eyes. "In any case, not every fight that happens is called in."

"True," I said. "But what if the fight ended in murder . . . someone else's murder . . . and that's what Terry was trying to cover up—washing away the evidence. Not that he'd have been able to do so. He had the washer set on hot water, which would just cook the blood's protein right into the shirt."

Chief Worthy's frown deepened. "Why would he do that? Why not just throw away the shirt?"

"Lots of reasons. Maybe he was afraid if he threw it away, it would easily be found. After all, the shirt had his name on it. Or maybe he panicked," I said. "From how he was talking to the Rhinegolds, that's certainly a possibility. Maybe he thought if he burned it somewhere, he'd attract too much attention."

"So, let me get this straight," Chief Worthy said. "You think that Terry got into a fight with someone—perhaps even killing them—and to hide the evidence, he bullied a key to your laundromat out of the Rhinegolds so he could wash away the evidence, but before he could do so, someone—not you—killed him."

Officer Cook was nodding slightly as if this made sense.

"That's exactly what I think," I said.

Worthy gave me his own gotcha grin.

"So . . . where's the body of Terry's victim? Don't you think if he'd killed someone last night, by now the body would be found, or at least the victim would be reported missing?"

"Not necessarily," I said calmly. "But you might want to check in with the Mayfairs and see if they are all accounted for. When I was over at the Mayfair house yesterday, the mood was pretty tense between Terry and the Mayfairs. Something about unfair contracts that date back a long way."

Even Chief Worthy looked startled at that.

"Well," I said, "you have my statement. So I'd kind of like to go now."

"I just want to verify: Your witnesses that you couldn't have been in your laundromat since discovering Terry last night are Sally, who you stayed with last night, the people at your church"—Chief Worthy paused and gave me a look that let me know something mean was about to come out of his mouth—"and your newest boyfriend. Levi Applegate." Worthy's smile spread into a sneer.

"Mr. Applegate is a new acquaintance," I said stiffly. "But, yes, he can verify all my whereabouts since meeting me at church this morning."

"Fine," Worthy said. He glanced at Officer Cook, who turned off the tape recorder. Then he gave me a look of dismissal.

But I stayed put, staring at Chief Worthy directly.

"Do you have something to add, Josie? Should we turn the tape recorder back on?"

"No," I said. "What I have to say has nothing to do with this case."

Worthy leaned back, crossing his arms across his chest. "Oh yeah? Well, then, why would I want to hear it?"

"Because you need to. This insane jealousy of yours is poisoning your life," I said.

He looked puzzled. "What? What are you talking about?"

Cook's eyebrows went up in a do-tell gesture.

"I'm talking about how we broke up in junior high because you dumped me to go with the football coach's daughter to get in his good graces," I said.

Worthy gave a stiff laugh. "So? That was, what, seventeen years ago?"

"Exactly. So you need to get over it."

"I need to get over it? Hmmm. I'm starting to think you haven't gotten over it."

"Oh, I'm over it, Johnny," I said, using the variation of his name I'd used back in junior high. "Way over it. Notice I've dated several men in the past few years, one seriously. That ended unpleasantly, but I managed to get over it, and if I can get over that, it's a no-brainer I'm over our little junior high romance."

Worthy looked a little pale, but sighed. "So why are you bringing this up?"

I stood up and leaned across the table so our faces were inches apart. "Because I do not appreciate your sneering tone in referencing the time I've spent this weekend with Mr. Levi Applegate. It is none of your business. But combining the fact that your most serious relationship was when you and I were thirteen with the fact that you are as unpleasant to me as possible makes me think you are not over the fact that you dumped me to try to move ahead in football."

I looked over at Officer Cook. "And don't let him fool you with glory day stories. His move didn't help him much. He was a lousy quarterback."

Officer Cook pressed his lips together, trying, I think, not to laugh.

"But you know what?" I said, looking back at Worthy. "I think you always thought that I'd try to get you back. And I didn't. Because even then I knew I had to trust someone to be in a real relationship.

"And I think that bugs you. And you're jealous when I have dates and boyfriends. And really, it's stunted your emotional growth. So here's a suggestion, Johnny. Forgive yourself. Forgive yourself for being a junior high jerk. Most people are jerks in junior high, at least at one time or another, but they move on.

"Maybe I was kind of a jerk for ratting you out in the school newspaper, too, but for pity's sake . . . I told you I was sorry long ago, and I don't need to do so again, and I've forgiven myself and moved on.

"So just do that—forgive yourself, and move on, and try . . . just try . . . to have a real relationship sometime in say the next, oh, year or so. I don't think that's too much of a stretch goal for you. It will make you a happier, better person. And probably a better chief of police, too."

I stood up and started toward the door.

"Josie!"

I turned and looked. Chief Worthy's face was flaming red with anger and embarrassment, and yeah, I felt a little sorry for him. But enough. I'd put up with him belittling me for seventeen years.

"Chief Worthy," I said, "you know how to reach me if you

need to ask me more questions. Next time, though, I will bring an attorney."

And I opened the door and walked out.

Levi was waiting for me. We walked to his car, silently, and after we got in, he didn't start up his car right away.

I leaned my head back against the passenger's seat and shut my eyes.

After a few seconds, Levi said, "You OK? Do I need to go back and take on Chief Worthy for police brutality?"

"No," I said. "It was fine. But I need to call my attorney in the morning. I've really only hired him to take care of paperwork pertaining to Guy's guardianship, so I don't know how much help he can be if I'm really in trouble."

"I'll call Stillwater's counsel and see who she knows in criminal law, maybe in Columbus."

"Thank you," I said, not at all shocked that Levi would offer to help in such a way.

"Are you feeling ill? Is Elroy's mama's chicken getting to you?"

I opened my eyes, sat up fast, and looked at him, horri-fied. "No, of course not. Are you sick? Oh, goodness, that would just break Elroy and his mama's heart . . ."

I stopped. Levi was grinning. I gave him a gentle whack on the arm, and he grinned even more.

"Don't scare me like that," I said.

"Well, don't scare me like that," Levi said. "You were a million miles from me."

"It's just . . . I'm free to go back to my apartment, but I just don't feel up to it . . . and I can't go to Sally's because her boys are coming home tonight, and . . ."

"I understand," Levi said. "You just don't feel comfort-able in your own apartment right now."

Tears pricked my eyes. I sniffled. "Will I ever? I paid so much, worked so hard, to make it just what I wanted, with the custom bookshelves, and the whirlpool tub, and the walk-in closet with the laundry chute to the laundromat below . . ."

Levi took my hands, and that did it. I started crying.

"Oh, Josie, it'll feel like home again. You'll just need some time," he said. "In the meantime, maybe you shouldn't be there, at least until this crime is solved." Levi thought for a second, then brightened. "I know what you can do!"

If he said he'd spend the night with me, or invited me to spend the night with him at the Red Horse, I would have burst out weeping. Not with pleasure, as much as I was already wondering what we'd be like in bed together, but in disappointment, because it was just too soon to find out, and I wanted him to know that without me having to say so.

"Why don't you come up to Stillwater, and stay in the guest apartment? No one is using it now," Levi said. "And I didn't use it just in case a resident's family member needed it. That's you."

On the second story of Stillwater's original building—a farmhouse—there's a tiny efficiency apartment meant for temporary lodging for parents or guardians who are visiting from out of town and unable to secure lodging elsewhere.

"After all," Levi said, "Stillwater is kind of your home away from home as it is, and that might be healing to you."

Turned out I burst out weeping anyway, just out of sheer gratitude, as I thanked Levi for his brilliant suggestion. He was quiet while I finished my crying jag, and it didn't even feel particularly awkward as he held me, even with the gearshift between us.

And then he drove me back to my apartment so I could put together an overnight bag.

15

"So, did you have sex?"

"Cherry! I am *so* not answering that," I said.

"Aha!" Cherry said, clearly pleased with herself. "You and Levi did have sex!"

At the next intersection—Possum Creek Road and Sweet Potato Ridge, country roads that made an X in the midst of cornfields and cow pasture—I stomped on the brake harder than strictly necessary. Cherry's head whiplashed forward, and she gave an oof when it bounced against my van's passenger side headrest, more from dismay that my action had bounced her perfectly coiffed 'do out of place than from anything else.

I put my van in park, turned it off, and twisted around in my seat to look at Cherry, knowing we could sit there for a good five to ten minutes before another vehicle would come along either Sweet Potato Ridge or Possum Creek Road, and even then, I stood a three-in-four chance that the vehicle— probably a truck—wouldn't come up behind me, and if it did, its driver would wait a full minute before honking at me.

Such are the benefits of traveling rural territory.

So I gave Cherry a full-on glare. "Fine. Levi and I had sex. Twenty times. First we had sex on the couch. Then in the bed. Then with me leaning over an ironing board—"

Cherry glared right back at me. "I'd let you go on but you'd only embarrass yourself. You can't describe what you haven't experienced. And you didn't have sex at all, not even once, did you?"

I tossed my hands in the air, accidentally bringing one hand down on the horn, causing it to toot, and a second later, a cow near the fence to jerk for just a second out of its somnambulant state.

"Sorry," I said, meaning it for the cow, although of course she couldn't hear me since my truck windows were rolled up. But it made me feel better, anyway.

"You got me there," I went on, now addressing Cherry. "I did not have sex with Levi."

Cherry gave me an exasperated look. "Well, for pity's sake, why not? He's single; you're single. He's new in town and probably lonely. You're lonely."

"I'm not lonely. Just single," I said. "Big difference."

"He's a hottie," Cherry said, ignoring me. "And you're . . ."

She paused just long enough that I thought she was going to say, "nottie," but instead she finished lamely, "And, well, you're lonely."

"I already said I'm not lonely!"

"But you two looked so cute together! So . . . comfortable! So meant to be!" she wailed.

"All the more reason not to jump his bones for wild sex within hours of meeting him," I said, turning around and starting my truck again.

"No, no, no," Cherry said. "That's all the more reason *to* jump his bones for wild sex."

I sighed. "Could you please just pay attention to the directions and navigate us to Rhonda Farris's apartment?"

I flipped on the right turn signal—just in case a car materialized out of either the cornfield, the cow pasture, or the thin air above me—and turned right.

"Turn right on Sweet Potato Ridge," Cherry said, in a mechanical voice that was meant to mimic, I think, one of the new GPS navigators.

God help drivers everywhere if Cherry's voice—or persona—ever did end up in a GPS navigator.

"I already *did* turn right," I said, exasperated, even though it was only 9:30 on a Monday morning. "I know how to get from Paradise to Masonville. I just need you to help me once we get to Masonville to get to Rhonda's apartment complex—what's it called again?"

"Whispering Woods," Cherry said, again with the mechanical GPS voice.

I sighed.

It was going to be a long day, if this was the start.

I'd driven down from Stillwater to Paradise, to pick up Cherry. We then got our go cups of coffee from Sandy's Restaurant, and hit the road, hoping to get to Masonville around 11:00.

We'd debated about calling Rhonda ahead of time to let her know we were coming.

On the one hand, I was pretty sure that if she knew we were coming to ask questions about Terry Tuxworth, she'd want nothing to do with us. After all, her behavior upon leaving Paradise had to be, in hindsight, pretty embarrassing. It couldn't have been very pleasant to be postcoitus in the Red Horse Motel, probably asleep or half dozing, and have the police burst in demanding to know everything you knew about your one-night stand.

On the other hand, I didn't like the idea of driving all the way to Masonville only to discover Rhonda wasn't at her new home, forcing us to while away hours hoping to catch her in.

After all, there was only so much of each other's company Cherry and I could stand without Sally as a buffer, and Sally had a carpentry gig (replacing a busted screen door at Mrs. Beavy's house) to fill her hours this morning while her boys were in school, before she went in to open up the Bar-None for its afternoon hours.

And besides, I had a 2:00 p.m. appointment with an attorney—a Ms. Susan Grey—that Stillwater's attorney had highly recommended. Levi had made good on his promise to ask for references first thing this morning. My meeting with Ms. Grey was in Masonville, too.

So Cherry had hit upon a plan. She'd called up Rhonda early this morning, apologized for waking her, explained that she'd gotten the phone number from T-Bone, and she was so sorry Rhonda hadn't had a chance to say good-bye before leaving.

She had, Cherry told Rhonda, put together a care package of her favorite hair and nail products as a good luck gift, and since it was her day off and she had some shopping to do in Masonville, could she bring it by midmorning, say 11:00?

Never mind that Rhonda hadn't been that great of a customer, or that Cherry had never been that nice before to her customers . . . Rhonda fell for it.

I guess when your love life is a mess and you're starting a new job, a care package of hair and nail products is so tantalizing you don't consider the giver's possible ulterior motives.

And it was a tantalizing care package—the shampoo and conditioner and nail polishes all done up in a wicker basket, finished with cellophane wrap, red ribbon, and a big red bow.

For last-minute care packages Cherry had quite a bit of flair.

So I found myself thinking . . . Cherry had done a wonderful job with the package . . . and she was clever in how she'd gotten Rhonda to agree to meet . . . and she was taking her day off to help me out . . . and she so wanted to help . . .

I sighed again, and snuck a look over at Cherry.

She was impervious to my sigh. Didn't even flinch or glance my way. Just stared down at the directions.

And she was starting to look a little sickly green around the mouth, even through her Fabulous Pore-Filling Foundation. If she kept staring down like that, pretty soon Cherry would be carsick.

And some stains and odors are next to impossible for even a stain expert like me to get out.

"Fine," I said, as we passed a small green metal sign that said MASONVILLE—13. We had thirteen miles before I really needed Cherry to give me directions, and I knew that if she wasn't her usual cheerful yet over-the-top self, we'd never ferret the information we wanted out of Rhonda, because Rhonda would be too distracted by wondering what was up with Cherry to really tell us anything. "I'll tell you what happened with Levi and me last night."

Cherry twisted in her seat, and the directions to Rhonda's apartment fell to the floor. "All right! I'm listening!"

I glanced at her. She was grinning. Her ears would have been wagging, if that were possible.

"We talked," I said flatly.

A tiny silence. Then, Cherry: "You talked? All you did was talk?"

"That's right," I said. "After our meeting at the Bar-None,

Levi took me back to the church, and I picked up my car. We went back to my place." I filled her in on my bloody find in washer 25 and what happened after that at the police station. Cherry made me happier with her when she giggled and said, "You go, girl," when I got to the part about telling off Worthy. I went on. "Levi packed up some food basics from my kitchen—enough to get me through a few days, anyway, without a grocery run—and I packed up some clothes, toiletries, books, and a few essential pieces of paperwork—mostly the info I need about Guy in case there is an emergency—and then we drove up to Stillwater.

"He helped me get everything into the guest apartment at Stillwater, and while I put away clothes, groceries, and everything else, Levi made a few phone calls and set up my two o'clock appointment with the lawyer, Susan Grey.

"Then I offered to make us a light dinner from what I had on hand and he accepted. I made BLT sandwiches and mac-n-cheese from a box."

"Not exactly candlelight dinner fare," Cherry said, just a note of disapproval in her voice. And did that voice sound a wee bit like Mrs. Oglevee's? Yeah.

"No," I said matter-of-factly. "But we weren't quite in the mood to go out and we weren't in the mood to part company, either, and so we ate and then . . . we talked.

"First, we talked about where Levi wants to live. He'd at first thought about an apartment in Masonville, but now he's thinking maybe he'll buy in Paradise, since he likes the town. Then we started talking about our childhoods and upbringings.

"Somewhere in there I remembered I'd brought along a half-full bottle of Chardonnay, so I poured wine for us in paper cups, and we sipped that and talked some more—about anything and everything. What we want in life, funny memories, even the goofy topics that used to keep us up as teenagers—remember those?"

"Yeah," Cherry said, wistfully. "Could there be life on other planets? What if there's an alternate timeline and you could see how your life would be different if you'd made a different decision?"

"Exactly. And we talked about books and movies we love, pets we've had, family stuff," I said. "We talked until two this morning." I yawned, picked up my go cup of coffee and had another sip, then put it back in my cup holder. "Then Levi gave me a good-night kiss on the cheek, and left."

I didn't think I needed to mention that I lay awake for at least another hour after that, thinking about him.

"Sorry to disappoint you," I said, "but that was it. We just . . . talked."

Cherry sniffled. I glanced over at her.

"Are you kidding?" she said, her voice wavering. She sniffled again. Her mascara was in definite danger of having a run-in with her rouge. "That's the most romantic thing I've heard in a long time."

I stared at the ribbon of road. In the distance, I could see the outer rim of Masonville, indicated by signs for a Mc-Donald's, a Wal-Mart and a BP gas station—franchises that hadn't made it to Paradise.

But my thoughts were on Cherry. If she could surprise me, then anyone could. I just hoped Rhonda had some surprising information that would help turn the focus of the investigation into Terry Tuxworth's death away from me.

16

Whispering Woods apartments didn't live up to either component of its name.

There probably had been woods on the site where the apartments now stood, but they would have predated corn and soy fields, which themselves had been replaced by the apartments at about the time the Mayfair Sisters officially broke up as an act, if not as a family.

And since the apartment complex was on a main boulevard in Masonville, built between a highway overpass and a strip mall featuring a mega-grocery, there was definitely no whispering, either. In fact, in the apartment parking lot, we had to raise our voices to be heard over the constant thrum of traffic.

On the other hand, one lone, skinny maple grew in the thin strip of grass that was meant as a buffer between the parking lot and the boulevard. It looked a little sad, its limbs whipped back every time a car whizzed past, but maybe it would be a tough little maple and start a trend. It obviously hadn't been planted there on purpose, but it had survived anyway.

Rhonda, on the other hand, as the new occupant of apartment 6G, had a much happier interpretation of Whispering Woods than I did.

Even her instant wariness at seeing me at the door with Cherry only temporarily dampened her enthusiasm.

"Isn't it great?" Rhonda said, placing Cherry's gift basket on a kitchen table already laden with boxes and stacks of dishes. She'd gushed about how great the basket was as we'd come in, giving Cherry a hug and me a mere nod. "I have two bedrooms, an eat-in kitchen, and this big living room! And an assigned parking space!"

Rhonda gave us a tour of the apartment. The walls of each room were dingy white, dinged and scuffed. The worn carpet had probably started out beige, but was now a dull brown, blotchy with stains.

And she was enthusiastic about every single room.

Cherry and I enthused with her. To Rhonda, this apartment represented a fresh start and freedom.

Back in the living room, Rhonda moved boxes off an old green and brown plaid lumpy couch. She gestured that Cherry and I should sit on the couch, while she sat in a wicker rocking chair.

"I got the couch and rocker for free yesterday!" Rhonda said. "They were on the curb in a neighborhood near here, for junk day pickup today, can you believe it? The owner had a pickup truck and brought them here for me."

Cherry and I shared a glance. Oh no. Rhonda wasn't getting involved with someone again already, was she?

She smiled at us. "The owner was a woman," she said, correctly interpreting our glance. "She was glad to get rid of the pieces rather than paying the haul-away fee. I think the rocker just needs some spray paint and the couch a throw, don't you?"

"That's a clever idea," I said, thinking a brightly colored throw would make the couch look better but would do nothing to fix the spring poking in my behind.

"And the landlord says it's OK to repaint as long as I use a neutral—he'll even deduct the cost of the paint off my rent." Rhonda glanced around her new apartment nervously. "I think after my first month's pay, I'll be able to get some pretty throw rugs to cover the, you know, worst of the stains and rips in the carpet."

Suddenly Rhonda dropped her head into her hands. "Oh, Lord, what have I done!"

"Now, Rhonda," Cherry said soothingly, "your plans will make this place spiffy in no time!"

Rhonda looked up and glared at Cherry. "I'm not talking about my move here. Are you kidding? This place is great. Much better than living with T-Bone. He was such a slob. The trailer was always disgusting."

"Of course this place is great," I said, giving Cherry what I hoped was a subtle kick—although she winced. "I'm guessing you're referring to your, ah, exit from Paradise involving Terry Tuxworth."

Might as well get to the point of our visit. Rhonda had to know that was why I was interested in talking with her.

"Did you tell the police everything about your evening with Terry? I mean, that would be important for them to know about Terry's death?" I asked.

"Of course," Rhonda said, looking away.

Aha. She hadn't.

"I was just referring to my, ah, date with Terry," she said. "If it gets into the news that I was with him the night of his death—I mean—with him, you know, in *that* way, then my employer is going to be really unhappy. This is a privately owned company I'm working for, and the owners have made it clear they want everyone acting, you know, proper, even outside working hours. They could fire me over any old excuse and never have to admit it's because I was Terry Tuxworth's one-night stand the night he died!"

Rhonda started crying again. "I'd never have visited his hotel room if I'd known he'd be murdered later that night!"

While I was mentally sifting through the ethics of what Rhonda had just said—she was more concerned about what her new bosses would think of her for having a one-night-stand than she was about the fact a man had been brutally murdered—Cherry apparently saw an opportunity.

"So . . . you'd like to make sure it's in the news that you went by to visit Terry for some more, ah, understandable reason?" Cherry asked.

Both Rhonda and I gave Cherry startled looks.

Mine said: *Cherry, what are you thinking?* meaning, *Uh oh, what are you cooking up?*

Rhonda's said: *Cherry, what are you thinking?* meaning, *Really? You could get me off the hook somehow?*

"Of course I'd like that!" Rhonda said. "I'm just starting over with this new apartment, this new job. I just can't get fired and go back to Paradise; I just can't. It would kill me. But the police found me there, and it will be reported and people will just assume—"

"Nonsense," Cherry snapped. "Were you clothed when the police came?"

"Well, yes," Rhonda said. She blushed. "I'd put my clothes back on."

"Did you tell the police you put your clothes back on? Say anything that indicated you'd had them off?"

"No. I had on my jeans and T-shirt," Rhonda said, "and I'd fallen asleep in a guest chair. I screamed when the police burst in. I hadn't heard them knocking. I'm a pretty deep sleeper in any case, and I was extra tired from packing up, fighting with T-Bone, and then, ah, visiting Terry."

"But you didn't directly tell the police you'd come by to see Terry for the purpose of having sex with him," Cherry asked.

Rhonda blushed. I looked at Cherry, wondering if perhaps I should hire her as my legal counsel—never mind the fact she'd gone to cosmetology school. She had a purposeful look on her face, and I sensed she was getting to a point that would help both me and Rhonda.

"No," Rhonda was saying. "But of course they assumed." She sighed. "I don't know what I was thinking. I was mad at T-Bone and I wanted word to get back to him that he hadn't been my, uh, last stand before I left Paradise. Make him hurt for all the times he'd betrayed me."

I didn't mention that Sally had seen a new woman already taking up Rhonda's space at T-Bone's trailer.

"Doesn't matter what they assumed," Cherry said. "If there are no witnesses to your and Terry's liaison, and you were fully clothed when the police burst in, then we can come up with a story to feed to the media. After all, Josie here has media connections with her column."

I gave Cherry a what-the-heck? frown. I couldn't help Rhonda in this way, and even if I could . . .

"The deal is simple," Cherry said. "You, Rhonda, will tell us what you told the police—and more importantly what you might have skipped over telling the police that might help us figure out who killed Terry, because Josie here is currently on the hook for the murder."

Rhonda gasped and stared at me. "Really?"

"Really," I said.

"Then Josie will let Caleb, her editor at the *Paradise Advertiser-Gazette*, know that you dropped by to see Terry on your way out of town for some reason we'll come up with later."

"But . . ." I started to protest. I didn't want to lie on Rhonda's behalf.

Cherry grabbed my arm and squeezed it. "You're on the hook, Josie, for murder."

I pressed my eyes shut. I thought about my laundromat business and my column and how hard I'd worked on both. I thought about Guy. I thought about my list of future goals—even my pie-in-the-sky idea to write a book about the history of laundry. I thought about . . . Levi.

This was so not the time for me to go off to jail on suspicion of a murder I didn't commit.

I opened my eyes. "Fine," I said. "We'll come up with something to save your reputation, Rhonda, but first you have to talk about what happened that night with Terry."

"I told the police I went by to see Terry because he'd invited me the night before, when I met him at the Bar-None. Then during our visit, he said he wanted to go out and pick up some beer. But he never came back. But really . . ."

She looked away, turning red.

"Come on," Cherry said gently. "We've all done things we're not proud of. But it's just us girls here right now."

Rhonda looked at us, took a deep breath. "I went to see Terry, just like I told the police. And Terry was very sweet to me. He had champagne, nice snacks, told me how pretty I was, and I felt like big stuff, in the motel room with a big-time music producer."

Never mind that the motel was the Red Horse. Or that the music producer was really small-time. And old enough to be Rhonda's father.

"But then he said he wanted me to put on something special," Rhonda said. "He went out to his car, opened the driver's side door—I watched him through the window—and pulled out what looked like just a wad of fabric. Then he shut the door and came back in and held up what he'd gotten out of his car—a tie-dyed slip dress."

I gasped. The Mayfair tie-dyed slip dresses. Terry had taken them from my van, after all. He had to have gotten them the previous afternoon, while I was inside at the Mayfairs', after he stormed out of their home. So he'd had all three tie-dyed slip dresses in the passenger seat of his car, at least until Rhonda showed up.

"I thought it was weird he'd want me to wear something like that," Rhonda was saying. "I mean—I've dressed up as a French maid, in leather, in fishnets—"

"OK, OK," I said. Really, I didn't need to know all about her past sexy outfits. "So did you put the dress on?"

She nodded. "I did." She looked shamefaced. "I didn't realize the dresses belonged to the Mayfair Sisters until we were well into making out. He started calling me Connie, and by the time I made the mental connection that he must mean Connie Mayfair, it was, well, too late to stop what we were doing because we were, ah, nearly done."

We all sat silently for a moment.

So . . . at the very least, Terry Tuxworth Jr. had lusted after Constance Mayfair. And he'd wanted Rhonda to dress up in the tie-dyed dress that had belonged to Constance to fulfill his fantasy.

Or . . . had Constance and Terry once had a real-life affair? What if Constance didn't want anyone to know? What if Terry had tried to blackmail her with their steamy past? Or what if Roger, Constance's husband, had found out after all?

Even if T-Bone hadn't killed Terry in a jealous rage, Roger might have.

"There were only two of the dresses used to murder Terry," I said, thinking out loud. "They must have been in the passenger's seat, and either for some reason Terry brought them in to my laundromat with him, or the killer saw the dresses in Terry's car, and brought them in . . ."

"I think I know where the third one might be," Rhonda said. "I was upset afterward, and pulled the dress off, snapping the shoulder strap. Terry was pretty upset by that, said he'd only taken the dresses to annoy the Mayfairs, and planned on returning the dresses for the auction."

Even the one Rhonda had worn? Ew. But maybe Terry's desire for Connie had been spurned, and this was some weird revenge, at least in his mind. Just based on the few times I'd met him, Terry seemed to be a few eggs shy of a full dozen, so maybe he'd used Rhonda as a fill-in for Connie . . . and planned to return the used dress as a mean-spirited prank. Of course, he couldn't have known Rhonda would actually come by his hotel room after all.

Maybe the dress was why he'd gone to my laundromat—to clean it before returning it?

But then I remembered the scene, the two slip dresses. I hadn't stared long, but I didn't recall a snapped strap. I shuddered and my stomach lurched as I remembered seeing Terry, lethally tethered to the Ironrite.

I also remembered finding his bloody shirt in the washer. He'd been interrupted before he could even add laundry detergent and water. By someone who'd come by my laundromat, and stopped spontaneously when they saw his car in the parking lot?

If so, had the sight of the dresses angered him or her for some reason—maybe one of the Mayfairs realized Terry had stolen the dresses just to upset them—and the person grabbed the dresses, and then went in? Or had the person hit

Terry on the head, and only then had a brilliant, macabre idea for how to finish him off, and gone back out for the slip dresses?

"Then he suddenly got upset, when he realized it was nearly nine o'clock," Rhonda was saying. "He said something about having an eight-thirty appointment that was going to make him a lot of money. He snatched the dress from me and left."

"Did he say who the appointment was with?" Cherry asked.

"Not directly," Rhonda said. "But he muttered something about thank God the person he was seeing being just the person to fix the dress."

"Moira Evans!" I exclaimed.

Cherry and Rhonda looked at me. "She's the seamstress I hired to repair the Mayfair costumes. Terry Tuxworth had an appointment with her?"

"I reckon so," Rhonda said. "I mean, he didn't say her name directly, but he definitely said the part about the person he was seeing could fix the dress."

"And you're sure he said the appointment would make him a lot of money?" I asked.

Rhonda nodded.

That implied Terry was blackmailing Moira. But that didn't make sense. After all, Moira barely had enough to get by.

But what if Moira had found something while working on the Mayfair costumes? After all, I'd found all kinds of things mixed in with the Mayfair costumes while laundering them. Poor Mrs. Mayfair's Alzheimer's had made her get confused and mix things up following her own bizarre notions of what should be packed together.

What if I'd missed something in one of the boxes . . .

something that Moira could use to blackmail Terry? Or . . . something to use to blackmail the Mayfairs?

Why, then, would she and Terry want to meet . . . unless . . . given Moira's ailing health, she'd rather just sell the information to Terry, whatever it was, and get fast cash quickly.

I had to talk to Moira.

I thought about the blood on Terry's shirt.

Oh, Lord.

I needed to check on her—fast.

I pulled my cell phone out of my purse and started dialing.

"Who are you calling?" Rhonda asked, startled.

I looked at her while the phone at the *Paradise Advertiser-Gazette* rang. Pick up, Caleb, pick up, I thought. I knew he was planning to interview Moira today for a feature on her experiences as a seamstress, to tie in with the Mayfair auction, and I was hoping he'd already been to see her and could tell me she was OK.

"Caleb Loudermilk," I said.

"But, Josie, we haven't figured out a face-saving story for Rhonda yet!" Cherry protested.

"Well, figure something out fast . . . Caleb! Hi! It's Josie. Yeah, I know Mondays are a terrible day for you. Now listen, have you been to see Moira Evans yet?"

17

While I talked to Caleb, Cherry helped Rhonda work out her story for the police so that she could tell it just like she'd told us, but leave out that she'd actually slept with Terry.

She would just say that he told her to put on the tie-dyed dress, saying it was Constance's, and she became upset. After he left—probably to meet with Moira given his comments—Rhonda just remained in the motel room, waiting for him to return so she could tell him off, but she fell back asleep.

(Truth be told, she got dressed after he left, and waited in the motel room to tell him off when he returned, but fell asleep.)

None of us could think of any reason the police really needed to know that Rhonda and Terry had slept together, and Rhonda was all set to call the Paradise police, when she got a stricken look on her face.

"Wait a minute," she said. "If I tell them I was upset with Terry after all, when last night I told them I wasn't, then I might become a suspect."

I gave Cherry a nervous look that said, *Do something.* If Rhonda backed out of making this call, then the police wouldn't know that Terry apparently planned to go to Moira's the night before. And I was worried about Moira. What if she had been trying to blackmail Terry? What if he'd hurt her? After all, somebody's blood was on the shirt he'd left in washer twenty-five in my laundromat.

"Hmmm," Cherry said. "That's a good point."

I glared at her as Rhonda snapped her cell phone shut. Her expression clamped closed, too. "If you tell the police what I just told you, I'm denying every word of it and sticking to my original story."

"Great," I fumed, poking at my crab Rangoon. After Rhonda ignored our pleas and protests and more or less threw us out of her apartment, Cherry and I had gone to Suzy Fu's Chinese Buffet for lunch before my meeting with attorney Susan Grey. "Now Rhonda will never talk to the police. And if I call up and say, Hey, I have this theory that maybe the blood on Terry's shirt is from Moira Evans, please go check on her because I'm worried maybe Terry murdered her over being blackmailed, then I'm really going to look suspicious."

I gave my crab Rangoon another poke and then gave up, pushing my plate aside. Normally I can eat a plateful of them, but my worries had made me lose my appetite.

"I think you're worrying too much," Cherry said, happily forking up a large bite of pork lo mein. "I mean, look at it this way . . . let's say something really did happen to Moira Evans. Won't Caleb find that out this afternoon when he goes over?"

I gave Cherry a hard look. "He said he's pressed to put Wednesday's newspaper to bed this afternoon. But he did agree to go to see Moira at five this afternoon, and I said I'd meet him at her house. Anyway, it's a big issue, what with the listing of all the auction items and a write-up about the concert. He finally got Candace to agree to an interview with him this morning. He pointed out that the Mayfairs would rather talk to him than be hounded by the media that will surely swoop down on Paradise this afternoon as word of Terry Tuxworth's murder spreads."

"Interesting," Cherry said. "So why would the Mayfairs rather talk to Caleb than the other reporters?"

"He promised Candace he'd play up the importance of the auction and concert as a way to raise money for her mama and pointed out that other reporters wouldn't care about that—they'd want every detail they could get about the Mayfair Sisters' relationship with Terry."

Cherry nodded. "I'm impressed. Did she fall for it?"

"Yes. Apparently he kept his word but did get her and her sisters to share a few details about Terry."

Cherry finished off her lo mein. "Like what?"

"He didn't say. He was just happy to get his scoop and was in the process of writing it up and taking care of the newspaper when I called," I said. "Moira Evans is low priority for him right now. He said he would go by about five."

I took a sip of hot tea, hoping to settle my stomach.

"Well," Cherry said, "look at it this way. If Terry did murder Moira, does it really matter what time Caleb goes to see her? It's not like he could save her by getting there earlier."

My stomach lurched after all. "Cherry! That's terrible! If my fear is right, then every minute counts in a murder investigation. And what if Terry didn't kill Moira? What if she's injured, bleeding, needing help? She lives alone and has no one to really check on her. She rarely leaves her house, so it could be days before neighbors would realize they hadn't seen Moira."

Cherry shook her head and started in on her General Tso's chicken. She swallowed, smacked her lips, and said, "Josie, you have an overactive imagination. Probably the blood on Terry's shirt is his own, from a shaving cut or something."

I thumped the table, and the crab Rangoon did a skip, hop, jump on my plate. "See? This is what I run into when I try to talk to Worthy."

Cherry looked horrified—offended, even—at the comparison. Good! I thought.

"Why would Terry shave late at night? If he had, wouldn't Rhonda have noticed the blood on his shirt? And even if he did cut himself shaving, there is no way that he'd get that much blood on his shirt." I leaned forward to Cherry. "I saw the shirt, Cherry. It was blood-soaked. And I saw Terry. That blood didn't come from him. He was trying to cover up something he did by coming to my laundromat to wash away the evidence."

Now Cherry pushed her plate away, suddenly not looking interested in her meal.

"Who has Terry encountered since he's been to Paradise that he might end up in a fight so big it could end in bloodshed—his or someone else's?"

I held out a finger for each name. "T-Bone, accounted for—Sally talked to him yesterday. Rhonda, obviously accounted for. Candace, Cornelia, and Constance, and Constance's husband, Roger—they're all accounted for, because Caleb just interviewed them."

"Even the husband?" Cherry said. "I thought Caleb was just interviewing the sisters."

"Caleb said Roger was there for the whole interview, which doesn't surprise me at all," I said. "He doesn't like to leave Constance's side."

Cherry waggled her eyebrows. "Well, what if he found out about Terry's interest in Constance? Maybe them being together again led to a rekindled romance." She pulled her plate back and snapped up a bite of General Tso's after all. Nothing like talk of illicit sex to rekindle Cherry's appetite.

"But Constance—actually, Cornelia, too—seemed to hate Terry. He profited his whole life from the unfair contract the Mayfairs' mother had her daughters sign with his father."

"Candace didn't seem to hate Terry?"

"I don't think Candace could hate anyone. She's too sweet, and too caught up in taking care of her mother."

"All the more reason to suspect her in Terry's death," Cherry said. "Never trust the sweet ones." If that was true, then Cherry would never be suspected for anything. "But I still say it happened like this: Constance and Terry rekindled a romance, or Constance let it slip to Roger that once upon a time Terry had hit on her and she didn't like it. So Roger got angry, and happened by your laundromat, saw Terry's car in the parking lot, and went in and killed him, and then finished him off with the tie-dyed dresses."

I cautiously picked up a crab Rangoon and nibbled. Mmmm. I was hungry, after all, and I admit that the fact of Terry's demise wasn't nearly so traumatic to me as the idea that Moira might be alone and hurt—or worse.

After finishing off my Rangoon, I said, "But there are several problems with that scenario. Why would Roger just happen by my laundromat?"

"Easy," Cherry said. "He was angry, driving around to work it off, and drove by your laundromat. It is on Main Street, after all. And there aren't that many other streets to wander up and down."

"Except Roger, Constance, and Cornelia are all staying

somewhere in Masonville," I said. "They didn't want to stay with Candace and Mrs. Mayfair, and they were very snooty about the idea of staying at the Red Horse."

Cherry frowned. "I don't like these people, the more I learn about them."

"Maybe they felt too much guilt, seeing their mama in such sad shape, and seeing how hard Candace had been working. And the Red Horse isn't for everyone, especially people who are used to room service," I said. "And even if Roger was upset about Constance and Terry, and wanted to drive around to shake it off, he wouldn't have driven all the way down here for that, not that late at night."

"Then it goes back to Candace," Cherry said. "Never trust the sweet ones." She pumped her straw up and down in her glass, tinkling the ice against the inside, for emphasis. "Maybe she left the house to take a walk, saw Terry's car in your laundromat parking lot, walked in to talk with him about releasing her and her sisters from the contract, and they got into an argument. She hit him, knocking him out, and then had the fiendish inspiration to finish him off with the tie-dyed slip dresses."

Cherry plucked my last crab Rangoon off my plate, swiped it through the orange-y red sweet-n-sour sauce. "Ta da!" she said, and popped the whole Rangoon into her mouth.

But I was already shaking my head. "Candace isn't strong enough to do in Terry. And even if she was, she would never leave her mother's side."

"Why not? Doesn't she have a night nurse?"

"Yes," I said, "but . . ."

"So she could easily leave the house knowing that the nurse would be there to take care of her mother if anything happened."

"Well . . . maybe," I said. "But none of this explains that blood on Terry's shirt. I'm just so worried about Moira . . ."

"Why does it have to be Moira Evans's blood on that shirt?" Cherry wanted to know.

"Because of the comment that Rhonda said Terry made. He was running late for an appointment . . . an appointment with someone who was going to make him a lot of money. Someone who could take care of the broken dress strap," I said. I fished an ice cube from my glass and popped it in my mouth and crunched on the cube. Cherry winced, and I knew what she was thinking: *Ice crunching is bad for your tooth enamel!* But we'd long ago agreed that she wouldn't nag me about that if I wouldn't nag her about the health risks of constantly wearing fake nails.

"Moira could definitely fix the strap," Cherry said, "but I don't see how she could make him a lot of money."

"I've been thinking about that," I said. "In several of the boxes of costumes were items that Mrs. Mayfair had apparently mixed in, items from when her daughters were younger. Envelopes with hair trimmings. School pictures and papers. It was like she'd created some odd filing system as the Alzheimer's set in that maybe made sense in her mind, using the boxes of singing costumes instead of the usual memento boxes."

"Awww," Cherry said, tearing up. She does have a soft heart, deep down.

"Yeah," I said. We were silent for a moment, in honor of Mrs. Mayfair. "Anyway, what if something got mixed in and I missed it? I mean, all the costumes came to me first, but at the end there, there were several that at first glance I knew needed to be repaired. Including the tie-dyed slip dresses and the pearl, silver, and gold dresses."

Cherry's eyes narrowed. "I still want that pearl one for my wedding dress."

"I know, Cherry, I know, but stay focused on what I'm saying, OK? What if something was mixed in that was of value and that's what Terry was after?"

"Like a diamond or something he could sell if he could get it from Moira?"

"I'm thinking more like . . . something that provided information he could use to keep the Mayfair Sisters from fighting the old contract. Or to blackmail them."

"But why wouldn't Moira just return it to the Mayfairs? I mean, she was reclusive and odd, but Moira never seemed to be mean. As far as anyone knew, she got along with Mrs. Mayfair just fine. And if she didn't, why not blackmail the Mayfairs directly?"

"Good questions," I said. "And truth be told, I don't know. Except maybe she couldn't bring herself to blackmail them directly. Or maybe she needed—or wanted—money fast. She could have asked herself, who else would pay to keep incriminating information hidden, and realized the Mayfairs' recording studio would. Then, she would have easily enough found Terry and set up a deal. Maybe that was why he really came to town."

We both thought about that for a few seconds, and then Cherry said, "Ice cream?"

I thought about the twenty pounds I need to lose, and then I thought about how stressful my life was at the moment, and I said, "Sure."

We made our way to the soft-serve ice cream bar and created ice cream sundaes. Only in our part of the country, I'm betting, will you find a soft-serve ice cream bar at a Chinese buffet. But the lack of authenticity didn't stop me from heaping on extra chocolate sauce and sprinkles. Somehow, the sprinkles make the sundaes taste better. I have no idea why, since the sprinkles have no flavor except generally sweet.

Anyway, after we were partway through our sundaes, Cherry said, "But what could Moira have found in a bunch of old costumes that would be valuable enough to use as blackmail?"

"I don't know, but I'm sure it has to do with the Mayfair sisters' youth and singing career. Everything I found—and returned—to Candace was from decades ago. I'm hoping that in researching the Mayfairs' past more thoroughly, Winnie will come up with something useful that could be a clue," I said.

"I guess it's not like you can ask Candace—hey, notice anything missing that might have been useful to blackmail you and your sisters?" Cherry said.

"No. But I could ask Moira," I said. "Assuming she's OK."

I pushed my half-eaten sundae away, suddenly not hungry again.

"Josie, I'm sure she's fine," Cherry said. "That blood on Terry's shirt could have been, I don't know, from hitting an animal while he was out driving around, and he tried to save it, and panicked or something."

I gave her a look that said: *Oh, like Terry would do something like that.* "I'm sure the blood is being tested to see if it matches Terry's. Maybe somehow or another it was from him and I'm just overestimating how much blood I thought I saw on that shirt."

Cherry looked at her watch. "Tell you what. You have to get to your appointment with your attorney in half an hour. After that, you can go with Caleb to check on Moira. Have you tried calling her?"

I shook my head. "I figured out early on that Moira is one of these people who never answers the phone—she just lets the answer machine kick in and every few days checks for messages."

"How sad," Cherry said.

"Yeah," I said. "Hey, what are you going to do while I'm meeting my new attorney?"

I waited for Cherry's usual answer: retail therapy. But instead she looked at me and shrugged, even as her eyes twinkled.

"Cherry . . ." I said, a warning tone in my voice.

"Listen," she said, "it shouldn't be that hard to figure out where Constance, Roger, and Cornelia are staying here. And maybe someone wherever they are staying would know if one of them left the other night before Terry was murdered."

I gave her a long look.

Sometimes I underestimate my friend . . .

Cherry pulled my sundae dish toward her and started finishing off my ice cream.

And other times, I can predict her every move.

18

The building for Susan Grey, Attorney, wasn't far from the Chinese Buffet. I found it easily enough and admonished Cherry to wait for me in the waiting area.

When Susan's secretary called me back to see her, Cherry was happily lost in an issue of *Cosmopolitan*, which was not among the magazine options on the coffee table. No, the table offered tasteful selections like *National Geographic* and *Newsweek*. Cherry had pulled the *Cosmo* out of her over-sized orange leather purse, which was really a tote bag. And from the smile on her face, she'd gone right to the article listed on the front cover: "Ten Dirty Secrets for Driving Your Man Wild."

Was she grinning because she'd already applied those secrets? Or because she was learning something new? Only she and Dean knew for sure . . . and I wasn't asking. In any case, Cherry didn't even look up when I stood up to follow the secretary back to the office of my soon-to-be attorney.

Ms. Grey was dressed in a fuchsia suit—much more colorful than her name suggested—and was as crisply confident and professional as I'd hoped she'd be, because just the thought of being a suspect in a murder case terrified me.

I told her everything—all about my involvement with the Mayfairs, about finding Terry Tuxworth in my laundromat, about my conversations with Chief Worthy, even about how he and I hadn't exactly been on good terms since junior high.

She took notes, nodded a lot, and didn't say much—until the end of our meeting, during which she admonished me not to do any investigating on my own (turns out, she'd researched me and found several articles citing my past forays into amateur detective work) and not to have any more conversations with the police without her presence.

I nodded seriously and meant it, sincerely, when I said I would take her advice to heart.

Then I left her office. I stood in the waiting area and stared at the chair where Cherry should have been, but wasn't.

"Your friend left right after you went into Ms. Grey's office," the secretary said. I whirled around and looked at him. He gave me a little smirk. "Told me to tell you she'd be waiting at the library."

"The library?" I echoed.

"There's a branch across the street," he said.

Of course. I knew that. I'd been to it before. I was just so overwhelmed by my situation, I hadn't paid any attention.

"I guess she felt she needed some new reading material," he said.

I turned and looked at him. "Why of course," I said. "How could I forget? Cherry mentioned she'd use this time to go check out *Crime and Punishment*. For our book club."

The secretary lifted his eyebrows in a look that indicated he doubted the likes of Cherry and me would ever read such a thing.

I thought about adding that the book was by Fyodor Dostoevsky, in case he ever wanted to read it, but then I reminded myself that it was never a good idea to antagonize secretaries or receptionists.

I found Cherry in the reference section of the library, sitting at a table, again reading her issue of *Cosmopolitan*. She seemed pretty absorbed in its contents.

I sat down in a chair across from her, and she didn't even notice, until I leaned across the table and hissed, "So what's dirty secret number seven?"

She startled and dropped the magazine, then frowned at me.

"I haven't even gotten to secret four yet," she said, "because I've been busily researching just for you."

"Thanks," I said, "but I'm not quite to the dirty secret stage with anyone at the moment."

"That's not what I meant," Cherry said, primly closing the magazine and dropping it back into her orange tote bag. "I mean, I've figured out where Constance, Cornelia, and Roger are staying."

I shook my head. "I just promised my attorney I wouldn't do any investigating on my own."

Cherry went on as if she hadn't heard me. "It wasn't that hard to figure out, to tell you the truth. I just thought, based on what you told me about the Mayfairs, where would they be most likely to stay? And the answer would be at one of the most expensive, elegant places in this town. Which pretty much narrows it down to the two bed-and-breakfasts in town.

"So I came over here and asked the reference librarian to help me get the phone numbers. I called both and pretended to have an important delivery for Cornelia Mayfair, since I couldn't remember Roger's and Constance's last name," Cherry said. "The first place, no luck, but the second bed-and-breakfast, bingo!"

She opened up her bag and plucked out a piece of paper, turned it around on the table so I could look at it.

The paper read: Concord House B&B, and gave an address and directions from the library. It was, at most, a five-minute drive.

What could we learn if we went there? It wasn't like we could just walk up to the bed-and-breakfast owner and demand to know the comings and goings of the guests. We couldn't say, "Hey, did Constance, Cornelia, or Roger happen to leave the premises Saturday night at, oh, say, nine p.m. or so, just in time to drive back to Paradise, stumble across Terry Tuxworth at Toadfern's Laundromat, and murder him?"

How would the owner even necessarily know if any of the guests had left at night?

Still, even though I didn't see how it would really help me, I was tempted . . . really tempted.

But I said, "Cherry, didn't you just hear me? I promised my attorney I wouldn't do any investigating."

Cherry grinned. "I know you did. But I didn't make that promise."

I groaned, knowing that somehow or another I was going to end up at that bed-and-breakfast, supporting whatever Cherry's kooky plan might be.

She stood up. "Let's go."

I remained seated. "Do you mean go, as in go back to Paradise, like we're supposed to do, or go, as in go to the bed-and-breakfast, which we shouldn't do at all?"

"I mean go, as in go to the copies-and-signs-made-while-you-wait shop just down the road," Cherry said. "I have directions to that, too. Libraries are really helpful!"

I'd been telling her that for years. But at that moment, I wished I hadn't.

"This isn't going to work, you know," I said, for the fifth time since we'd left the library.

I'd said it once after we left the library, while Cherry explained her plan, twice at the copy/sign shop, once on the drive to the city park, just two streets away from the Concord House, and now, again, as we stood outside my van in the parking lot.

"Of course it will," Cherry said confidently. "Just look at that!"

I stared at the side of my van. Where my laundromat's name and logo had been airbrushed was now a large magnet, proclaiming: "Deputy Dean's Security Systems, Inc."

Cherry had had business cards made to match.

"Dean will kill you if he finds out," I said.

"Oh, pshaw," Cherry said. "How will he find out? Besides, he's talked about starting his security consulting business on the side, after we're back from our honeymoon, of course, and settled in. That's how I got this idea. Besides, we can reuse the magnet and business cards, so the expense is OK."

Dean's always nervous about Cherry's tendency to overspend.

"Cherry," I said, "you had a fake phone number and address put on the business cards." She'd also had her name, followed by the title "Vice President of Marketing" put on the cards.

"True," Cherry said, "but they were cheap compared to the magnet, and we can use that again." She pointed to a bench. "Now, you just set there and wait," she said.

I stood rooted in my spot.

"You're not mentioning my name," I said.

"Of course not," Cherry reassured me.

"And you'll be careful with my van," I said.

"Absolutely."

"What if the Mayfairs are there and they recognize my van? The magnet isn't going to fool them."

Cherry gave me a look. "Josie, it's a big white van. How many of those can there be?"

"What if they recognize the license plate?"

"You really think the Mayfairs have been memorizing your license plate number? Who does stuff like that?"

Well, I did know a Stillwater resident who remembered license plate numbers after a glance. He was also able to calculate the distance between any two points in the U.S., within seconds.

But I saw her point.

I sighed. "Now, look, if this starts to go badly, you'll make an excuse to leave right away, right? Like if the bed-and-breakfast owner gets suspicious."

Cherry gave me a look of incredulousness. "Why would the owner get suspicious? Don't I look like the vice president of marketing at Deputy Dean's Security Systems, Inc.?"

Cherry—in her orange capris, white flip-flops, white blouse, orange and white polka-dotted headband, orange tote bag, and big hoop earrings—asked this with complete seriousness, and then blew a big, pink, bubble gum bubble.

There wasn't a thing I could say to that.

I went over to the park bench and sat down.

"This isn't going to work, you know."

I groaned and looked up at Mrs. Oglevee, who smiled as she repeated my earlier words to Cherry.

Great. In my nice, hot, sunny spot on the park bench—

where I had settled to watch the happy sight of some kids swinging—I had fallen asleep.

I was probably slumped over and drooling. Pretty soon a police officer would come along and arrest me for loitering. Or the sight of me would scare one of the kids.

Or a bird would poop on my head.

"Why do you always think so negatively?" Mrs. Oglevee said. She was swinging on a swing set. She was also wearing an old-fashioned schoolgirl dress—the kind of pinafore my aunt made me wear for my elementary school pictures, even though the photos just were from the neck up—and black patent leather Mary Jane–style shoes, lace-trimmed anklets, and a blond wig styled with bangs and braided pig-tails.

Her getup should have disturbed me, but what was really alarming was that there wasn't just one Mrs. Oglevee . . . there were three. The two clones swung, too, and they were humming, something vaguely familiar.

Yet what was somehow really disturbing to me was a fourth swing, empty, just barely swaying back and forth.

Now, I wondered, why should that bother me?

"Josie! I asked you a question! Why do you always think so negatively?"

Well, Mrs. Oglevee's voice and attitude certainly hadn't regressed to that of a young girl.

"I'm not thinking negatively."

"Yes, you are," she said. "You think Cherry won't find anything out."

My eyebrows went up at that. What? When had Mrs. Oglevee ever defended the likes of Cherry?

I admit it. I was a little jealous.

"And you think things can't possibly work out with you and Levi," she went on.

"Now, wait a minute," I said. "I've not even known Levi for seventy-two hours!"

Mrs. Oglevee hmmphed. "How long did you know Owen?"

"OK, that's unfair," I protested.

"Why? You assume that you can only know you've found your soul mate after a certain length of time?"

"And you assume knowing a person is your soul mate is a love-at-first-sight proposition?" I shot back.

"Depends," Mrs. Oglevee said . . . and started humming along with her two clones. The fourth swing just wavered pathetically.

"What is that you're humming, anyway?" I asked, annoyed. "And what makes you think Levi's—"

Something landed on my shoulder. I started flailing. No way was I going to be victim to a bird poop attack in Masonville City Park . . .

I woke up.

The something on my shoulder was Cherry's hand.

I stared up at Cherry.

She grinned at me as I sat up. "It worked!"

I stayed on the park bench for a second, staring at the swing set just yards in front of me, and gasped.

There were four swings on the set. Three were still. One was swaying back and forth.

I gasped.

"What?" said Cherry.

"That swing . . . that's moving . . ."

"What of it? A little girl just jumped off." Cherry pointed and I looked. A small child—brunette ponytail, shorts, T-shirt, I was relieved to see—walked off, hand in hand with her mother.

"Are you OK?" Cherry asked.

"Yeah, fine. I just had a . . . dream. There was this song . . ."

I shrugged, stood up, and we started back to my van.

"I can't wait to tell you how it happened," Cherry was babbling.

I held up a finger in a one-minute sign and then pulled the Deputy Dean's Security Systems, Inc. magnet off the side of my van.

There, I thought as I gazed with satisfaction at Toadfern's Laundromat Services and my logo—a toad atop a laundry basket.

At least something in my life was back to normal.

Cherry told me about her undercover detective work at the Concord House B&B as we drove back to Paradise.

"It was so simple!" she raved. "I just explained how I was visiting all the upscale places in Masonville—the B&B owner, Martha Winslow, seemed to really like that characterization of her business. Then I gently pointed out that her business was only blocks away from a high-crime area of Masonville. And I wondered if I could review her business's security system because of course upscale customers like hers would want to know that they, and their possessions, would be really safe."

"And she told you how her security system worked?" I asked, aghast. Why, for all Martha Winslow knew, Cherry was just using a fake van sign and business cards to worm her way into inside knowledge of the B&B!

Which, of course, she was.

"Of course not," Cherry said. "She told me all about how the building had really good locks, and that of course she had a safe for customers who wanted to use it. I just smiled and nodded at that, waiting for her to say something that would give me a good hook to start asking about her current guests—particularly the Mayfairs.

"Then she said she had lighting and a security camera in the parking lot because they had had vandalism problems in the past. And I hooked right into that. I asked how much time passed before the images were erased and she said weekly, resetting at five p.m. every Wednesday—the idea being that no customer would wait more than a week to complain that something happened to his or her vehicle in the B&B parking lot.

"So I casually asked, well, do you mind showing me some of the film, starting at, oh a random time—say nine p.m. Saturday night.

"She took me back to her office and started showing me, fast forwarding through, and saying how she hadn't heard any activity in the B&B after that hour.

"But soon enough, I saw a figure coming out to the parking lot—a man. I gasped and said, 'Oh no, is he about to key that nice car?'"

Cherry giggled.

"You knew he wasn't going to do any such thing," I said, in an admonishing tone. Making that poor B&B owner nervous. On the other hand, if Cherry found out something that would help me . . .

"Of course," Cherry said. "But it worked. Martha backed the film up and played it on regular speed and we both acted very relieved at the fact that the man was just getting in his car."

"Did you get a look at him? The car?"

"Well, the film was taken at nine-thirty-two at night, according to the time stamp. But here's what I saw," Cherry said, and described the car and the man.

Her description of the man could have been Roger . . . or another man at the B&B. But the convertible he drove . . . well, there weren't any other convertibles in the parking lot, according to what Cherry saw on the film, so it had to be his, right?

"The good news is the camera lingered long enough—and the lighting in the parking lot was good enough, that I even caught the license number," she said, "A vanity plate that says: BYEBYEU."

"That's Roger and Constance's car, all right," I said. "What did he do?"

"He got in, drove off," Cherry said.

My heart did a double thump. OK. Roger had left the B&B at the right time to get to Paradise in time to connect up with Terry, get in a fight, and kill him. But they couldn't have planned to meet there. After all, Terry's action of stuffing his bloodied shirt in a washer just before he was murdered didn't suggest a planned meeting. And there was no reason to meet at my laundromat.

Plus the circumstances of Terry's murder suggested an act of passion.

"Well, how did he seem?" I asked. "Was he in a hurry? Did he seem upset? Distracted?"

"The camera caught him just for maybe ten seconds, from a distance, before moving to another section of the lot," Cherry said. "So it's hard to say—but he seemed, well, fine."

"Oh," I said, disappointed.

"On the other hand . . ." Cherry started.

I glanced at her as we neared the outskirts—meaning soy and cornfields with farmhouses I recognized—of Paradise.

"Don't be coy with me," I said. "What?"

"Well, I said something about how odd it was that a guest would be leaving that late at night, and was Martha sure that was a guest? Maybe it was someone trying to steal the car? And she said no, the man was a guest. She remembered he'd asked her about where was the closest pharmacy as his wife had forgotten some medicine and he needed to go get it."

Hmmm. Roger had had to go to a pharmacy for his wife,

Constance. And he hadn't looked particularly in a rush or upset as he was leaving. So all we really knew was that, yes, he had left the B&B at a time that would sync up with Terry's killing—if Roger had driven to Paradise.

But there was no reason to believe he'd have driven there. "Any chance you asked to see the tape at, say, midnight? About the time Roger might have returned to the B&B, if he'd really gone to Paradise instead?" I asked, hopeful.

"No," Cherry said. "By then Martha was getting restless. I just gave her a card, thanked her for her time, and told her that her security system looked great but I'd write up a free proposal of suggestions about how Deputy Dean's Security could help her make her system even better, for less money."

I cut her a look. "You know, Dean really will be upset if he ever finds out. And also there's no way you can follow up on that promise to Martha."

Cherry shrugged. "I didn't give her a time frame," she said. "Eventually, who knows? Deputy Dean's Security might just get back to her."

I took Cherry by her home, thanking her as I dropped her off. I wasn't sure I'd learned anything that would help me; it wasn't like I could go to Chief Worthy and tell him I'd found out, through Cherry's playacting as vice president of marketing for a security systems company that didn't exist—that Roger had left his B&B to go to a Masonville pharmacy at 9:30 or so on the night of Terry's murder, and expect him to bring Roger in for questioning based on that.

After dropping off Cherry, I told myself I'd go by my laundromat and apartment and reopen. I'd start by cleaning all the fingerprinting dust in my supply room/office.

But the center of Paradise was a mess, traffic wise—especially around my laundromat. Three TV crews were filming in front of my laundromat, and I knew if I tried to go in, I'd be attacked by reporters asking me questions. And I had no desire to deal with being on TV as a murder suspect or as the owner of a business where a grisly murder had just happened.

It wasn't like I could reopen for my customers, and I had a place to stay, so I pulled a U on Main Street and hurried over to Plum, to connect up with Caleb for our interview with Moira Evans.

Caleb was parked outside the house and waiting for me when I pulled up. He watched, with amusement, as I pulled out the big "Deputy Dean's Security Systems, Inc." magnet and slapped it back over the Toadfern's Laundromat title and logo on the side of my van.

"What's that all about?" he asked.

"Camouflage," I said. "I just drove past my laundromat, and the place is crawling with media types." I shuddered. "I just don't want to talk to any of those vultures. The magnet is cover until I get back out of town."

Caleb lifted an eyebrow. "Oh, thanks. I feel so loved."

I punched his arm. "I don't mean you," I said, as we walked up to the front porch. "You're OK. Besides, you're in print media. It's the TV types that scare me."

Caleb poked the doorbell. We heard it chime inside. "Just so long as you save all your exclusives for me," he said.

I didn't reply to his playful banter, ripe with innuendo, as I would have a few days ago, even after we'd stopped dating. I just stared at the screen door over the regular door, whose green paint, I noted, was peeling.

"I meant that in the strictest news sense," Caleb said quietly.

I looked at him. He gave me a real smile that was only tinged with sadness and could-have-beens. "I know you've just met him, but I could see the connection between you and Levi at the Bar-None," Caleb added. "And I'm happy for you, Josie." He gave my arm a little squeeze.

I looked back at the peeling patch of green paint. "Thanks," I said. I poked the doorbell again. Moira was slow, but usually not this slow.

"So . . . why the Deputy Dean's magnet, really?" Caleb asked. "I sense Cherry was involved."

I smiled. "Of course." I tugged on his arm. "I'll tell you about it quickly while we go to the back of the house. Moira's sewing room is at the back of the house, and she didn't always hear the front bell. I had to go around to the back several times."

Still, I felt a sense of uneasiness curling in my stomach as we walked around the yard—just a bit patchy and overgrown—to the back. I tried to push it away as I told Caleb about what Sally had learned at the B&B.

I finished telling him as we got to the back door. The screen was shut but the back door was open just a bit.

I knocked on the door frame. "Yoo hoo!" I hollered. "Moira, it's me, Josie!"

No answer.

"Josie," Caleb said softly, "I think we'd better go in."

He moved to the side, and pulled me to where he'd been standing, and then pointed.

I saw, just on the other side of the door, Moira's right shoe and ankle—unmoving.

Caleb was already dialing 911 as I yanked open the screen door, shoved the back door, and stepped in.

My mouth gaped and I gasped and gagged all at once as I saw the rest of Moira, and the smell of death in the small, dark, hot kitchen overtook me.

Moira was on her green and white tiled floor, the front of her blouse crusted with dried blood. She'd been stabbed to death.

19

What happened directly after Caleb and I discovered poor Moira Evans is still a blur, and truth be told, I'm kind of hoping it stays that way.

I do remember talking with the police at the scene of the crime.

I vaguely remember somehow or another ending up at the Paradise Police Department and ending up, again, in the interrogation room with Chief Worthy and Officer Franklin Cook, just one day after I'd been in that room with them talking about Terry Tuxworth's murder.

Of course, during that interrogation, I'd been a lot calmer and had even unloaded my opinion of Chief Worthy's attitude toward me, after all these years.

But finding Moira Evans like that . . . someone I'd known all my life . . .

I wasn't able to be my usual calm self. I just kept thinking about how she died so violently. I wondered if she'd died right away, or had fallen to the floor, and suffered, unable to get to a phone for help.

I wondered how many days would have gone by if Caleb and I hadn't shown up to talk with her before someone would have thought to check on her. A few days? A week? Even longer?

It made me feel guilty and horrified, all at once.

So I was semihysterical through the whole interview with Police Chief Worthy. I insisted that Worthy should order DNA testing on the blood on the Terry Tuxworth shirt in my laundromat washer to see if it matched Moira's blood.

I told Worthy what Rhonda had told us, leaving out the part about her sleeping with Terry (I had at least the presence of mind to stick to the PG version of Rhonda's evening with Terry that Cherry and I had cooked up for her). I told him that Rhonda would probably deny telling Cherry and me about that.

I shared how I'd noticed that the boxes of costumes I'd received had, mixed in between the dresses and scarves and blouses and skirts, mementos of the Mayfair women's lives from when they were girls, as if Mrs. Mayfair had set up in her head some kind of sentimental filing system only she could understand.

I told Worthy that Rhonda had said Terry complained he was late for an appointment with someone who would make him a lot of money. I added my theory that, no, Terry couldn't make much of anything off of poor Moira . . . but what if she'd found sensitive information mixed in with the costumes, information she was willing to sell Terry? And what if he wanted the information but didn't want to pay for it and risk her continually demanding more or trying to sell the information to a higher bidder?

Or . . . what if Moira had lured Terry to her house and then tried to blackmail him, based on something she'd found . . . maybe something that Mrs. Mayfair had forgotten that could put an end to the "in perpetuity" contract Terry's father had signed with the Mayfair Sisters' mother?

I even told Worthy about how Cherry had found out that Roger had left the B&B around 9:30 the night Terry Tuxworth was found murdered in my laundromat.

I let everything I knew, everything I'd been thinking about this case just spill out. I even let my emotions spill over. I had to stop several times to cry, then pull it back together, and blow my nose.

Finding poor Moira like that . . . brutally stabbed . . . just shook the truth right out of me.

And what was really amazing was that Chief John Worthy listened, without interrupting, or being sarcastic, or mocking me.

He just listened solemnly, took notes, let me take my time.

Guess I should have told him off years before.

The days following our terrible discovery were fairly quiet, at least for me.

I stayed at Stillwater, taking comfort in the quiet refuge of Guy's home. Everyone was kind to me there and didn't ask questions.

Only Cherry, Sally, Winnie, and Caleb—back in Paradise—knew where I was staying, but they were good and loyal friends and didn't tell members of the media, who by now were swarming around the Mayfair house, my laundromat, and Moira Evans's house.

The media frenzy was so bad that Candace had moved her mother early to the Alzheimer's home and had temporarily taken up residence in the Concord B&B, Cherry told me she'd learned from Dean—who had of course forgiven her when she confessed to him that she'd used the idea of his future business to gather information about Roger, Cornelia, and Constance's comings and goings at the B&B.

I spent a lot of time in the guest room at Stillwater—Guy would have been too confused by seeing me suddenly there all the time—and I napped and read.

Levi and I went out to dinner in Masonville and went for walks at the state park and got to know each other better and better. I kept waiting for our relationship to cool, after its initial heat, but it didn't.

I talked several times to my attorney, Susan Grey, who admonished me, again, to keep my nose out of the investigation.

Which, strictly speaking, I did.

However, through the grapevine, Sally learned that Rhonda did in fact deny what I'd told Chief Worthy she'd said about Terry's comments about being late for an appointment that would make him a lot of money.

So it was her word against mine and Cherry's (who backed me up).

The next round of news from Sally was even more depressing: The police were holding Clint Evans, Moira's grandson, on suspicion of Moira's murder. Clint had come back to Moira's house after I observed his blowup. The neighbors across the street had heard them fighting again in the early evening of Terry's murder. Clint had wanted her to give him cash and some jewelry to sell at a pawnshop, and she'd refused.

Clint had been seen storming away from the house, angry, and a crying Moira had gone back inside.

When the police went to interview Clint, they found illegal drugs, and jewelry that he confessed was his grandmother's, stolen on previous visits but that he hadn't been able to pawn for as much as he needed. He was shocked to find out about his grandmother's murder, breaking down in sobs, and swore he hadn't killed her.

I also learned—this time from Caleb, who was selling news stories freelance to the AP and other wires—that Terry's bloody shirt, and a sample of Moira's blood, had been sent to the Ohio Bureau of Criminal Identification and Investigation. But it would take two or more weeks to find out if there was a match.

In the meantime, Clint was the prime suspect in his grandmother's murder . . . unless it turned out that his grandmother's blood was on Terry's shirt, in which case he'd end up being, Caleb told me he'd learned off the record, the prime suspect in Terry's murder, on the theory that he could have come back, found his grandmother murdered, found something that connected Terry to his grandmother, and then happened by my laundromat and saw Terry's car out front, and angrily confronted the man he believed killed his grandmother.

"And leave his grandmother's body for two days . . . or however long?" I protested when Caleb told me that.

Clint, he said, had a long criminal record. Maybe, since his grandmother was dead and nothing could be done about it, he'd panicked.

That seemed like a pretty unfair assessment. I felt Clint, whatever his troubles, was being set up. And even if that let me off the hook—for the time being—for Terry's murder, I didn't like that, so I called Susan Grey and asked her to represent Clint. I'd cover the fees somehow, I told her. I just couldn't believe that Clint had killed his grandmother or Terry.

Something was nagging at me . . . something I couldn't quite put together.

And so the week passed, until it was Friday evening, the

night of the Mayfair Sisters, farewell concert at the Licking Creek Lake State Park's amphitheater.

Levi and I decided to go with Cherry and Dean.

An hour before it was time to go, Winnie called me on my cell phone.

I almost didn't answer it because, well, I'd always been a perfectionist about answering in the past in case there was something wrong with Guy.

But I'd just looked in on him in the dining room, not ten minutes before, and he was fine.

Plus the whole Stillwater staff knew I was staying in the guest apartment, so they'd know how to find me if something was wrong with Guy. My plan was to stay at Stillwater through the weekend. I figured after the Mayfair Sisters' concert on Friday night and the auction on Saturday morning, the media would start to leave Paradise.

And then I'd have to make myself go back to my laundromat and apartment and be at peace with both, no matter what had happened to Terry.

The other reason I almost didn't answer my cell phone was that, truth be told, I was doing my nails. I'd just finished carefully applying eye makeup, even.

I know. Doesn't sound like me at all, does it?

But I had just put on a light taupe eye shadow, and a coat of dark brown mascara, and then moved on to doing a nice, soft, shell pink coat on my neatly filed nails. I wanted to look as nice as possible on my double date.

Still, I answered my cell phone anyway. Old habits die hard.

"Josie!" Winnie said, sounding breathless. "I'm so glad I caught you before you left for the concert. I figure once you're out with everyone else, and at the concert, it would be difficult to talk. Besides . . . I think you might want to know this before the concert."

"What did you find out?" I asked, my heart picking up speed into a double-time thump.

"Well, I started by digging through old newspaper clippings—almost all on microfiche—from the *Paradise Advertiser-Gazette* about the Mayfair family. I figured the national coverage wouldn't tell us anything we didn't already know about the Mayfairs, and I was right.

"And at first, I didn't really find anything new in the *Paradise Advertiser-Gazette*," Winnie went on. "So I started digging into the Tuxworth family—anything I could find about the business in particular.

"Since I was focusing on business news, I almost missed it, but fortunately, there was a mention of something very interesting at the end of an article about the Tuxworth Recording business . . . about Terry Tuxworth's daughter finding him."

We were quiet for a moment, as Winnie let that news sink in and as I mentally scrambled to see how this new piece of information might fit with the other pieces I had.

"Wait . . . Terry had a daughter, too? But I assumed Terry Jr. was his only child, since he inherited the business and no one mentioned any siblings," I said.

"Terry Sr. apparently thought so, too. But his daughter—JoBeth Anderson—always knew she'd been adopted. After her mother died, she was looking through old items and found an official copy of her birth certificate, naming her parents," Winnie said.

Now my heart was beating so hard I was having trouble breathing.

"Who . . ." I started.

"The article just says Terry Sr. is the father," Winnie said. "Apparently they had a nice enough reunion and he wasn't at all hostile toward her. The article said JoBeth had personal reasons for not connecting with her birth mother. And all Terry Tuxworth Sr. said was that he did have a brief affair with a woman in Nashville before getting married, but he had no idea he'd fathered a child. He was, however, glad to reconnect with her."

I pressed my eyes shut, and then—to heck with my home-done manicure—rubbed my eyelids. "Were you able to find out how to contact JoBeth?" My voice was gravelly.

"I did an Internet search on her, plus made a few phone calls to verify what I found," Winnie said, in a tone of voice that made me know the news would not be good. "JoBeth Anderson died about six months after connecting up with her birth father, Terry Tuxworth Sr. Pancreatic cancer. Apparently she knew she had cancer at the time she contacted Terry Sr. Knowing she was ill was one reason she wished to connect with her birth parents. It was, apparently, on her list of things to do before she passed away. So Terry Sr. knew when JoBeth contacted him that his daughter was very ill and had only a short time to live."

"When was this?" I asked.

"Three years ago," Winnie said. "About a year after Dora Mayfair was diagnosed with Alzheimer's."

"Do you suppose that's why JoBeth Anderson didn't want to push a connection with her birth mother?" I asked.

"That would be my guess," Winnie said. "Maybe she thought there would be no point. Or maybe she thought it would be cruel to pursue connecting with a woman who was already confused about life and her loved ones."

I swallowed hard and spared a kind thought for JoBeth Anderson. If Winnie's guess was right, then JoBeth had been kind and selfless to spare her birth mother from pain and confusion.

"But we can't know for sure, then, that JoBeth's mother was Dora Mayfair," I said.

"No, but it seems likely. Reading that article sparked my memory of something else I'd read in all those gossipy who's-visiting-who columns in the *Paradise Advertiser-Gazette*," Winnie said. The newspaper, much to Caleb's chagrin, still had guest columns like that. Someone's grandchildren and nieces and nephews would come into town for, say, a fifty-year-anniversary, and someone in the family would write up a guest piece for the local paper.

Caleb did not dare to refuse to run those pieces, any more than he would dare to get rid of news about Scouts and church carry-in suppers and youth sports events. The advertisers would pull out and the newspaper would fold.

And that was as it had been, probably since the first issue of the newspaper. Sure, run an in-depth article about the plans of the local water board if you must.

But don't leave out the good stuff!

"Anyway, there's a column about Terry Tuxworth visiting Paradise after he was home, following injury, after World War II. He wasn't from here, but he wanted, says the column, to visit Paradise, Ohio, because his good buddy Mayfair had said so many nice things about it. So, on his way back to Nashville, Terry stopped in town and told everyone how brave and smart their hometown hero, Mayfair, was being over in Germany. And there's even a picture of him with Dora Mayfair," Winnie said, "who married Bob Mayfair right before he left for the war. Dora lived with his parents, with frequent visits back to an aunt in North Carolina. Anyway, another year would pass after Terry's visit before he'd return."

I took that piece of information in, put it with all the others Winnie had given me, and said: "Let me guess. Nine months later would coincide with JoBeth Anderson's birth date."

"That's right," Winnie said. "But I'm not sure how any of this fits, exactly, with Terry Tuxworth Jr.'s and Moira Evans's murders."

"I'm not, either," I said. "Not yet."

"Um . . . Josie," Winnie said, sounding suddenly worried. "Be careful, OK?"

"What's there to worry about?" I asked in my most innocent-sounding voice. "I'm just going to a very public concert with three other people."

"Uh huh," Winnie said. "I know you. Just be careful. All right?"

"OK," I said. "And thanks for letting me know what you found out."

We said our good-byes and I snapped shut my cell phone.

I closed my eyes and thought about what I'd just learned from Winnie.

Mrs. Oglevee hadn't traipsed into my dreams for the whole week, but the images from my dream of her during my snooze at the Masonville City Park the previous Monday came to my mind now.

I saw her and the two clones of her, dressed in schoolgirl garb, swinging. I saw the empty fourth swing, eerily swaying to and fro.

Of course, the images symbolized the three Mayfair sisters everyone knew about . . . and the fourth half-sister no one knew about, until now, except Terry Tuxworth Sr. and Dora Mayfair.

But how could I have conjured that image . . . I still wasn't quite comfortable with the notion of Mrs. Oglevee's spirit literally visiting me in my dreams . . . before this news from Winnie?

And then I heard the tune that Mrs. Oglevee and her extra selves had been humming in my dream, so softly.

Finally, it hit me. That was the tune to the same song Candace sang . . . for love . . . over and over to her mother. The one song Mrs. Mayfair had ever written in her life: "Carolina Calling." A song that the Mayfair Sisters never sang as a group . . . that only Candace sang to soothe her confused, ailing mother.

I had assumed, as the words implied, that "Carolina Calling" had been about Dora's childhood days in North Carolina, and how she missed living there.

The words trailed through my mind: *Carolina, I hear you calling, but I can't answer, for I've gone a long way away, I knew you only for a moment, but my heart has never strayed . . .*

The true meaning of those words was suddenly clear.

Dora had given all her daughters names beginning with C. Probably she dreamed of naming her first child for the state she'd grown up in and missed as an adult.

But, because she was married to another man, she gave that child up for adoption. Maybe she even went back to her home state to stay with her aunt to have the baby before giving her up.

Maybe she even let Terry Tuxworth Sr. know that she'd gotten pregnant by him during his quick visit to Paradise.

My guess was he'd been glad that she had quietly given the child away, and that he was all too glad to have no more to do with his army buddy and his buddy's wife . . . until that wife became a widow and Terry learned about a regional singing act, the Mayfair Sisters, who were ripe for a recording contract.

I could just imagine him realizing that he had a golden opportunity to make a mint off the Mayfair Sisters. All he had to do was threaten Dora with revealing that there was, somewhere out there, a fourth Mayfair daughter. Maybe he even had proof—a pleading letter, for example—that he could use as blackmail.

And Dora would have wanted to avoid that for all kinds of reasons. Even though it was the 1960s, life was still conservative in our part of Ohio—and still is. Dora and her daughters would have been shunned.

Perhaps she feared that her daughters' careers would be ruined and no one else would sign them.

Dora would not have had anyone she could really turn to for help on how to get out of what she saw as Terry Tuxworth Sr.'s iron grip on her and her daughters' futures. And she probably thought any career in music would be better for them than none at all.

And so she'd signed the contract that locked the Mayfair Sisters in with Terry Tuxworth Sr.'s company in perpetuity.

But fast-forward several decades. The Mayfair Sisters find a good entertainment rights attorney to fight that contract, on the grounds that Tuxworth Recording has, in essence, been defunct by not doing any new recordings since their act wrapped up.

And then, somehow, Terry Tuxworth Jr. finds out just why Mama Mayfair agreed to such an unfair contract in the first place.

How? Something Dora mixed in the costumes years ago, when she started losing her grasp on reality? Something that ended up with Moira Evans, who saw a chance to make some money by selling whatever it was to Terry Tuxworth Jr.

That certainly fit what Cherry and I learned from Rhonda earlier in the week.

But there was something else.

Candace had been singing that song, "Carolina Calling," for months now to her poor mother to soothe her.

Dora had said to me on several occasions, "Is it you?"

And I'd heard her say it to her nurse, too.

What if Candace had figured out the truth . . . that the song referred not to a place, but to a person who, at the end of her life, Dora longed for, but could never see. At least not in this life.

Would Candace—little, ethereal-seeming Candace—kill to keep that truth hidden, to protect her mother's reputation, to protect the Mayfair Sisters' legacy, because it was the one thing her mother had been so proud of, no matter the financial and creative cost to her daughters?

There was a knock at the Stillwater guest apartment door.

I opened my eyes and realized that tears had welled behind my eyelids, and when I opened my eyes and rubbed away the tears, I smudged my carefully applied eye makeup.

So be it.

I opened the door anyway, glad to see Levi. And he looked thrilled to see me. I don't think he even noticed the smudged eye makeup.

20

Levi did notice, however, that I was quiet on the drive over to Licking Creek Lake State Park.

We were in the backseat of Dean's car. He took my hand and squeezed it. "You OK, Josie?" he asked, concern rounding out his voice.

I wanted to tell him what I'd learned from Winnie, the theory I'd put together about the truth behind Terry Jr.'s and Moira's brutal murders.

I wanted to tell him how sad I felt at the thought that Candace, the one who sang for love, was really behind their gory deaths.

But this time, this place wasn't right for it.

Besides, Cherry foiled the moment by twisting around in the front passenger seat and looking back at us.

"Are you carsick, Josie?" she asked.

"No, Cherry, I'm just thinking about the concert—"

"Give her a bag!" Dean exclaimed.

His car—a restored 1979 Chevy Camaro—was his automotive pride and joy, but it didn't stop Cherry from littering the passenger's side with fast-food and retailers' bags.

I looked at Levi. To his credit, he was not inching away from me. He just kept holding my hand and gave me a smile. But I said, anyway, "I got carsick when I was a kid. I haven't been carsick in years . . ."

My explanation was interrupted by Cherry tossing a small, plastic Walgreens bag back at me.

It fluttered onto my lap.

"Just in case," Cherry said.

Well, I thought, you work with what you're given. I'd been trying to think up a way to get Cherry away from the men once we arrived at the park, so I could tell her my plan.

"Cherry," I snapped, "that does it! I want to talk to you—privately—when we arrive at the park."

That made Levi give me a wary look. I'd just have to explain later, I thought.

"Are you really mad at me?" Cherry asked, wide-eyed.

Levi and Dean had gone on ahead to spread out our blankets for the concert. Our tickets were on the lawn section.

"Annoyed," I said, "because I really haven't been carsick since I was a kid, but that's not why I want to talk to you."

I pulled her out of the path of people streaming toward the park's amphitheater. The Mayfair Sisters' reunion show to benefit their mama was sold out, even the lawn section. Nearly a thousand people were eagerly attending.

We stood underneath a big oak tree. Cherry glanced down at the vines in which we stood—me in practical tennis shoes and her in high-heeled flip-flops.

"That's not poisoned ivy, is it?" Cherry asked.

"No," I said. "No one has poisoned that ivy. Do you mean poison ivy?"

Her eyes got wide.

"It's not that, either," I said. "Now listen to me, and focus!"

I summarized what I'd learned from Winnie, my theory, and my plan.

And then we went to find the dressing trailer behind the amphitheater that the Mayfair Sisters would be using as a greenroom and for costume changes between acts.

There's something special about a live performance that a CD or mp3 recording just can't capture . . . even if the recording is of a live performance.

Maybe it's the notion that anything can happen. Or the give-and-take of energy between the performers and the audience that creates its own invisible buzz if the connection is vital, alive, excited.

And for the first half of the Mayfair Sisters' reunion show, that was exactly what happened.

It wasn't just that the crowd enjoyed hearing their favorite tunes again, like "Sugar Daddy." It was that the sisters connected on stage, through their music, in a way that was genuine and energetic, no matter their varying motivations for singing or their private differences.

I understood, being part of the audience, why the Mayfair Sisters had been a big hit in their day in a way that hearing "Sugar Daddy" on the Bar-None's digital jukebox would never convey.

For the second to last song, Candace took the microphone and said, "As you all know, this is a benefit to help our dear mother, Dora Mayfair."

The crowd burst into applause. When the crowd settled down again, she went on: "All of us want to thank you so much for your help and generosity. And thank you, in advance, if you get a chance to attend tomorrow's auction."

Another cheer went up.

"Most of you don't know that our mother wanted to be a songwriter and was a fine singer herself. She gave us her love of music and taught us to sing. When we were growing up, she sang as a lullaby to us the one song she wrote as a young woman. It's called 'Carolina Calling' and is about missing her home state, North Carolina, although she loved Ohio, too. Anyway, instead of singing it in our usual harmony, we're going to sing it in unison," Candace said.

The crowd hushed, sensing something special. I felt chills so strong go through me that I feared for a second they'd levitate me off the blanket I shared with Levi.

The Mayfair Sisters gathered around one microphone.

"For our mama," Candace said, "Dora Mayfair."

And then the sisters sang, a cappella, as one voice: *Carolina, I hear you calling, but I can't answer, for I've gone a long way away, I knew you only for a moment, but my heart has never strayed . . .*

By the time they finished, there weren't any dry eyes. Dean and Levi were sniffling and wiping their eyes, too, which endeared them to me. Real men know when to let themselves cry.

The final note floated hauntingly over the crowd and then there was enthusiastic, but respectful, applause.

When that faded, Cornelia said, "Now, we're going to take an intermission, but first we want to leave you with something upbeat!"

Then the Mayfair Sisters launched into another popular hit, "Hey, Big Boy."

That was my and Cherry's cue.

We started getting up from our blankets.

"Where are you two going?" Dean asked.

"Bathroom," Cherry said.

"We want to beat the lines," I said.

We started hurrying away.

"It's just amazing how women always travel in pairs or packs to the bathroom," Dean said.

"Yeah," Levi agreed. "Even to Porta Potties!"

Cherry and I bypassed the Porta Potties, of course, and headed straight to the trailers behind the amphitheater. There were two trailers, both unlabeled.

We ducked into trees near the trailers, so we could get a view of which one the Mayfair Sisters entered, and which one the backup musicians entered.

Cherry stared down woefully at her high-heeled flip-flopped feet, again in ivy. "You're sure this isn't poisoned . . . I mean poison?"

"I'm sure," I said, not looking. "Now let's watch!"

The Mayfairs finished their last song before the break, then came off the side stairs of the stage, and quickly were escorted by guards hired just for the occasion. They entered the trailer nearer us—lucky break—as their hired band came down the other side of the stage and entered the trailer nearby.

"OK," I said. "You know what to do?"

Cherry whipped out her cell phone, hand at the ready to dial 911 if she heard me scream our code word—"Carolina!"—which we were pretty sure she could hear outside the trailer. After all, it was a trailer just like Sally's, and boy could we overhear some doozies at night from other trailers when we visited her home.

She was also instructed to holler at the guards that her friend had just gone in to attack the Mayfairs if she heard me scream the code word.

Bless her heart, Cherry hunkered down right in that ivy to

watch. I prayed that it wasn't poison ivy—it didn't look like it to me—and that, for once, she wasn't wearing thong underwear under her miniskirt.

Then I rushed up to the guards.

"I've got to get in there!" I hollered at the biggest, beefiest one nearest the trailer door. I assumed he was the guard in charge.

The guards didn't even crack a smile.

"No fans," said the big guard.

"I'm not a fan," I said. "I'm Josie Toadfern, and I was responsible for fixing up the Mayfair Sisters' costumes, and I rushed over here because I realized that there's a problem with the next set of costumes they're going to be wearing."

Mr. Muscles, as I was now dubbing him in my mind, since his biceps were putting some serious stress on his black T-shirt sleeves, just stared down at me, not at all impressed.

I poked him on the chest. It was like ramming my forefinger into concrete, but I kept poking for dramatic effect, even though it made me wince.

"Listen to me, I have to tell the sisters, or at the beginning of the next act, there's going to be a costume malfunction to rival Janet Jackson's at the '04 Super Bowl . . . times three!" I said.

That, at least, made Mr. Muscles's forehead twitch.

I folded my arms.

"Fine," I said. "I'll just tell Candace, Cornelia, and Constance later that I tried to warn them, but—"

Mr. Muscles looked at the smaller guard on the other side of the door and jerked his head toward the trailer. While the smaller guard went in, Mr. Muscles and I held an impromptu staring contest.

Mr. Muscles was about to win, but then the other guard

popped out and muttered something that made Mr. Muscles glance away from me.

I'd have enjoyed the small victory, but I was nervous about what would happen once I entered that trailer.

Mr. Muscles looked at me. "Go in," he said.

I went up the three steps to the door, entered, and shut the door behind me.

Candace was in the trailer's living room, sitting on the couch, sipping what I guessed was chamomile tea with lemon and honey, from the fragrance coming from her mug.

She looked at me. "Hi, Josie," she said. "Cornelia and Constance are in the bedrooms, resting. We have about ten minutes to talk."

I sat down on a chair across from her.

She smiled at me. "I'm guessing our costumes are just fine."

I nodded. "As far as I know. But I knew as soon as this concert was over, you'd be gone."

"Yes," she said. "As we've said, none of us can bear to watch the auction. Now, you must have something important to ask me, or you wouldn't have found a way into our trailer."

I gulped. "That song . . . 'Carolina Calling' . . . it's about your half-sister, isn't it? The daughter your mother had with Terry Tuxworth Sr. before you were ever born. The daughter he used to blackmail your mom into signing an unfair contract on her other daughters' behalf. And, I'm guessing, Terry Tuxworth Jr. found proof of Carolina's—or JoBeth Anderson's—existence and was planning to use that to try to con you and your sisters into doing yet another recording under that contract, thinking you'd agree to save the purity of your legacy."

Candace took a sip of her tea, the mug in her hands perfectly steady. "You figured it out, Josie," she said. "But you don't have the proof that Terry has—or, rather, had."

I gulped again. "I'm guessing he got that proof from poor Moira Evans." I didn't have to point out that her mama had mixed personal items in with the costumes; I'd returned several such items to her. I had passed several boxes directly to Moira, for her to inspect for mending needs. Moira could have found the proof mixed in one of those boxes.

Candace nodded. "He told us she had proof, that she was planning to sell it to him. Carolina's birth certificate—the original copy."

What would I have done with it if I'd found it? Certainly not blackmail anyone. I'd have just quietly returned it to Candace, maybe nosed around for the story because of my natural curiosity. Would Moira and Terry still be alive if that had happened?

Or, I thought, my gut crunching on itself . . . would I be the one brutally murdered?

Terry's bloody shirt made me think he'd murdered Moira, perhaps because she'd decided to keep the proof for herself, or perhaps because she'd upped her price for the proof.

And then, while he tried to get rid of that evidence at my laundromat, someone . . . someone in this trailer . . . had murdered him.

Cornelia, Constance, and Roger had all stayed at the Concord B&B. Sure, Roger had left the B&B that night, but just to go to a pharmacy.

Candace was the only one who stayed in Paradise, who took a nightly walk after the night nurse came . . .

"Your walk," I said softly, "the one you took each night after the night nurse came, did it take you by my laundromat? Did you see Terry's car there, decide to confront him?"

Suddenly Candace's eyes went wide. Her hand shook, and she spilled some of her tea.

And I knew, looking in her eyes, that she hadn't killed Terry at all . . . that she was horrified at the very idea I would think that of her.

"No," she whispered, "no, Josie, you can't think . . . I wasn't even upset at him knowing the truth about Carolina. In this day and age, who'd really care? My audience wouldn't."

"But what about your sisters?"

"They were upset," Candace admitted. "They seemed to feel their target audience—or ours, because they hadn't given up on a reunion—would be put off by this revelation, enough to hurt sales. But I can't believe either of them would . . ."

Her heartfelt denial was interrupted by Roger bursting out of a room in the small bedroom hallway.

"Damn it!" he exclaimed.

We looked at him.

"Constance forgot her asthma inhaler again . . . and now I'm supposed to try to get all the way back to our B&B for it?" he was ranting. "Just go to a pharmacy, she says, when she knows I couldn't get it refilled with an out-of-state scrip the other night, because she insists on using a local pharmacy back home and not a national chain." He thumped his hands in raging frustration against his thighs. "She knows how annoying it was for me to drive all the way back to Paradise—"

And then Roger stopped, staring at Candace and me staring at him in stunned realization.

And in an instant, he knew that we knew, and he bolted for the front door of the trailer.

I jumped up and started after him, shouting as loudly as I could, "Carolina!"

Epilogue

As it turned out, Cherry, outside the Mayfair trailer, hadn't been kneeling in poison ivy . . . she'd been kneeling in poison sumac.

And, yeah, she'd been wearing thong underwear.

Not only that, she'd lost her balance and sat in the sumac, and began itching painfully within minutes.

So by the time Roger ran out of the Mayfair trailer, Cherry was already jumping up and down and hooting and hollering, much to the annoyance of Mr. Muscles and his colleague.

The three of them blocked Roger's hurried exit, and Cherry heard me continually screaming "Carolina," so she tackled Roger as he ran out—and sprained her left ankle in the process, because of the three-inch spike heels she'd insisted on wearing to the concert. She caught the heel in a gopher hole just as she tackled him.

So, in the end, Cherry caught Roger because of her costume choices of spike heels, miniskirt, no pantyhose, and thong underwear, in combination with poison sumac and gopher holes at the Licking Creek Lake State Park.

Roger ended up confessing that he had in fact gone back to Paradise the previous Saturday night to get his wife Constance's asthma inhaler. While driving back, though, he saw Terry's purple sports car in my laundromat parking lot.

Roger went in to confront Terry and they got into a fight over the unfair contract. Roger said Terry taunted him with the truth about Carolina, and even showed him the birth certificate he said he'd purchased from "an interested party." (The birth certificate was later found in Roger's belongings back at the Concord B&B.)

Roger lost his temper and hit Terry with the health chair. Roger hurried back to his car, but, under the parking lot lights, noticed the two tie dye dresses in Terry's car's passenger seat as he started to get in his own car. That infuriated him even more—that Terry took the dresses just to annoy—and suddenly he had a creative, deadly idea for how to use them to finish off Terry. He hoped that Terry's demise would finally let his wife do the recordings she wanted to do with her sisters—never mind that Candace had no intention of doing recordings as anything other than a solo act. The torn dress was found at the bottom of a trash can in the bathroom at Moira's, where Terry must have stuffed it after killing Moira. Later, her grandson also verified the black T-shirt Terry was found in was his, left in his old bedroom.

A few weeks later, the DNA testing of Terry's bloody shirt and Moira's blood came back as a match. We'll never know for sure, but everyone agrees that Moira probably tried to withhold the certificate and raise her price, hoping to have money to help herself as well as her grandson, Clint, and that Terry lost his temper and stabbed her with the kitchen knife, in a spontaneous violent outburst that would only an hour or so later be echoed in his own demise. Then, he'd taken the certificate.

Eight months have passed since that fateful farewell Mayfair concert.

For about a week, the Mayfair sisters—all four—were just about the only news—with the national media occasionally interrupting itself to provide quick updates about things like, oh, foreign policy crises, areas of the world where famine and water shortages are taking a calamitous toll on the population, health care and education issues—things like that.

Anyway, Constance and Cornelia got an extra flash of fame, which they leveraged by cosigning a tell-all book deal. That meant they got a boost of fortune, too. Candace refused to have anything to do with the book, although she's mentioned in it, of course. Winnie read the book—*The Mayfairs: An American Tale of Tragedy and Triumph*—and told me that it was a pretty good read, although it didn't really provide any insight into the sisters' lives and how being such young stars had an impact on their overall lives.

The last media report about the sisters was that the book had been a flash-in-the-pan success . . . and that Constance was divorcing Roger, who is serving time for killing Terry.

With Terry dead, and no one to fight for his estate—since he didn't have any children—a court ruled that after his estate was settled, royalties from the old Mayfair Sisters' recordings now go back to the sisters. And the sisters are free to make new recording deals.

But without Candace, it turns out no one is really interested in making new Mayfair Sisters' recordings—despite the brief flash of fame the media attention and book deal created—and Candace isn't interested in relaunching their group.

I've stayed in touch with Candace, who says Constance and Cornelia aren't speaking to her because of her refusal to cash in on their old act and on the sensationalism around Terry's death—and the revelation of the fourth Mayfair sister.

But Candace seems at peace with that. She just released a solo CD, called *Carolina Calling*, which she again recorded herself and sells through her Web site. Any proceeds over cost go toward her mom's care and to a charity that helps single moms. It's Candace's way of trying to make something good come out of the ordeal of her mother's young life and the tough decisions she had to make.

So Candace still sings for love.

And speaking of love . . . Cherry, Sally, and I had triple weddings this past Christmas!

See, Cherry said there was no way she was going to get married with her ankle all bound up and her private areas itching from the poison sumac. So her and Dean's July 4 wedding had to be postponed.

Meanwhile, Levi and I realized we really were falling in love. About a week after the Mayfair concert, I moved back into my apartment and reopened my laundromat, and learned to overcome—I'm proud to say—the queasy feelings I had at first about working and living in a building where someone was murdered.

I've spent my life building up the business my aunt and uncle willed me, and I wasn't about to walk away from it because of Terry. Besides, I helped bring his killer to justice, so I figure he owes it to me not to haunt me, and so far he hasn't.

Levi rented a trailer in Sally's Happy Trails trailer court. That gave him an easy enough commute to Stillwater, gave us space when we needed it, and yet made dating simple. We saw each other most every day and managed to have a few fights and get over them by the time Labor Day rolled around, which was when Levi proposed.

I happily said yes! to a man I knew was not only my soul mate, but would always completely understand—and share—my devotion as Guy's caretaker.

And on the same Labor Day weekend, Sally got stuck in traffic on Interstate 70. She was on her way with her triplets to the Children's Museum in Indianapolis for a rare minivacation with her sons, when traffic came to a literal stop because of a trailer disconnecting from the cab and spewing its contents—cartons of canned fruit cocktail—across the highway.

The traffic was stopped for an hour and a half, during which everyone turned off their cars and trucks and got out and walked around and chatted, kind of like a spontaneous backyard barbeque, just with no barbeque.

Sally was having a hard time keeping Harry, Barry, and Larry occupied and cool in her car, so she'd gotten out with them and was trying to get them to walk beside her, but they kept trying to dart across the meridian.

Fortunately, Eddie Kalaman came along. Eddie's a trucker, and the boys took an instant liking to him, minding his admonition to listen to their mother.

Then Eddie and Sally took an instant liking to each other, and exchanged contact information. And it turned out Eddie lives in Masonville . . . at the Whispering Woods apartments, at that!

So Eddie and Sally fell in love, and Eddie and Sally's boys took a liking to one another. Eddie and Sally became engaged during Halloween, after the boys came back from trick-or-treating and were divvying up their candy, right there in Sally's kitchen.

As she put it later, how could she say no to a man who patiently convinced three boys to stop squabbling over how to divide ten Charleston Chew candy bars (Eddie's solution: Give one to your mother because she takes such great care of you, and that leaves three for each of you . . . but not all at once) and who also, she says, has a very cute behind? So she said yes.

And that's how we came to have the first triple wedding

ceremony at the Methodist church in Paradise. Probably the first triple wedding ceremony in Mason County. Maybe even in all of Ohio.

We all had our hair and nails done by the stylists at Cherry's salon. We each wore white dresses—because what bride doesn't deserve to wear white—which we found at Macey's Bridal at the Masonville Outlet Mall. Dean didn't even grumble, because Cherry was able to return the original dress to the flea market, due to the dress's neckline molting all its feathers.

Our grooms rented tuxes, and we drew names for which of Sally's triplets would be our personal ring bearer. (Sally got Larry, Cherry drew Harry, and I had Barry.) Our ring bearers behaved perfectly, like adorable little men.

We came down the aisles simultaneously, Cherry down the middle—because she wouldn't have it any other way and Sally and I didn't want to argue with her—and Sally down the right aisle and me down the left. The altar area was already so full—with three grooms waiting nervously up there—and the pastor, and then the three of us—that we decided we'd not only be brides, but we'd also consider ourselves to be one another's bridesmaids.

Afterward, our triple reception was held at the Bar-None. The place was packed with hundreds of well-wishers.

Even Chief John Worthy came . . . with a date. And he was even nice to me and looked like, finally, he might end up being happy himself. I was so happy that I didn't feel a mite of grumpiness toward him.

Levi and I went to Siesta Key, Florida, for our honeymoon, at a renovated mom-n-pop motel that was just a hundred-yard walk from the gulf, at half the price of the beachfront resorts. We had a wonderful time.

Cherry and Dean went to Gatlinburg as planned, and Sally and Eddie surprised us all by going to Cancun.

Now we're all back in Paradise.

Cherry moved into Dean's house, and Eddie moved into Sally's trailer, but it's so crowded with the five of them and Bozo the dog that they're buying a house on Plum Street, walking distance from my laundromat.

Levi and I have settled into the apartment over my laundromat. As he said, it's beautiful and convenient and plenty big for the two of us . . . and any Toadfern-Applegates that might come along in the future. The near future, I'm hoping.

We're so happy that I no longer feel any uneasiness about Terry's murder in the storeroom, especially since for a wedding present Levi had the whole room retiled and painted.

So, no ghosts in my life . . . well, except Mrs. Oglevee. Assuming she's a spirit come to poke through into my dreams from the afterlife, and not just my unconscious taking on a weird persona. In any case, I've finally accepted that for whatever reason, she's going to be popping into my dreams to nag me every now and again. Of late, it's to tell me I'm not getting any younger and it's time to get to work on making Toadfern-Applegate babies.

I just smile at her and say, "Well, honey, we are . . . but it's not exactly work." Infuriates her every time, but she always comes back.

I guess she's nagging about that because I haven't stumbled across any murders in the past eight months, so she can't nag me about either solving cases or staying out of them (depending on the circumstances).

I'm not sure what to make of that. After all, in the course of one year, I was involved in six murder investigations. I was starting to get used to this as my life's fate.

But there's a saying that life's what happens when you're making other plans, and I have to say that as exciting—and scary—as it was to be part of those investigations, I'll be just fine if I never have to help solve another murder investigation.

After all, I have a great, new marriage; my best friends are happily settled now, too; Guy is doing fine; and as a bonus, my stain-busting column really did end up taking off at a national level.

See, Caleb finally got so many great stories out of the Mayfair Sisters that he was hired by the *Chicago Tribune*. His editor happens to be friends with an editor at one of the few national column and comic syndicates, and the syndicate editor liked my column so much that he made a great offer.

I learned my lesson from the Mayfairs' experience, though, and had an entertainment rights attorney review the contract before I signed it. After a few changes, I finally did, and my column has gone national—with a twist. It not only includes stain-fighting tips, but household hints as well, with a focus on keeping homemaking cheap, fast, and simple, so it's now called "Josie's Tidy Tips: Stain-Busting & More."

My column's gotten so popular, in fact, that there's talk of me going on national TV talk shows! And I've even found the confidence to actually work on my book on laundry history. I'm all the way up to the chapter on washboards, now. And I think I'll have a chapter on ironing machines, too.

Anyway, I have far more fame and fortune than I ever thought I'd have in my life as just a simple, small-town Ohio laundromat owner with stain-removal know-how.

But still, I pray that, like Candace, I keep doing what I love to do most—help people stay a leap ahead of dirt and disorder—because of, well, love.

I don't think that will be a problem. After all, I live in Paradise, surrounded by the people I most cherish and who cherish me, and I know they will always keep me focused on the things that matter most: family, friends, and whenever possible, generous dollops of love and laughter.

Josie's Tidy Tips: Stain-Busting & More!

by Josie Toadfern
Stain Expert and Owner of Toadfern's Laundromat
(824 Main Street, Paradise, Ohio)
(Distributed by Happy Feet Syndicate)

Welcome to this, my first nationally published column!

I look forward to sharing my tips every week that will make laundry and housekeeping simpler, faster, and cheaper.

And more comfortable, too.

And what's more comfortable than fluffy towels?

Now, truth be told, no towel will stay fluffy forever. But you can prolong your towels' usefulness and fluffiness with these cost-saving tips:

1. Skip the liquid fabric softener! This causes the towel's fibers to grease down. If you've been using liquid fabric softener on your towels, wash them again and add a cup of white vinegar to the wash.

2. It's tempting to overfill a washer with just "one more towel," but resist the temptation. Again, that wears down the towel's fibers, and also adds to the wear and tear on your washer—a cost in the long run.

3. Do use dryer sheets in the dryer if you wish—but here's another cost-saving tip. I find using half a dryer sheet is as effective as using a whole one.

4. BONUS TIP: Reuse the used dryer sheet to dust and remove lint or pet hair from clothing or upholstery! Once the dryer sheet has been used once, it won't have enough softener to gunk up furniture or

clothing, but it will have enough "pull" left to take care of pesky dust and pet hair!

5. It's nice to hang out towels to air dry on sunny days, but keep the towels fluffy by shaking them out before you hang them out and again after you take them off the line.

I also want to share ironing tips with you. With today's new permanent-press fabrics, ironing may seem a thing of the past. It's hard to believe that not long ago, women (and, I suppose, a few men) ironed with heavy cast-iron irons, called sad irons, or even large, bulky machines called mangles.

Today's irons are much more lightweight and easy to use—kind of ironic, considering ironing is no longer such a, well, pressing problem.

But many natural fabrics, such as silk, cotton, and wool, need touching up. A few tips for keeping your clothing smooth and wrinkle-free:

1. Be sure to set your iron's heat according to the fabric guide on the iron. Too much heat can ruin lighter fabrics; not enough makes the task impossible.

2. For shirts and blouses, do the collar first, then sleeves, and then the bodice and back. Move the ironed material away from you as you finish a section to keep from rewrinkling the material.

3. If you don't want a crease in the sleeve, but don't have a sleeve board, just make one using a rolled-up towel.

4. It's easier to iron slightly damp clothes, so make your own ironing spray by pouring distilled water

into a spray bottle and adding a few drops of essential oil (available at health food stores) in your diuijdfavorite scent (I prefer lavender!) and shaking well. Then lightly mist the item to be ironed.

5. If you're ironing fragile or dark items, use a pressing cloth between the material and the iron—any clean, old bit of sheet or pillowcase will do.

6. Iron cotton and silk right side up, polyester from either side, and other materials inside-out. Just remember this tip: When in doubt, inside-out!

Until next week, may your whites never yellow and your colors never fade.

Love,
Josie Toadfern-Applegate

SHARON SHORT's

sensational Laundromat owner and stain-busting sleuth
JOSIE TOADFERN

Tie Dyed and Dead
978-0-06-079328-9

When a customer's dresses go missing, only to reappear in a more deadly fashion, Josie is the prime suspect in a murder.

Murder Unfolds
978-0-06-079327-3

When the daughter of Josie's deceased junior high school teacher claims her mother was murdered, suddenly more than unpleasant school memories keep Josie up nights.

Hung Out to Die
978-0-06-079324-1

When a dead body is tossed into the explosive chaos of bitter feelings at Josie's family's Thanksgiving dinner, she has to prove her disreputable Dad innocent of murder.

Death in the Cards
978-0-06-053798-2

An upcoming "Psychic Fair" has brought all manner of mystics and soothsayers to Paradise, Ohio. It doesn't take a crystal ball to predict that murder will ultimately foul the fair.

Death by Deep Dish Pie
978-0-06-053797-5

Josie eagerly awaits the town's annual Founders Day celebration and its pie-eating contest. But when a pie-making bigwig suspiciously drops dead after sampling the company's latest wares, Josie leaps into action.

Death of a Domestic Diva
978-0-06-053795-1

When a world famous domestic doyenne shows up in Paradise, Josie is shocked. But rapidly spreading rumors of the insufferable icon's immoral—and quite possibly illegal—carryings-on have sparked Josie's curiosity.

**Sign up for the FREE
HarperCollins monthly
mystery newsletter,**

The Scene of the Crime,

**and get to know your favorite authors,
win free books, and be the first to learn
about the best new mysteries going on sale.**

To register, simply go to www.HarperCollins.com, visit our mystery chan
page, and at the bottom of the page, enter your email address where
states "Sign up for our mystery newsletter." Then you can tap into mont
Hot Reads, check out our award nominees, sneak a peek at upcom
titles, and discover the best whodunits each and every month.

Get to know the magnificent mystery author
of HarperCollins and sign up today!

MYN 0